D1043615

Queen of Swords Press LLC

FEB   2019

Other books by Alex Acks/Alex Wells

Hunger Makes the Wolf (Angry Robot Books)

Blood Binds the Pack (Angry Robot Books)

MURDER

ON THE

TITANIA

and Other Steam-Powered Adventures

Alex Acks

MURDER ON THE TITANIA AND OTHER
STEAM-POWERED ADVENTURES

Copyright © 2018 by Alex Acks

Queen of Swords Press LLC
Minneapolis, MN
www.queenofswordpress.com

Published in the United States of America

ALL RIGHTS RESERVED

No part of this book may be reproduced in
any form or by any electronic or mechanical
means, including information storage
and retrieval systems, without written
permission from the author, except for the
use of brief quotations in a book review.

This book is a work of fiction. Names, characters, places and incidents are
products of the author's imagination. Any resemblance to real people or current
events is purely coincidental.

Cover Design By: KaNaXa Design

Interior Design by Terry Roy

ISBN 978-0-9981082-7-8

"Murder on the Titania," "The Curious Case of Miss Clementine Nimowitz
(And Her Exceedingly Tiny Dog)" "The Jade Tiger" and "The Ugly Tin Orrery"
all previously appeared in *Sausages, Steam and the Bad Thing* by Rachael Acks.
Musa Publishing, 2015.

Contents

Contents

1
Murder on the *Titania*

THE AIRSHIP *TITANIA*, JEWEL of Her Royal Highness the
Grand Duchess Sophronia Victoria Saint-Clair of New
York's fleet, floated above the murky Manhattan skyline,
tethered to the spire of the Empire State Building by a set of thin
ropes and a ramp made of deceptively delicate-looking beams of
brass etched to look like lace. Within the *Titania's* observation
deck stood Colonel Geoffrey Douglas, decorated soldier, veteran
of the Canadian front, and newly hired Chief of Security for
His Royal Highness, the Grand Duke of Denver. Geoff was a
man of action and daring by his very nature; it grated on him
to be trapped within a cage, even one made with lush carpeting
to go with the steel and glass. He drummed his fingers on the
brass railing that edged the deck and watched as cranes belching
columns of steam loaded the last of the cargo.

A porter threaded through the crates, head low and shoulders
hunched. Geoff tensed, hand firm on the railing as the man
approached the set of crates bearing the seal of the Grand Duke.

The porter's hands fluttered furtively at his pockets, and Geoff smoothed one hand down his jacket, pausing at the reassuring shape of his service revolver, but all the porter produced was a cheroot and nothing more offensive.

The porter continued on without pause, glancing over his shoulder as he smoked while on duty. Geoff blew a sigh out through his neatly trimmed officers mustache and went back to drumming his fingers.

He longed to be in the thick of things, making certain that all was in place, that not a single order had gone astray. One did not leave the placement of a fortune in custom-made jewelry, the wedding set for the Grand Duke's only daughter, to the vagaries of chance. But like many other great houses, the Grand Duke's had been troubled by thieves and pirates—clever ones at that— and Geoff's healthy sense of paranoia had been shrieking that his every move might be watched from the moment he'd picked the jewelry up.

Even worse, shortly before he'd picked up the jewelry he'd received worrying intelligence that the most dastardly of the Grand Duke's enemies, a Captain Ramos, may even have been spotted just north of the Duchy of Charlotte, far from his normal Western stomping grounds—suspiciously proximal to Geoff's current location. And with North America divided as it was, into bickering sovereign grand duchies and a scattering of smaller client domains dotting the continental wasteland, getting security information, let alone *cooperation* from other generals or security chiefs was an exercise in frustration.

"Sir?"

He glanced over his shoulder at the steward, who waited behind him, clad in an impeccable, deep indigo coat. The steward touched his cap with great deference.

"Yes?" Geoff straightened, squaring his shoulders. He was not a large man, but he was accustomed to command and knew the use of a stern carriage to command respect. He still maintained his light brown hair in military trim as well; he thought it provided a subtle reminder that he was not to be trifled with.

"Just wanted to let you know, sir, we've finished loading all of your baggage."

"And you've sent the safe to my room?"

"Yes, sir. Saw to it myself."

Geoff nodded and pulled his watch from his vest pocket to check the time. "Will we be underway soon?"

"Yes, sir. There's just a little loading left to do, and the doctor's making his final rounds. We'll be casting off right on schedule."

"Glad to hear it."

"Ah, and speak of the devil, sir…"

Geoff turned to face the man who had descended to the deck. He was tall and thin, with dirty blond hair that gave his clean-shaven face a sallow cast. His jacket was a sober, dark brown and his shirt collar was impeccably starched.

"Excuse me," Geoff said, "I don't think I've had the pleasure before. Colonel Geoffrey Douglas, formerly of Her Royal Highness Luella's Expeditionary Forces."

"Dr. Matthew Lehmacher," the man said, followed by a polite bow. "I'm sorry to trouble you, but I'm doing the final passenger inspection."

"Of course."

"Thank you." The doctor closed the distance between them and took a small brass-rimmed magnifying lens from his pocket. His prominent brow and sharp nose made his expression overly serious as he peered through the lens into Geoff's gray eyes. He twisted the outer rim of the glass back and forth a few times, tinting it from blue to amber and back, then nodded to himself. "And if I may check your pulse, Colonel?"

Geoff offered the doctor his left wrist. "I trust everything is in order?"

"No sign of Infection, I'm pleased to say." The doctor smiled, wrapping cold fingers around Geoff's wrist for a few seconds. "And you seem pleasingly alive, in case you were concerned."

He chuckled. "How comforting. I often worry I might've become exanimate without noticing. I trust the other passengers have fared just as well?"

"They have, by the grace of God." The words sounded like a recitation rather than a true expression of relief. He extracted a list from his pocket, scanning over it quickly. "And it seems that you were my last appointment, Colonel. This ship is stuffed to the gills, so to speak, but I've seen everyone at last." He turned toward the steward, still at the door. "Please let the captain know that I've completed my inspection and we are able to proceed."

"Yes, sir!" The steward disappeared up the stairs, his footsteps muffled by the expensive burgundy carpet that covered the metal decking.

"Forgive me for saying so, but you don't quite look the part of ship's doctor," Geoff said.

"Quite observant, Colonel; I'm certainly no man of the Navy. I'm actually a passenger, myself, but was called on to perform this duty."

Geoff nodded. "I see. Well, I hope that you'll find Denver agreeable."

"It's been two years since I last visited, but unless it's changed drastically I think I'll find it quite agreeable." The doctor's smile edged toward sly. "And if I may ask...I noticed that you're His Grace's Chief of Security. A bit far afield, are you not?"

"A bit. In my case, most decidedly on business. More than that, I am not at liberty to say." Geoff examined the man's face carefully, trying to find the source of that slyness. He'd found Denver agreeable before, but for what? Most likely the statement was innocent, the interest in Geoff's role likewise innocent, but that curiosity prickled at senses already on edge.

"Ah, I understand. I didn't mean to pry."

Geoff nodded, though before he could speak, the sound of a gong being struck three times echoed through the ship. "Oh, at last." While he respected the Grand Duchy of New York for its rich history, and at times, overly rich culture, he would be happy to leave it behind. The air was no less smoky in the wide valley that housed Denver, but at least it lacked the ever-present humidity that made New York's chemical fog a living, malevolent presence.

The doctor moved forward to look out the windows as the *Titania* cast off her moorings and lifted away from the spire of the Empire State Building. "Not to worry, Colonel. In twenty-four hours, you'll be safely home. With luck, there will even be some decent entertainment to be had between now and then."

"With luck," Geoff agreed as he watched the last of the skyscrapers fall away under the haze of distance and humidity. "They've filled the tennis courts and the theater with cargo, but I have heard that the string quartet is still in residence at least."

"Perhaps a little after dinner dancing? I couldn't help but notice a number of our fellow passengers are unattached females."

Geoff laughed, shaking his head. "Not much of a dancer, I'm afraid," he said, tapping his cane on the floor. "I don't just carry this for fashion. But I still enjoy the music."

"Oh, I see." The doctor nodded wisely. "Childhood mishap, or...?"

"War injury, I'm afraid. Canadian front." *Mishap* would be the far kinder answer for them both, but Geoff was not a man given to dishonesty for the sake of something so transient as social comfort.

"Oh. I hadn't realized..."

"Quite all right, Doctor."

"Simply a break?"

The continued curiosity, while understandable, was most unwelcome. Geoff cleared his throat, not wanting the man to imagine a leg twisted and scored by burns as a legacy of the removal of infected flesh. "A bad break."

"Surely they took better care of you brave boys than that."

"They did the best they could, but it was in days before we turned the tide, and resources were limited." Surviving those difficult months had earned him his share of medals and glory, not that those could replace full use of a leg. Geoff cleared his throat, posture going a bit stiff.

"My apologies, Colonel. I ought not to have pried, but professional curiosity will get the better of me every time. I don't suppose there's anything..." He reached out to rest his hand on Geoff's shoulder.

Geoff stared at that hand until the doctor moved it away. "I manage well enough, so long as the criminal and mischievous aren't overly swift." It was Dr. Lehmacher's turn to clear his throat in a bit of awkward conversational punctuation. "I'll make sure to take in an extra dance or two in your honor then. It's a decent enough excuse."

WHILE ALL ACCOMMODATIONS ON the *Titania* were luxurious by Geoff's personal standards, he was in one of the smaller interior cabins, which shared toilet facilities. Still, the furniture was rich and comfortable, and the royal-blue carpet obviously new; the cabin smelled faintly of the dye that had been used on it. The small safe he'd brought on board made a strange sort of end table next to the narrow bed that took up one wall, a perfect place for his brandy snifter. He busied himself until dinner by reading a book he'd picked up in New York, a collection of fascinating essays about how humanity might have progressed without the scourge of Infection throwing society into disarray. When it was time to get dressed, he took out his dinner suit, a sober, charcoal-gray cloth with a woolen vest of forest green reminiscent of his Expeditionary Forces uniform.

The doors to the dining room were open when he arrived, the passengers already moving to their seats with all seemly haste. Inside, portraits done in oils graced the richly papered walls, with the Grand Duchess of New York occupying the place of honor. A steward carefully directed Geoff to his seat at one of the lesser tables, five of its six seats already taken. He recognized one of the occupants immediately.

Dr. Lehmacher rose to his feet. "Ah, Colonel, I had hoped you'd be joining us all for dinner." He smiled, pointing to the chair next to him. "Our numbers are a bit uneven, but I hope you'll find this seat acceptable."

"Of course. The cook on the *Titania* is without compare, and I would hate to miss out on making the acquaintance of my fellow travelers."

"Please, allow me to introduce you," Lehmacher said, turning toward the couple who were to his left along the round table. "Colonel Geoffrey Douglas, may I present my dear friends, Lord and Lady Caraway of Manhattan."

He bowed to the Lord and kissed the lady's hand, as was appropriate. Lord Caraway was a younger man, his black cheeks cleanly shaven, his dark, tightly curled hair barely under control in the absence of a hat. A golden pin, shaped like an owl, sat on the right lapel of his jacket. He wore a dark suit with a deep red silk vest; his lady was dressed similarly in black and red, a string of gemstones laced through her hair. The lady was small and thin, her dark brown hair making her face look even paler by comparison. Still, she smiled prettily at Geoff when he kissed her hand.

"Professor David Jefferson, fresh from a guest lecturing stint in Berlin," the doctor continued, introducing the man to Lord Caraway's left. "He's traveling to your home duchy to give a series of public lectures on chemistry, I believe."

"Indeed," the professor said. He was an older gentleman, his white hair and beard neatly trimmed. "I promise not to lecture during dinner tonight, however."

Dr. Lehmacher indicated the lady who would be at Geoff's right, sandwiched between him and the professor. "And this is Miss Isadora Alvarez of Santa Fe."

The woman, barely more than a girl, giggled nervously as Geoff took her hand. She was pretty enough, her rich brown hair trying to escape from a feathered headband to sweep across the lighter skin of her neck. Her dress was a rather unfortunate pale blue, however, and showed her to be surprisingly plump for her young age. "Please, Colonel, feel free to call me Dory." Her voice was high and breathy. "Even if we're only to be traveling companions for a day, there's no need to be so formal."

"As you wish, Miss Dory." Geoff didn't care for the overly familiar way she spoke, but he was not so cruel as to censure a young lady in public.

"Dr. Lehmacher has told us that you're His Grace's chief of security," Lord Caraway said. "That sounds like a rather exciting job."

"A bit. Though I've only recently been brought in to his service."

"Isn't it dangerous?" Dory asked, her hands fluttering nervously before she clasped them in front of her chest. "I've heard there are all sorts of awful people about."

"Perhaps there's a little danger." Geoff smiled kindly. "But I think that risks must be taken if order is to prevail. Most of the criminals that might threaten the Grand Duke are, to put it bluntly, simple hooligans. The former chief of security became a bit complacent, I fear. But that will change."

"And besides," Dr. Lehmacher said, "I can't imagine any danger from thieves compares to what you saw on the Canadian Front."

Damn the man anyway. Geoff cleared his throat, ducking his chin slightly as Lady Caraway and Dory exclaimed over that revelation. "Perhaps. I'm certain I shall soon find out. Professor, if you don't mind me asking, which area of chemistry do you find of interest?" He had no desire to speak of an uncomfortable past, and hoped the professor would be kind enough to act as a diversion.

"All areas, of course!" the professor said, laughing. "In particular, I am interested in the nature of things biochemical as they can be applied to modern medicine. That is, in fact, how Dr. Lehmacher and I came to be acquainted. He attended my home university. As did Lord Caraway, actually; I introduced the gentlemen."

"A long-standing set of friendships, then."

"Oh indeed. The stories I could tell." The professor tilted his wine glass and smiled impishly. "And well might, yet."

"Lucky for the delicate ears of the ladies and the tender state of my pride, they're bringing food to stop your mouth," Dr. Lehmacher said, laughing.

THE FIRST COURSE WAS oxtail soup and oysters, brought out by a bevy of waiters in neat white coats. Whatever her other flaws, Dory's table manners were impeccable; Geoff felt slightly ashamed at the quick stab of relief that ran through him at that.

"Miss Dory," he said, "I know that Dr. Lehmacher had said you were from Santa Fe, but I can't help but notice you're a bit far from home now."

"Oh, yes, Colonel. My parents thought it best I become a little more worldly, so they sent me to school abroad. But now that I've been engaged to a gentleman of good standing, it's most definitely time for me to return home." She giggled, though not too loudly.

"How delightful. Which school did you attend?"

With half an ear, he listened to her chatter about the plays she had seen in Europe and the museums she had gone to, her voice melding in with the sound of the string quartet tucked away in one corner of the dining room. He was far more curious about the Caraways. Lord Caraway spoke a great deal to the professor and doctor both; their mutual enthusiasm seemed to be about all things scientific, particularly the new generators being designed that would apparently revolutionize the protection of farm fields. Lady Caraway said little and only picked at her food, lips going paler and thinner with each passing moment as the men shamelessly ignored her. While male enthusiasm for certain topics was understandable, Geoff quite disapproved of the overt rudeness of it; surely they could have waited until after dinner when it was time for brandy and cigars.

As the second course was delivered, Geoff attempted to engage the lady in conversation. "Did you attend university as well?" While it was unusual, it wasn't unheard of for ladies to take a few classes in the more academically gentle areas to aid them in finding eligible men of their social stratum.

"I did not, I'm afraid," Lady Caraway said, shoulders relaxing slightly. "Though I had a bit of private tutoring in literature. Poetry is where I excelled."

Dory, listening in, giggled. "Oh, so you did not know what sort of horrid school friends you'd be getting along with your husband?"

Lady Caraway's lips went thin, her face pale. "Excuse me," she said, rising. "I don't feel well." The men at the table barely had time to stand before she rushed from the dining room.

"Will your wife be all right?" Geoff asked as they all sat back down.

"I think so," Lord Caraway said. "She sometimes finds air travel disagreeable. My theory is that she's unusually susceptible to changes in atmospheric pressure." He inclined his head toward Dr. Lehmacher. "Though sir, if you would be so kind as to look in on her later, we would both be greatly obliged."

"Of course. As soon as dinner has finished."

"Oh, I hope she'll be all right," Dory said quietly. "You don't think it was what I said, do you?"

"I'm certain that she will be. And I'm certain not, when it was such a mild joke about merry gentlemen. Though I am sure she appreciates your well wishes. Would you care for some wine?" Soon he had the table drinking a toast to the lady's good health. Only Geoff wasn't so certain that it was a question of health; the lady hadn't looked so much ill as deeply upset.

GEOFF SAT UP WITH a gasp, disoriented for a moment in the darkness, recognizing neither the bed nor the thin strip of light leaking in under the door. He heard only snapping tree branches, the crack of distant guns, shouts, and screams as the Infected slammed into his company's defensive lines.

No, he realized, those sounds were in his mind, mixed with someone pounding frantically at his door, rescuing him from a thoroughly unpleasant dream. He took three deep breaths to calm himself and then felt along the wall to find the lamp and turn it back on.

"A moment," he shouted. "A moment if you please. I'm awake. Let me make myself decent." He slipped from bed and quickly dressed. His shirt was rumpled, collar and cuffs undone, and his tie nowhere to be found, but he deemed it good enough for the ungodly hour.

There was a young officer other side of the door, face pale, ginger hair disheveled. His uniform had a lieutenant's stripes on the shoulder.

"What is so important that it couldn't wait for a decent hour?" Geoff demanded.

"Something awful's happened, sir. Captain told me to fetch you quick as I could—"

"Is it my luggage?"

The lieutenant shook his head, swallowing hard. "No, sir, it isn't. It's much worse."

Geoff nodded and dug his lorgnette from his traveling case. The little device was rather battered and showing its age, but still serviceable. "Then you'd best show me the way, Lieutenant...?"

"Collins, sir."

Geoff followed Lieutenant Collins along several hallways and down two flights of stairs. Soon they were at the top of another set of stairs, these a plain metal that clearly led down to the crew quarters.

There was a small crowd gathered at the bottom of the stairs, most of them dressed in the uniforms of the crew or servants. More to Geoff's interest, there was a body sprawled untidily across the deck plates, a pool of dark red spread out in a halo from the back of its head. The head itself was turned at an unnatural angle, far back and to the side.

It took only a moment for his sleep-muzzled mind to place who it was at the bottom of the stairs: Lord Caraway. It made little sense for the man to be in this area of the ship, but the truth was inescapable: he was very much there and very much dead.

"Move away," Geoff said, carefully descending the stairs without touching the railings, Lieutenant Collins at his heels. "All of you, move. Be about your business." He used the same tone that had once made hardened soldiers snap to; it had the desired effect and most of the gawkers scattered down the hallway.

He stepped over the body, carefully skirting the pool of liquid blood, its color still fresh and vibrant, and squatted down painfully to take a better look at what had once been Lord Caraway. The earthy smell was still far too reminiscent of the soup of blood and dirt that he'd waded through in battlefield after battlefield in the wilds of Canada, and it turned his stomach.

He had to remind himself that there should be no possibility of Infection; Dr. Lehmacher had cleared everyone before takeoff. Besides, the fall had clearly destroyed the unfortunate lord's head. Still, Geoff lifted the lorgnette to his face after snapping the red and blue filters into place. Much to his relief, the blood looked normal, rather than alive with Infection. Unfortunately, anything of use to answering this mystery with ease was merciless in its absence. No stray hairs, odd fingerprints, or otherwise essential pieces of evidence made themselves apparent. The railing for the stairs was a smear of layer upon layer of prints, utterly useless.

"When was he found?"

"Just now, sir. Soon as he was seen, they sent a guard to the captain, who sent me to get you. Couldn't be more than five, perhaps ten minutes."

"Has anyone touched him?"

"Don't know, sir. It'd be powerful rude, though, wouldn't it?"

Geoff shook his head, a wry laugh escaping his lips. "Death often is, Lieutenant Collins."

From down the hall, a woman called her own answer. "No sir, he ain't been touched since I was in the hall at least."

"Thank you." Geoff nodded, not looking up.

Lord Caraway's face was fixed in a look of surprise, mouth open and eyes staring. Streaks of blood came from his eyes, but it didn't look as if anyone had hit him; probably it was from the impact on the unforgiving deck. More interesting was the state of the man's clothing; while he had his jacket on, his shirt was unbuttoned all the way down the front. Geoff carefully lifted the sides of the coat, checking to see if there was anything in the pockets: nothing. Geoff lifted the man's hands, first his right and then his left. His fingernails were torn, and on his left hand, a band of slightly lighter colored skin showed where his wedding ring was missing.

He put the lorgnette away in his coat pocket and turned to the lieutenant. "Go fetch Dr. Lehmacher. Quietly. I wish him to examine the body before it is removed."

"Yes, sir!" Lieutenant Collins raced back up the stairs.

Geoff straightened, rubbing his hands idly on his pants, hoping to scrub away the faintly waxy feel of dead flesh. He walked down the hall to the two women, who on closer observation stood like guards in front of a cabin door. "Did either of you see what transpired?"

"No sir," the older of the two women said. "Didn't see nothing but the poor gentleman already in such a sad state. We was woken up out of a sound sleep by the hue and cry."

"What hue and cry?"

"The lady who found him, sir. She was in quite a bad way, so Mary and I, we decided it best to let her sit in our cabin so she could collect herself. She didn't want no company, poor lamb."

"Very kind of you both. If I might speak with her…?"

"Of course, sir." A light tap on the cabin door received and answer, muffled quaver, the sound of a woman badly shaken. A moment later, she opened the door.

Of all the people Geoff might have expected, Dory was perhaps the last. She was in a terrible state, her hair in complete disarray and her eyes and nose red from crying. She wore a plain, simple dress of cream-colored cotton, suitable for light exercise.

"Colonel Douglas?" she quavered.

"Miss Dory, are you quite all right? Here, please take my handkerchief."

Dory took the bit of cloth with shaking hands. Rather than put it to any sort of use, she simply clutched at it as if it were a lifeline. "Is Lord Caraway… Is he…?"

"I'm afraid so," Geoff said. "At the risk of causing you further upset, I must ask… Did you see anything?"

Dory shook her head, covering her face with the handkerchief for a moment. "I was just taking a…a walk, since I've never been able to sleep on ships like this. I get too excited! And I thought it wouldn't do any harm to explore a bit, as long as I was quiet and careful, so I came down the other stairs and walked across the hall and saw…and saw…Oh there was blood! It was so awful!" Her voice rose to a wail and she began crying again.

That at least explained how she had come to be down in the crew quarters, Geoff thought, even as he squirmed uncomfortably at the sound of her distress. He'd never had cause to deal with many women socially, let alone young, fragile females. He knew he ought to do *something* but wasn't quite certain what. "Did you see anyone else?"

Dory gulped loudly, still hiding her face in the handkerchief. "No. No one at all. I just…I screamed, and I woke everyone up, and I feel awful about that, but I didn't know what else to do!"

"You did nothing wrong, Miss Dory. It's a good thing you raised the alert. We wouldn't want to leave poor Lord Caraway just lying there any longer than necessary."

Dory sniffled, nodding her head. "He's in such a state," she wailed. "Has someone covered him up, at least?"

"We will soon." That the girl hadn't seen anyone near the felled lord told him little, other than that the perpetrator had likely escaped before she happened across the terrible scene. Of more interest was how the man had come to be in such a state of undress. It was possible he had been carrying on some sort of clandestine, dishonorable affair with one of the servants— that could explain Lady Caraway's upset at his inattention—but it seemed just as obvious that he had been robbed, either pre- or postmortem. Either way, it was at least a starting point for an investigation. And since the captain had specifically sent for him, it seemed obvious that the investigation was indeed his to conduct.

More footsteps sounded on the metal deck plates. Geoff leaned back to glance out of the room, catching sight of Lieutenant Collins with Dr. Lehmacher in tow. The doctor's face was pale. He looked shaken, even a little ill—as one might expect a man to look upon receiving news of the sudden and violent death of an acquaintance. "I brought him, sir," Lieutenant Collins called.

"Good man. I've got another errand for you now. Go check up on Lady Caraway. I'm afraid that you will have to wake her, but it's quite urgent. Let her know that I will be up shortly to see her. And breathe not a word of this affair."

"Yes, sir." Lieutenant Collins hurried away again.

"Dr. Lehmacher, are you quite all right?" Geoff asked.

"As well as can be expected, under the circumstances," the doctor assured him, though his voice was as wan as his face. He had changed his clothes since dinner, but was in as similar a state of disarray as Geoff.

"As the only doctor aboard, I'm afraid this sad duty falls to you. I need you to examine the body and see if there is anything to be found regarding the cause of Lord Caraway's death…beyond the obvious."

The doctor nodded. "I will endeavor to do my best," he said, his voice catching. "Though it shall break my heart as I do."

"Carry on." Geoff looked away, not wanting to see another man so undone by grief. "Miss Dory, will you be quite all right if I leave you alone for a few minutes?"

She nodded, sniffling into the handkerchief. "I think so, Colonel."

"Brave girl." Geoff headed back in to the hall. He gave the women whose room Dory was using a somewhat flat smile. "May I trouble you for some paper?"

"Yes, sir, of course." The woman went into her room, murmured something to Dory, and then returned with a few pieces of cheap, plain stationary. "Will these do?"

"Yes, perfectly." He pulled his pen from the inner pocket of his coat. "If I could trouble you for your name…?" He took down her name, and that of her friend, and made note that they'd noticed nothing untoward. He then asked the older woman— Mrs. Ivers—to take him up and down the hall, letting him know who lived in each of the small cabins. He knocked on each door, but most were deserted; the occupants had either been awoken and taken themselves elsewhere when Geoff had shown up, or were already at work. He would have the guards find those people later.

Those that were still in their cabins, muzzy from interrupted sleep, and many in something of a temper because of it, were not terribly helpful. Most had heard nothing until Dory screamed. A few recalled perhaps hearing a few people out in the hallway in the hours before that, but considered it nothing unusual, since the running of an airship was a twenty-four-hour operation, and crew members sometimes returned to their quarters at odd hours.

The man nearest to the fateful set of stairs, an old cook's assistant who was obviously hard of hearing, thought he might have heard someone drop something on the floor a few minutes before Dory's scream, but hadn't thought anything of it. The stairs, he said with no small degree of bitterness, were far too steep and narrow to be safe, and he'd lost his baggage down them a few times in the past.

Opposite the cabin of the cook's assistant, Geoff was about to knock on the door when Mrs. Ivers said, "That one's empty, sir. Normally where the third cook's assistant hangs his hat, but they got in to an awful row before we left New York and he cleared out. I heard there weren't time to hire a new one, since the chef's a bit fussy about his help." She shrugged one shoulder slightly. "A locked and empty room's no consequence, right?"

"I would agree, Mrs. Ivers, but these are quite unusual circumstances." Geoff tried the doorknob. To his surprise, it turned easily under his hand, and he pushed the door open.

"Well, that can't be right at all. 'Twas supposed to be locked. Maybe the steward forgot."

"Perhaps." Geoff stepped in the doorway, wrinkling his nose at the sour tang of sweat, and something much saltier and muskier, which he recognized courtesy of the few brushes he'd had with houses of ill repute during his time in the Expeditionary Forces. "It appears to have seen recent use." While the room was for the most part bare, containing no personal effects and only the most basic of furniture, the narrow bed was in disarray.

"What is it? Have you found a clue?" Dory called from out in the hallway, sounding much recovered. Geoff turned to look at Mrs. Ivers, doing his best to fill the doorway and block the view of what was inside.

"If you please, Mrs. Ivers," he murmured. "I hardly think this is a suitable sight for a young lady of good breeding."

She made a sound suspiciously like a snort, though she covered it with one hand. "As you say, sir. Been a lot of unsuitable things going on recently." But she did back away and take gentle charge of Dory, moving her farther down the hall.

Geoff gave the room a more thorough examination, but there was little to see. There was no blood apparent when he checked the area through the filtered lenses of the lorgnette, and he stopped short of pawing through the rumpled sheets, not wanting to touch them. He turned the lamp back down and shut the door behind him. By now there were a few guardsmen loitering in the hall. "I want this door locked now and the room left undisturbed," he told the nearest.

A picture of the events began to form in his mind. That Lord Caraway had been involved in some sort of affair seemed obvious. That he had been robbed seemed also obvious. It was possible, he thought, that the man had given chase to his robber and gotten pushed down the stairs for his trouble. That meant the person he most wanted to talk to was whatever woman had been with Lord Caraway at the time, either one of the crew or passengers.

Still deep in thought, he moved back down the hallway, to where Caraway had met his end. The doctor stood to one side now; two rather broad young men were lifting the unfortunate lord onto a set of canvas sheets.

"Did you find anything, Doctor?" Geoff asked.

The man stood stock-still, face white, one hand curled over his mouth. He did not seem to hear.

"Dr. Lehmacher?" Geoff gently touched his elbow.

"What? Oh." Dr. Lehmacher blinked watery eyes. "I am sorry, Colonel. Just…I…oh, this is terrible. Seeing it…seeing it has left me quite unmanned, I'm afraid."

"I can only imagine, knowing of your friendship. But for the sake of that friendship, Doctor, you must offer me your best work and observation on this topic."

"Yes. You are right. I must…I owe it to him." Dr. Lehmacher nodded and cleared his throat, visibly struggling to regain control of his expression. His throat worked uselessly for a moment before he spoke, words barely above a whisper but at the least steady and clinical. "He fell down the stairs backward and snapped his neck cleanly, opening three fractures in his skull as well. I don't think he had time even to suffer." His voice shook as he said the last word and he took a moment to compose himself, his lips setting in a thin line. "I think he must have been grasping the railings, and quite tightly, when he was pushed."

"Then you do not think it was a simple fall."

The doctor paled, licking his lips. "I can think of no other reason for the state of his fingernails." He took a deep breath. "Now, if you don't mind, Colonel, I think there's a decanter of brandy in my room calling my name."

"I understand, Doctor. As much as it pains me to say, have care to not make yourself insensible."

"Oh, I shall," the doctor said. "I only wish to be somewhat… numb."

Geoff nodded, watching Dr. Lehmacher turn and walk slowly down to the other end of the hall, shoulders hunched and footsteps heavy. Such obvious grief was too painful to watch, and he owed it to the doctor to avert his eyes. Geoff himself had lost so many dear friends during the battles in Canada that he wondered if perhaps he'd become a bit numb to it. Or perhaps it was that an officer had to maintain his stiff upper lip at all costs, while a civilian doctor could afford to be a bit softer about such things. Geoff shook his head and returned to Mrs. Ivers's room.

He beckoned the older lady out into the hall. "You seem quite well acquainted with your fellow crew members."

"Could say so, sir." She raised an eyebrow at him, obviously waiting for him to get to the point.

It made him distinctly uncomfortable to speak so frankly, but the pursuit of justice was far more important, and Mrs. Ivers had already shown herself to be a very pragmatic woman. Those of the lower classes tended to be, in his experience. "Are there any among the serving girls that might…carry out affairs with the gentlemen passengers?"

She sucked at her teeth. "Aye, a few names spring to mind."

He offered her his pen and one of her own sheets of paper. "If you would be so good to write those names down, and then…" Of course, nearly everyone was a suspect, but it was useful to have a starting point for inquiries. As Mrs. Ivers began to make her list, he looked into her cabin. "Miss Dory, have you recovered from your shock sufficiently to return to your quarters?"

She nodded. "I think so, Colonel. If you would be so good as to escort me?"

"Of course, that was my intention." He offered Dory his arm as Mrs. Ivers returned his pen and the paper, now folded in half. "Mrs. Ivers, you have my deep gratitude for the many services you have done for me this morning. I will make certain that the captain is informed."

"Bless you, sir," Mrs. Ivers said, ducking into a rough little curtsey. "'Twas the least I could do. Take care, Miss Dory."

Dory was strangely silent for part of their walk back to the passenger deck. As they approached the hallway leading to the quarters for the wealthiest passengers, however, she hesitated. "Colonel?"

"Yes?"

"Do you think that Lady Caraway will be all right? Do you think…maybe I should check on her? Of course I haven't known her that long, but we had such lovely conversations before dinner that I almost feel as if we've known each other for years."

"I am intending to check in on her personally." Geoff remembered the wan look on the woman's face as she left the dining room, already suspecting her husband had done their marriage harm before being struck this terrible blow. "Perhaps your presence might be of some comfort to the lady, if you feel up to the task yourself, of course." While the presence of a bystander made his task a little more difficult, it was also a necessity. It would be most unsuitable for him to be in the lady's private room for any length of time without some sort of chaperon. In a pinch, Dory would have to do.

Dory smiled, trying to draw her plump frame up a little taller and squaring her soft shoulders. "I may have had a nasty shock, Colonel, but it has not rendered me selfish or mean. I doubt I can be of much comfort in the face of such a horrible loss, but I will do my best."

HE KNOCKED LIGHTLY ON the door, which was made of black walnut, a much finer, thicker wood than that of the servant's cabins. For a moment, he wondered if the lieutenant hadn't woken the lady; then the door swung open soundlessly, revealing Lady Caraway. She was obviously still dressed to sleep, a scarlet brocade dressing gown carelessly tied over her white sleeping nightgown. The brilliant color only made her look more wan, bordering on jaundiced. Her eyes were red and puffy and her hair in complete disarray, but she was otherwise composed.

Geoff quickly averted his gaze. "Lady Caraway, I'm afraid to be the bearer of ill news."

"Please, come in, Colonel, Miss Dory," she said, standing aside. "Unless you have news that outmatches the death of my husband, it can hardly be worse." She walked a trifle unsteadily over to the small grouping of richly embroidered couches that comprised the sitting area. Geoff hazarded a quick glance around the room but saw nothing untoward; the door that led to the bedroom of the luxurious cabin was firmly shut. The curtains on one side of the room were drawn back, revealing the night sky outside, stars hanging above, a soft gray carpet of clouds beneath them, and the *Titania's* sleek oval form a darker smudge cast by the moonlight.

"I'm sorry, Lady Caraway. Did Lieutenant Collins disturb you with the news? He may be an officer, but he's not so old I wouldn't gladly box his ears for such an affront."

Her eyes widened with a hint of surprise. She quickly shook her head. "No, please don't stir yourself on my behalf. I'd rather be told ill news at once than be kept in suspense."

"I see."

"I am sorry that such a terrible thing has befallen you," Dory said, sitting down with surprising delicacy on the edge of one couch. "Please, is there anything I can get for you?"

"If you could ring for some tea, that would be lovely," the lady said. Dory immediately stood and went to the corner where the small telephone sat. She wound it up quickly and then called in their request before returning to her seat.

"I am afraid that I must ask you a few questions," Geoff said. "I do not wish to intrude, but it is necessary. When did your husband return from dinner?"

"I'm not entirely certain. I was feeling unwell, as you may recall. I came back to our room to sleep. I know that he returned at some point, since I remember him kissing me on the cheek to say good night. But I was far too tired and overwhelmed."

"And then I suppose you do not recall him later leaving?"

"I'm afraid not. I wish that I could be of help, Colonel. I really do."

"Did he have any enemies? Or perhaps have an altercation, even a minor one, in the short time we've been on this ship?"

"Of course not. My husband was a kind and generous man. He never had a harsh word for anyone." For a moment she closed her eyes tightly, her voice shaking with emotion.

There was a soft knock at the door; Dory answered it and returned with a tea tray. She poured a cup of tea for Lady Caraway and offered one to Geoff, which he refused.

"Was he—" Geoff paused, not quite able to bring himself to ask about an affair so directly, not when confronted by her pale face "—acting at all strangely?" he finished a bit lamely.

She stared at him.

Taking it as incomprehension, he tried again. "Did he often absent himself at odd hours?"

"Colonel, please!" Lady Caraway's hand shook; she would have spilled her tea into her lap if Dory hadn't moved quickly to steady her. "There is nothing I can say to help you. Nothing unusual or out of place. I've been asleep all night. If only I hadn't been, maybe I could have prevented this somehow!"

Dory gave him a long look, murmuring, "It's all right," to the lady.

Perhaps she did know something, but as distraught as she seemed, he wouldn't find out anything useful now, and he had no desire to push the lady into another attack of the sort they'd seen at dinner. He rose to his feet. "If you will excuse me ladies, I need not upset you further, I think. Please, do let me know if you remember anything at all."

"I won't," Lady Caraway said, her voice harsh with tears. "I won't."

Geoff bowed to the ladies and left the room quickly. As he left the room, he ran into the doctor; he caught the man before he could fall, but barely. He held on to the doctor's jacket of deep maroon cotton broadcloth, until he was certain that the man was steady on his feet. He caught a sour whiff of alcohol in the process; the doctor hadn't been joking about the brandy in his room. "Doctor."

"Colonel." Dr. Lehmacher attempted a rather unsteady bow. "Have you just been to see Lady Caraway? Is she all right? Did she...see anything?"

"I think she's quite shaken. And was solidly asleep all evening, so I'm afraid she is of no help to our investigation."

The doctor nodded, swaying dangerously in time with the motion. "I am sorry to hear that. I thought maybe I should look in on her."

"I think the only thing you ought to look in on right now is your pillow, dear fellow. You're in no state to minister to anyone's health at the moment."

The doctor leaned against the wall. "Perhaps you're right."

"It's been a terrible night for us all, I'm sure. Miss Dory is with Lady Caraway now; I'm sure if things take a worrying turn, she will fetch you. Go to bed, man."

"Yes...yes, you're right." The doctor nodded, his head not quite straight on his neck. "I'll go to bed. And you ought to as well, Colonel."

"Oh, I will, fear not." Geoff waited until Dr. Lehmacher was well on his way back down the hall before leaving. Doing his best to ignore the steadily increasing twinge in his leg, he followed the labyrinth of corridors to the bridge.

It was a marvel of modern technology, gleaming brass and lovingly polished wood, thousands of dials and levers and wheels that regulated every aspect of life on board the great airship. Officers in sober blue with shining brass buttons moved back and forth between the instrument panels. Even more impressive was the view, a one hundred and eighty degree panorama of the sky, with the stars and moon ahead and the silent clouds entirely cloaking the landscape far below. The colors of false dawn were just beginning to flow over the wind-stirred tops, the sun itself still hiding behind the distant curve of the horizon.

Little could he enjoy these wonders, however, with a mind spun in circles by too many questions. It seemed obvious that Lord Caraway had been conducting some sort of affair. Was his mistress married and her husband on board, thus making this a death caused by impassioned vengeance? Had he been robbed perhaps, as he left his clandestine rendezvous in a crime of opportunity? Or was there another hidden dimension to this bit of robbery? Absurd though it seemed, he could not put the potential presence of the notorious pirate Captain Ramos entirely from his mind.

"Ah, Colonel...I have been expecting you," Captain MacConnell said. He was a large man, almost too tall for the corridors of his own ship, and well built besides. His red-brown hair and neat beard were salted with white. "Has the matter been resolved?"

"Not yet," Geoff said, frowning. "Murder is far more complex than guarding my employer's property from common thieves." As worried as he had been over his new job, it was nothing compared to the strain of dealing with Lord Caraway's death. That sort of thing had most decidedly not been in the job description.

"So it is true. A damned shame." The captain gave him a little half bow. "And please, don't think me unappreciative. You are far more qualified to handle this matter than any of the guards, or I would never have troubled you."

Feeling slightly mollified, Geoff cleared his throat. "Indeed. I understand you have been put in an awkward position, Captain."

"Any service that I and my crew can render is yours. I want this matter resolved before we unload at port."

"We are in agreement. I shouldn't like to give the murderer the chance to escape." And into his new home duchy no less—that wouldn't do at all. He cleared his throat again, refocusing his mind on the details of the matter at hand. "I've a list of all the crew that live in that hallway. I need to know where they were all of last night, and if any saw unusual comings or goings around cabin number...let me see...one fifty-one. And of course if anyone saw Lord Caraway or any other person of interest moving about near that fateful hour. This second list is...Captain, it should go without saying, but I am compelled to speak even so. I trust our conversation will be kept in the strictest confidence?" He waited for the captain to nod before continuing. "I have gathered the names of women in your crew who may have...loose moral character. Lord Caraway was involved in some sort of affair, and the woman involved must be found." He held out the lists to the captain. "I do not think I need to see to each of them personally if you believe your guards are up to the task. I will only need to question the ones who are inconsistent or otherwise suspicious."

"I'll see that it is done." The captain hesitated, and then asked, "Was there nothing of interest or worth found on the body? No clues at all?"

Geoff gave him a thin smile. "I'm afraid this is no penny dreadful mystery, Captain. Perhaps the most interesting fact is that nothing was found on him at all...barely his own clothing, even. I think he may have been robbed, though if that was the motivation behind his death, I cannot say." He considered. "Yes, I think you ought to have your guards search the cabins belonging to the servants and see if any have possessions that they ought not have."

"That will be done as well, then. Is there anything further?"

"No, I think not. Before I can find the next turn in the path, I need more information."

"I will see to it that you have that information." The captain glanced at the ornate clock that sat in the panels near the ship's wheel, above the compass. "You've still got a few hours before breakfast will be served. Perhaps you should take some rest in the meantime, Colonel, while the guards do the legwork for you. You look like you've been used rather hard, if you take my meaning."

"Indeed I do. Though I doubt I'll be able to sleep, with so many suppositions rattling around in my head." He rubbed one hand against his cheek, grimacing at the scratch of unruly stubble. "I think I can be convinced to at least retire briefly in order to attend to my toilet." He took his leave of the captain and returned to his room, his mind swirling with the image of Lord Caraway's head surrounded by a sticky halo of blood.

AFTER SHAVING, GEOFF INTENDED to lie down on the cabin's small bed, just to close his eyes for a few minutes before it was time to prepare for breakfast. He'd barely undone the buttons on his vest, however, when there was more knocking on his door. He opened it quickly; this time it was one of the stewards on the other side. "Yes?"

"If you'll come with me, sir, we've found something we think you ought to see," the steward said, touching his cap respectfully.

Geoff's eyebrows went up a little with surprise. "That was quite fast, wasn't it?"

"Our guards, sir, they don't mess about their business." He led Geoff back down to the crew quarters. A guard stood outside one of the cabin doors, at attention. Another guard was inside the small cabin, where a rather disreputable-looking deckhand sat on the bed.

The man glared at Geoff. He rose and said, "You've got no right—"

"Shut it," the guard said. "Or I'll hold you down for the gentleman."

Geoff frowned. "What have you found, officer?"

"We were doing the cabin search as ordered, sir, and found some stolen property in the possession of this...gentleman." The guard offered Geoff a cigar box.

"And this 'gentleman's' name?" Geoff asked as he opened the box.

"Stark," the deckhand spat out.

"Mr. Stark." Out of habit, Geoff added, "A pleasure, I'm sure." He examined the inside of the cigar box with great interest. Most of the shining contents were obviously the property of women. The pocket watch, however, was a different matter. Using his pen, Geoff lifted the pocket watch up carefully by its chain. It was badly dented, its face cracked, and the hands no longer moved. The time was stopped at two sixteen. "Where did you come by this?"

"Found it," the man said.

"Found it on the body of a dead man, I gather," Geoff said mildly.

"I ain't no grave robber," the man said, drawing himself up.

"No, sir, you are a thief, and now it would seem a murderer."

"I didn't kill no one!" the deckhand shouted. "I found it, just found it. I didn't see no body!"

Geoff snorted, shaking his head. He reached for his handkerchief, but remembered that he'd given it to Dory. "Your handkerchief, if you please," he said to the guard. "Thank you." He wrapped the watch up, put it in his pocket, and then favored the deckhand with a narrow-eyed look. "There'll be a noose waiting for you in the Grand Duchy of Denver."

"I said I didn't kill no one! I found it fair and square."

Geoff began to poke through the cigar box again with his pen, ignoring the deckhand. He turned up the golden owl pin that Lord Caraway had worn to dinner; it was half coated with blackened, dried blood. "Show me your hands," he ordered the deckhand.

The deckhand said something vile; the guard cuffed him across the jaw, and then yanked up his hands for Geoff to inspect. The man had obviously not washed his hands in quite some time; dirt and grease streaked them, creating smudged rims around his fingernails. Geoff took the lorgnette back from his pocket and peered at the man's hands from every angle, but found no shining trace of blood.

It was possible, of course, that this man had committed the crime and just worn gloves in order to do so, discarding them later. In such a case, a dense layer of dirt would provide a fine sort of alibi. Geoff glanced at the deckhand again, considering the man's low breeding and mean countenance. While he knew criminals were by no means stupid as a class—otherwise there would be no need for men like himself—the chances that this deckhand possessed the necessary forethought seemed vanishingly slim.

"Either way, you'll be spending time in gaol when we arrive," he said, holding up the pin. "You say that you found this? If you want to save yourself from a long drop with a swift stop, you had better show me where."

The deckhand gave him a hate-filled glare, of which Geoff took no notice. He could almost see the rusty processes of the man's brain working, taking him to the inevitable conclusion that ten years in a work crew was preferable to dancing at the end of a rope. It took a depressingly long time for him to figure that out. "Fine," he snarled. "If your boys'll let me up."

Muttering dire curses, the deckhand took them to the staircase, and then led them up two floors. Near the toilets, reserved for use by the passengers, there was a small potted plant on a decorative table. "In here," he said, pointing at the plant's pot. Geoff bent to examine it, turning the pot to take advantage of the lamp on the wall; it only took him a moment to find the spot of blood on the inside of the rim. He nodded to himself. "Get him out of my sight," he said to the guard. "I've got no further use for him."

The deckhand squirmed and spat as he was dragged away, until the guard struck him again and grabbed him by the hair. Geoff paid scant attention. It made little sense that Lord Caraway's valuables had been dumped so carelessly; it was becoming obvious that theft had not been the murderer's true aim, but rather the appearance of it. He dug carefully through the top layer of dirt in the plant's pot, but found no sign of the man's wedding band either.

Frowning to himself, he went into the men's toilet, checking around it thoroughly. The sink and counter had been wiped down recently, showing a smear of dry water spots. Grimacing, he examined the toilet and was gratified to discover a tiny smudge of blood, fresh enough to sparkle for the lorgnette. He compared the mark to those his own hands might make and concluded that the mark had likely been made by the side of a man's thumb, grasping the chain to flush.

"Unexpected," he said, straightening up. "That certainly changes everything." Knowing that the perpetrator had intended murder, not mere thievery, set his sights on a new class of suspects: the passengers, all men of good breeding. That knowledge left him no less determined, but distinctly less comfortable. Why would a murderer immediately feel the need to use the toilet, especially before washing the evidence from his hands?

Frowning to himself in thought, he returned to the bridge and handed the cigar box to Captain MacConnell, thinking it best that it be kept in the ship's safe until it could be turned over to the regular police force in Denver. The captain eyed the contents of the little box with raised eyebrows, stirring through them with one blunt finger before frowning. "Did you find anything else in the plant?"

"No, nothing." Geoff frowned, something in the captain's question rousing his suspicion. "What did you expect me to find?"

"Some sort of clue, I suppose. Nothing in particular." The captain turned away.

Geoff's temper, already frayed by a night of stress and little sleep, snapped. He whipped his cane around as if it was his old saber, slamming it into the brass railing to the side of the captain.

The railing rang like a bell; as the sound died out, the bridge was silent. "I do not appreciate having my efforts hampered by half-truths. I cannot possibly solve our mutual problem if I am not in full possession of the facts!"

Captain MacConnell turned back toward him, face darkened with anger. "You go too far, Colonel."

"No, sir, you do. Twice you have asked me if I found something, without specifying what, and were disappointed when I said no."

"I have done nothing of the sort." The captain crossed his arms over his chest, face going pale.

Geoff flicked his cane up to point at the man's nose. No matter how fatigued he felt, his hand was still rock steady. "What is it that you are so desperate for me to find, Captain?"

The captain opened his mouth, but shut it quickly as Geoff's glare intensified. At last, he looked away. "My master key for the ship. Lord Caraway and I have been friends for quite some time. He asked to borrow it so that he could make use of a few rooms privately. As he is—" he caught himself "—was a trustworthy, dear friend, I allowed him to do so."

"You allowed someone to borrow the master key for the ship," Geoff repeated, dumbfounded. It was a breach of security that took his breath away; the master key opened every door on the ship, including the vulnerable engine rooms and the cargo holds. He dropped the tip of the can back down on the floor, needing to lean on it.

"Perhaps now you understand why I was somewhat reticent in sharing that information."

"Do you realize what risk you've put us all at?" Geoff demanded.

"If I had it to do over again, I would certainly make a different decision," Captain MacConnell snapped.

Geoff passed one hand over his forehead, trying to think. "Did anyone know that Lord Caraway had the key?"

"I doubt it. He gave me his word he would be discreet, and his word has never been broken. Perhaps his wife."

"Who is an innocent victim in this sordid mess," Geoff said bitterly. "So the key may be in possession of someone completely unknown. You had better post every guard you have at your disposal, and now."

"I had hoped it would turn up with Lord Caraway's missing possessions. I can offer nothing further."

"I see." Geoff turned to leave, his back stiff.

"Colonel, I would appreciate it if you could keep my own indiscretion from becoming a matter of public record."

Geoff had no reply for that. Instead, he gave the captain a long, intense look, and stalked off the bridge. This new problem was almost too much to bear and put his primary mission on this cursed airship in grave danger. It was possible, he thought, that whoever was in possession of the key might not know what he had; in that case, it was imperative to keep that fact quiet while simultaneously leaving no stone unturned in the search. But how to accomplish that particular feat was beyond him, when now even the guards themselves might be suspect; more well-bred men than they had turned to criminal efforts in the past when such a golden opportunity presented itself.

He was so lost in thought as he walked that the ship's bell ringing to announce breakfast startled him quite badly. Breakfast. He ought to have breakfast. The mind could not operate without fuel.

As he passed by the passenger cabins, following the scent of bacon toward the dining room, he caught sight of Lieutenant Collins and Professor Jefferson. Both were men with whom he'd intended to speak. It seemed both felicitous and suspicious to see them together in urgent conversation.

"Gentlemen?"

"Ah, Colonel, sir. Was the lady all right? She looked a bit under the weather when I woke her up," Lieutenant Collins said.

"Terrible business," Professor Jefferson agreed. "Just terrible." At the narrow-eyed gaze Geoff directed at him, he hastened to add, "Matthew came by my cabin after he'd discharged his duties to you. He was quite distraught, poor man. They were such good friends."

Geoff frowned. "As all right as can be expected, though no thanks to you, Lieutenant. I told you to breathe not a word of the tragedy to her."

"But I didn't, sir!" the lieutenant said, sounding quite affronted.

How then, could the lady have already been acquainted with the tragic events? Perhaps Dr. Lehmacher had seen fit to inform her. The man had seemed quite undone, and some had a sad tendency to share their distress with all around them. Though if that were the case, it was also a sad reflection on the doctor that Lady Caraway had taken her husband's death with far more poise and grace than he.

"Was she already awake when you went by her cabin?" Geoff asked.

"I should think so, sir. She wasn't quick to answer the door and looked a frightful mess."

Geoff nodded, looking at Professor Jefferson. "You seem a bit troubled yourself, sir."

The professor sighed. "While I shudder to seem too small-minded in the face of such tragedy, I think someone's gone through my cabin. It's so subtle I admit that it might all be in my imagination, but I could have sworn that things were a bit rearranged in my absence last night. I thought it best to inform the lieutenant of the possibility, even if it just turns out to be the wandering mind of an old man as the cause."

"You may not be as out of sorts as you think, Professor. A few hours ago, a thief was caught by the guardsmen aboard and I interviewed him myself. I think it best that you check over your belongings carefully and make certain none are missing. I've turned over the property the thief had on him to the captain." Geoff smiled tightly. "But rest assured, you shan't be troubled by a thief again this trip."

"Excellent work, Colonel, and you even out of your home Duchy," the professor said, clapping Geoff on the back.

"Glad to know it, sir, though a black mark on us that we didn't catch him before now," Lieutenant Collins said, looking far less cheerful about the subject.

Geoff then took the opportunity to question the professor delicately about Lord Caraway's disposition the previous night, but the gentleman had noticed nothing at all untoward. Satisfied that there was nothing else to be learned, Geoff excused himself when his stomach uttered a rather undignified grumble, one that all three of them were at least able to laugh about.

"Hard work, catching thieves," Lieutenant Collins said.

"And there seem no end to criminals wanting to be caught." The work on the *Titania* would be a mere first act for the greater array of challenges waiting in Denver, including the greatest challenge of capturing Captain Ramos, who had taken down his predecessor. Geoff bowed to the two men and quickly resumed his journey to the dining room.

Breakfast was a much less formal affair, and the passengers had dressed accordingly, in more comfortable suits and dresses that would allow them to stroll around the ship after eating. There were also far fewer people present than there had been for dinner. Geoff looked over the dining room, searching for a familiar face. Unsurprisingly, Lady Caraway was absent; he doubted she would want to be seen in public for the rest of the short journey. Dr. Lehmacher, too, was absent, though as tired and drunk as the man had seemed the night before, Geoff was not surprised.

Geoff did spot Dory, seated at a mostly empty table, wearing a dress in a nearly flattering shade of lilac. She met his gaze, which really gave him no choice but to sit with her and make inconsequential small talk until the waiters had brought their breakfast plates and they'd begun eating.

"I am surprised to see you up and about, Miss Dory," he said, "rather than sleeping late after your adventures last night."

"It seems like a great many people have chosen to sleep in. But…if I'm already too nervous to sleep much to begin with, I can hardly bring myself to even lie down again after such events."

He kept his voice low. "Is Lady Caraway all right?"

"As well as can be expected. I sat with her for quite some time before she said she was feeling unwell again and wished to be alone." She sighed. "I am planning to look in on her again after we finish eating. I'm rather worried."

He nodded. "If you wouldn't mind my presence, I should like to come along. I've recovered Lord Caraway's pocket watch and lapel pin; I thought perhaps she might like them back." It would also afford him the opportunity to ask her about the key, though he doubted she would be of any help. Lord Caraway had used a room in the crew quarters that was supposed to be locked; there was little doubt that he'd had the key with him at the time of his death.

"Oh!" Dory exclaimed, and then quickly quieted as some of the other diners glanced toward her. "Did you find the horrible person that…you know?"

"We apprehended the thief," Geoff said, after a moment of consideration. "I think that the man who committed the act is a different person, however. So you must remain cautious."

"Oh my…" Dory covered her mouth with her hand for a moment, her eyes wide with shock. "How terrible."

But she rallied and continued,, "I…Well, don't tell anyone this, but I did a bit of eavesdropping before you arrived to entertain me. No one's talking about the incident. I think, perhaps, it has been kept under wraps?"

"If the captain has managed to do so, he deserves a medal." Geoff allowed himself a bitter smile; he had little doubt the captain was frantically doing damage control behind the scenes, considering his personal, if peripheral, involvement.

"But I'm sure Lady Caraway will be much relieved. She was most concerned last night that this terrible business would reflect badly on her family. She made me promise three times that I would not tell a soul."

"You're telling me."

Dory laughed. "Don't be silly. Since you already no doubt know far more than I, speaking with you isn't breaking her confidence."

Geoff couldn't help but laugh at that. "If only I did know far more than you. I'm afraid that we're both still equally in the dark."

"I'm certain that you shall prevail," Dory said, setting her teacup down quite firmly.

THEY FINISHED THEIR BREAKFAST with less heavy conversation. Geoff offered Dory his arm and escorted her from the dining room. Together, they went down the hallway to Lady Caraway's suite. Geoff knocked on the door, again, a third time. There was no answer.

"Maybe she's still resting," Dory said.

"Perhaps. Though if she said she was feeling unwell...I find that a bit worrying."

Dory nodded. For a moment, she contemplated the door, her expression suspiciously like a pout. "Well, there can't be any harm in trying the doorknob. I don't recall hearing her lock up after me, so she may have forgotten." The knob turned under her hand and she opened the door slowly, calling, "Lady Caraway? I'm terribly sorry to intrude, but we're a bit worried about you..."

The sitting room was as it had been the night before, the tea tray still on the table and the curtains drawn back. Geoff followed Dory inside, shielding his eyes from the sudden brightness and closing the door behind them. He felt cold, the skin of his forehead prickling; there was another possible explanation for the door being unlocked, and he didn't like it one bit.

"Now I'm very worried." Dory hesitated. "Do you think perhaps I should…" She pointed toward the bedroom.

"I think that would be a very good idea. In case she has taken ill."

"And the worst she can do is shout at me, I suppose. Please stay back. I don't want to cause her more embarrassment."

"Of course." Geoff edged back toward the door, averting his eyes for good measure. He swallowed against a throat gone suddenly dry.

Dory tapped on the bedroom door. When there was no response, she opened the door a crack, and then more fully. "Lady Caraway? Lady…Colonel, I think something is wrong, she—Oh no!"

Geoff hurried inside the doorway to the sound of Dory's shriek. He had just enough time to take in the scene—Lady Caraway curled up among a nest of bedcovers, hands knotted into claws at her chest, Dory backing away in horror—before Dory collapsed down into a swoon.

Geoff tried to catch her, but his hold wasn't secure and she was heavier than expected. He almost fell down himself, and ended up having to lower her to the floor in an undignified jumble. Her skirts were in disarray, and he caught a flash of a surprisingly shapely leg before he realized that he really ought to look away.

"Miss Dory? Miss Dory?" He bent to pat her face, but there was no response. He hurried from the room as quickly as his leg would allow, and burst into the hallway. He dimly remembered which room he'd seen Dr. Lehmacher near; he half ran down the hall to it and pounded on the door.

There was a muffled crash inside, followed by a curse. The doctor jerked the door open. He looked worse than he had the night before, if it was possible, his eyes sunk deeply into his skull. For a moment, the doctor gaped at him before stammering, "Colonel?"

"Get your medical bag. Something's happened to Lady Caraway, and Miss Dory has collapsed."

To his credit, the doctor didn't pause to ask any more questions. He ducked back in to his room—another crash, as if he'd tripped over something, followed by a curse—and reappeared a moment later with a black leather bag in his hands.

Dory was sprawled on the floor where he'd left her, insensible. Dr. Lehmacher hesitated a moment, looking at the girl, and Geoff impatiently waved him toward Lady Caraway, who appeared to be in a much more dire condition. He knelt down by Dory and felt her forehead—cool and perhaps a little clammy—and then, trying not to look, twitched the corner of her skirt back down to cover her legs properly. "How is she?" he asked the doctor.

Lehmacher straightened up, his expression blank. "Beyond my help, I'm afraid. It appears that the lady passed away during the night." He left the bedside and knelt on the carpet next to Dory, checking her pulse. "At least our friend, here, I can help." He reached into his black leather bag and drew out a small vial of smelling salts. Waving that near Dory's nose had the desired effect. She jerked into wakefulness, sneezing in a most undignified manner.

"Colonel? Doctor?" she asked, bewildered.

"Here, come along," Geoff said, taking her arm to help her up. "I'm afraid you've had another nasty shock."

Dory struggled to her feet. Upon looking at poor Lady Caraway, curled up in her bed, and she began to cry. "I must be cursed," she wailed. "I must be."

"Now, no need for that," Geoff said. "Come along." He gently led her from the room and helped her to one of the couches in the sitting room. Once she was settled, though still crying disconsolately, he took a moment to use the telephone to call for the guards. He checked the bottles that sat in the room's small cabinet, selected the brandy, and poured a small glass for Dory. "Here, drink this. Will you be all right if I step into the other room?"

She nodded, sniffling.

When he returned to Lady Caraway's bedroom, Dr. Lehmacher had rolled her onto her back and was looking into her eyes. Geoff sniffed delicately at the air; along with the smells that invariably accompanied death, he caught a hint of cloying sweetness. The top of the room's chest of drawers was in disarray. He delicately picked up a perfume bottle and sniffed at it, but the odor wasn't quite the same. "What killed her?"

"I think she suffered some sort of nervous attack. Or perhaps her heart gave out. See how even in death she clutches at her chest?" Dr. Lehmacher shook his head. "Perhaps the death of her husband was too much for her; her health has always been a bit tenuous." He took a moment to button the cuffs of his shirt; he hadn't grabbed a jacket in the rush out of his room, though he wore his gloves.

Geoff came to the doctor's side for a closer look. She showed none of the signs that he associated with violent death; her eyes were unblemished, and there were no obvious bruises. "A true tragedy for her family." He had seen someone suffering a heart palpitation once; they had tripped and stumbled, and he supposed that could account for the mess on top of the chest of drawers, though that seemed too easy—just like assuming that she'd simply forgotten to lock her cabin's door. As he leaned over her, he caught another whiff of that cloying sweetness, but it was gone quickly. "Can you tell how long she's been dead?"

"Her muscles have begun to go stiff. But not so much that she cannot be moved. Three, perhaps four hours."

Long after he had taken his leave of the lady and Dory, then. He looked at the doctor for a moment, peering hard at the man. He was pale, but composed. "I must laud your professionalism."

"After the tragedy that pulled me from my bed early this morning, I confess to finding myself somewhat numb."

"I understand. Thank you for your help."

"Indeed," the doctor said. "I'll go check on Miss Dory, with your leave. There's nothing to be done here."

Geoff waved the man off before bending to examine Lady Caraway a bit more closely. He lifted one of her hands, and noted that that there was something under her fingernails. He scraped a bit of it out with his penknife; it appeared to be skin. Geoff frowned. The lorgnette confirmed a trace of blood as well, and another small spot on the lady's sleeve, though when he rolled it up there was nothing but a miniscule bruise at the crook of her elbow.

There were means of murder that could make death look natural, and natural enough to fool a doctor who was distracted by personal grief; it would be naive to not consider that fact. He walked out of the bedroom to see that the guards had arrived. "I think I'd best go talk to Captain MacConnell."

Dr. Lehmacher nodded. "Of course. I'm going to escort Miss Dory to her room, then, and get her settled."

"Thank you, sir." He took his leave and returned to the bridge.

Captain MacConnell greeted him as cordially as ever, though he couldn't hide the concern in his eyes. "Colonel, we're about eight hours from port now. Have you had any success finding the culprit?"

"The matter remains murky," Geoff admitted. "And I also bear unhappy news; Lady Caraway is now dead, Captain."

The man took a step back, grabbing onto the railing that surrounded the ship's wheel for support. "Foul play?"

"Perhaps," Geoff said. "I haven't ruled out the possibility."

The captain shook his head. "This is insane."

"It may well be." Geoff tapped his cane against the deck plates. "Whoever is now in possession of your key did the deed, I believe. It must be found."

"The crew has been searched, and nothing has turned up. Though if the murderer is clever, the key could be hidden nearly anywhere."

Geoff shook his head sharply. "Not the crew. The passengers."

Captain MacConnell looked nothing short of horrified. "With all due respect—"

Geoff cut him off with a sharp wave of his hand. "The deed was done by one of the passengers. I am certain of it."

The captain still shook his head. "There are many powerful people amongst the passengers, Colonel. They will take offense—"

"Then you tell them that I ordered the searches, under the authority of the Grand Duke. If you must, wait until we're in the duchy's air space. Use whatever excuse you must." He paused, pinching the bridge of his nose. "Give me a passenger manifest.

I'll attempt to divine some likely suspects so that we're not just shooting in the dark."

"If you're certain there's no other way..."

"It's that, or risk letting a murderer escape."

Captain MacConnell bowed his head. "Let us hope that we need not turn over too many stones."

As Geoff left the bridge and moved down the hall, a steward ran after him, a sheaf of papers in his hand. Geoff took the passenger lists with a bare nod of acknowledgment, scanning over them quickly. No names leaped out at him. His mind swirled, trying to form connections between the missing key, the murder, the second possible murder...Breakfast, he thought, that was the place to start. He doubted the murderer would be so cold-blooded as to calmly go to breakfast after killing twice. And considering the state of the crew cabin, perhaps he needed to examine which passengers were married. It seemed likely Lord Caraway had been stepping out with a married woman, and thus his death was an act of revenge. But why, then, kill the Lady Caraway as well?

There were too many factors for an exhausted mind unaccustomed to such problems to tie together at once. He needed to write the facts down, see everything together and connected like the strands of a spider web in black and white. Then the answer might present itself, or at least a reasonable avenue of investigation.

At the thought of writing, he automatically reached into his pocket, his fingers searching for his pen. He encountered nothing. Geoff paused, trying to recall when he'd last had it; he knew that he'd put it in his pocket before leaving his room for breakfast, and could think of no incident during the meal that would have caused him to lose it. But later, when they'd found Lady Caraway's body, when Dory had fallen in to a faint, they'd been tangled up for a moment, and perhaps...He changed course, heading for that cabin instead.

The guard at the door nodded to him, stepping aside. He walked purposefully into the bedroom, glancing around, eying the carpet in particular. At first he noticed nothing, but when he moved to change his angle of view, a glint of silver caught his eye. He knelt down and reached under the chest of drawers to retrieve his pen from where it had rolled.

There was something caught in the clip on the pen's cap. Geoff stood, examining the small scrap of cloth. The edges were ragged, as if it had been torn from a much larger piece. He held it close to the lamp, examining the color—a dark maroon—and the cloth—a thick cotton.

Geoff's eyes narrowed as he recalled the color of Dr. Lehmacher's jacket, which he had seen the night before as he left Lady Caraway's room. And this morning, the good doctor had been wearing gloves, even though he'd forgotten his jacket in his room. Gloves, he thought, to hide scratches; to hide the marks left behind by a woman struggling for her life with an assailant who stood behind her, driving him back into the chest of drawers, knocking over all of the perfume bottles...

"Fool! You blind, blind fool." Then he recalled where the doctor had said he would be: escorting Dory back to her room. He bolted for the door.

"Sir?" the guard asked.

"You have a passenger list. Tell me which cabin belongs to Miss Isadora Alvarez!" Geoff yanked his own copy of the list from his pocket, fumbling through sheets he'd already put out of order.

The guard fumbled his own list from his breast pocket. "Cabin 5C, sir."

"Follow me," Geoff commanded. Not glancing back to see if the man was doing as told, he hurried down the hallway, scattering papers as he went. He didn't pause at Dory's door, but twisted the knob and flung the door open, sending it crashing against the wall.

Dory's cabin was barely bigger than his own. The tiny floor space was covered by a man sprawled across it: Dr. Lehmacher. The doctor's bag sat open on the small desk. Geoff caught a heavy whiff of the same cloying scent he'd caught in Lady Carraway's room.

Geoff paused to check the doctor's pulse. The man was still alive, but unresponsive, even to being slapped. The glove had been pulled from one of his hands, revealing the angry red scratches that Geoff now expected. A golden wedding band glittered on that hand as well, too big for the finger that it encircled.

Still trying to make sense of it, Geoff looked at the doctor's black bag. In its shadow, there was a dark glass bottle, and a crumpled handkerchief. He checked the label on the bottle: chloroform. Cautiously, he prodded the handkerchief, catching another cloying whiff that left him dizzy.

The handkerchief was his, the one he'd loaned to Dory last night. Taunting him.

"Sir?" the guard said.

"Whatever alert you can call, do it," Geoff snapped, hot rage crawling up his spine. "Don't let anyone in or out of this room. And find the woman. *Now.*"

Geoff lurched from the cabin, slamming the door behind him, his mind racing. That a woman had done all this was bizarre and completely unexpected, but it had to be her. And it was too soon, he thought, too soon for someone so clever to reveal themselves, for that was what it had to be: intentional. Why else leave the doctor displayed so prominently in her cabin? Why else place his handkerchief just so? Unless she had another way to escape, a way that left nothing to chance discovery.

He began to limp down the hall, faster and faster, as his thoughts reached that conclusion, that inescapable conclusion. It took him past baffled guards, crew members, and other passengers. He ignored anything that they said, heading like an arrow for the cargo bay.

The hefty, gasketed door was unlocked, an accusation of guilt in and of itself, but was still difficult to open; the air was under much greater pressure in the living area of the ship than it was in the cargo bay. Growling with effort and anger, he yanked it open and stalked into the bay.

It was noisy with the rush of the wind outside; his breath frosted in the far too thin air as he wound his way through the dim, orderly rows of crates stacked ten feet high. He was out of breath and dizzy when he reached the end.

The cargo bay doors were open, showing brilliant blue sky and white clouds. At the open doors, a woman stood, face covered with a leather air mask and goggles. All she had in common with the girl he had known as "Dory" was her hair, dark brown and wild in the howling wind. She wore men's clothing, a scarlet frock coat, and brown buckskin pants. Even her posture had changed, her shoulders taking an aggressive set. She carried a cloth satchel strapped across her chest.

And of all insolent things, she was waiting, obviously waiting. When she caught sight of him, she offered him a bow, unhooking the mask so she could speak, not in the least out of breath in the thin air. He lunged toward her, but she danced back.

"Come forward again and I shall throw myself out of this airship," she said, her voice much lower than the tone she had used as Dory. "And then you shan't have anyone to prosecute."

"You!" Geoff shouted. "Murderer!"

"Hardly," the woman said. "Murder is just the sort of unreasoning crime of passion that I find deeply abhorrent."

"Liar! As if I'm to believe anything you say!"

"When you look over your evidence, you'll see it line up if you don't willfully blind yourself to it. But I will do you the courtesy of explaining the bare bones of the events, dearest Colonel." The woman leaned casually against the arm of the loading crane. "Lord Caraway had the captain's master key because he wished to have a secret rendezvous with a lover. They met in the crew quarters because there were no other empty cabins or private rooms to be had. His wife, suspicious, followed, and caught them in the act. When he tried to give chase, in her rage, she pushed him down the stairs, and then took his wedding ring for reasons of her own."

"I hardly think such a frail woman…"

"Hardly think is correct," she said, her tone bitter. "You waste so much time underestimating us, Colonel, and do your treasured cause of law and order no service by discounting fifty percent of the population as suspects. I have no doubt that you know the sort of strength that can be bestowed by the unreasoning rage of the betrayed. Women are just as capable of that feeling." She dismissed his further attempt at protest with a flick of her fingers. "His lover, terrified of discovery, attempted to make it look like a robbery, taking his obvious jewelry and running in blind panic."

"And that was you."

"Don't be stupid. That was Dr. Lehmacher."

"That—that—that's unnatural!" The very thought of it left him feeling sick, but a traitorous corner of his mind said that sick might indeed be the explanation for the smudge of blood in the men's toilet. He'd seen many a pale recruit lose their composure and their last meal upon the death of a friend, let alone a…And that was where he stopped that thought.

She looked at him coldly. "Judge as you like. I tend to think that murder is a crime against nature, and the rest is none of your concern. Anyway, it was mere luck that I happened upon Lord Caraway's body and liberated the master key before raising the alarm. It saved me a great deal of trouble." She glanced out the cargo bay doors. "Later, the good doctor confronted Lady Caraway and saw to her demise, though out of desire for revenge or desire to protect himself from blackmail, I cannot guess. My money would be on revenge, since it was he who took Lord Caraway's wedding ring from her. If you examine her body carefully, you'll find a needle mark where he injected air into one of her veins after first pacifying her with chloroform."

"Then what was your part in this?" Geoff demanded. Already, he cursed himself for not seeing things that seemed so obvious in retrospect, for being so trusting of the wrong people. It was a lesson he would not soon forget.

"Only the most superficial. I had other matters to attend to on this ship and just so happened to be in the right place at the right time, I suppose you could say. Though it was jolly fun to give you a hand."

"What other business?" He could already guess, his gut sinking.

She smiled. "Oh, but that would be telling. You'll find out soon enough." Again, that quick glance out the doors. "I do hope to hear that when you hang Lehmacher, it will be for his actions as a murderer rather than his poor decision to help a married man commit adultery."

"Or you'll do what?" Geoff managed something like a smirk, edging forward.

"If you wish me to make your life a bigger misery than your predecessor's was, I'll be happy to oblige. And now I must take my leave."

"My predecessor? Wait…who are you?"

"Captain Ramos, at your service." She bowed mockingly, as a man would.

"Impossible!" Captain Ramos was discussed like the top prey for big game hunters among the upper echelons of security, but always in terms of who would achieve undying fame by taking *him* down.

But perhaps that had been one more bit unconscionable ego on the part of a field inhabited by men.

"Obviously not impossible, as I stand before you." She smirked. "But perhaps highly improbable." Without a backward glance, she jumped from the cargo bay doors. He caught one instant of her shape against the sky, perfect and streamlined like a diver, and then she was gone.

Geoff let out a shout of horror, all but forgetting his anger for a moment. He lunged forward as if he could stop her, barely catching himself against the support from the loading crane to stop from tumbling out the doors himself. For a moment, the support post sang with tension, and he realized that there was a thin silk rope, colored gray to make it difficult to see, tied securely there. For a moment, he stared at the taut line. Suddenly it went slack. Geoff reeled the rope in, already knowing what would be at the end: nothing. Heart racing, he leaned out as far as he could, trying to see where she might have been gone. The roaring wind whipped his hair around his head. He saw only a rapidly dispersing trail of white smoke and steam.

There was nothing else to be done; he shut the cargo bay doors with the nearby pressure wheel before he slumped down to the floor, breathing heavily. "We'll see whose life ends up a misery," he said. "I don't give up easily."

ANOTHER CRAFT FLEW BELOW the airship, this one held aloft by wings and the power of a steam generator, instead of lighter than air gas. It was precisely where it was supposed to be, and at the right time, much to the approval of Marta Ramos, known until lately to the colonel as "Dory."

The thin rope stopped her free fall from the *Titania* about six feet above the little aeroplane. For a dizzying moment she swung back and forth; with perfect timing, she released the clip that held the rope to the harness she wore under her jacket and landed on top of the plane's wing, catching herself on the handholds. Grinning, she scrambled down into the copilot's seat, closing the glass canopy behind her.

"You can take us down now, Simms," she said.

"Aye, sir." Meriwether Octavian Simms, known by preference as simply "Simms," let the plane drop away from the airship, and then pointed its nose toward the still-distant mountains that lay west of the Grand Duchy of Denver. "You get everything you went in for?"

"Possibly even more." Marta unslung her satchel and opened it up, removing several leather-bound journals and a set of carefully folded papers. "I took the liberty of raiding Professor Jefferson's belongings since I've found some of his research rather interesting. And I hadn't realized it, but the dear man was actually on board to meet up with one Dr. Lehmacher. He'd recently been in Germany and had some secret papers to hand over, so I took those as well." She paused for a second, her lips curling into an amused smile. "That gentleman certainly won't have use for them. It's likely just some inbred idiot slighting another inbred idiot, but it could turn out to be useful."

"That's not quite what I meant, sir."

Marta was already paging through one of the journals, eying the chemical formulae therein. "Do stop being so obtuse, Simms."

The pilot snorted. "The jewels. You know, the ones the Grand Duke got for his daughter? The whole point of this jolly little adventure of yours? *Those* jewels?"

"Oh, those. Must you always be so concerned with money?"

"I may not be as good at math as you, but I know that jewels sell for money, and money equals food, thank you very much. And we've got no shortage of mouths to feed back home."

"Our financial situation has never been so desperate as that, I'm sure, so you needn't be dramatic." She dug back into the satchel. "You'd think that he'd invest in a more intelligent security chief and a better safe to transport them in." She came out with two black velvet boxes and opened one. "See? Here they are..." Her voice trailed off as she examined them. "Hm."

"Hm, what? What's that mean?"

Marta pulled a small magnifying glass from a pocket in her coat and examined the glittering jewelry that sat in the box. Suddenly, she laughed.

"I don't like it when you laugh like that," Simms said. "Particularly not when you're supposed to be answering my question."

"These are fake," Marta said, still laughing. "Lovely fakes... Certainly not cheap, well-crafted and the like, enough to pass cursory inspection. But fake nonetheless."

Simms started cursing, banging his hand on the control panel. They abruptly dropped two hundred feet in altitude before he got his temper and the aeroplane back under control. "So this has all been a complete waste?" he shouted.

"Don't be stupid. All the lovely data I've collected is far more valuable if you ask me, even if the payoff isn't immediate." She ignored what Simms muttered, snapping the box closed and dropping it back in to her satchel. "And you can give these to Dolly for costume jewelry."

Simms stopped shouting, somewhat mollified at the thought of giving his daughter such an apparently extravagant gift.

"I also solved two murders. Just for a lark."

"You—you *what?*"

"Stimulation for the mind, Simms. You ought to try it."

"You're talking about the lives of two people."

"It wasn't anyone you knew, if that's any comfort." She raised an eyebrow at his colorful protest. "Just two of the nobility caught up in sex and scandal. And I suppose that I should give credit where it's due. The Grand Duke's chief of security did help me out a bit with the legwork."

"You were hanging around with *him?*"

"Yet here I sit, uncaptured and capable of annoying you." Marta returned to the leather-bound journals, still chuckling quietly. "Perhaps this new chief of security isn't as dim as I thought he would be. It was quite fun."

"The things you think are fun…"

Marta waved one hand, dismissing the words. "Let me know when you're prepared to have a new conversation. That one has grown tiresome." When no new remark was forthcoming, she turned her attention back to the newly acquired books, seeking occupation for her mind as Simms guided the tiny aeroplane toward their home deep in the Rocky Mountains.

Captain Ramos was not a woman who took well to boredom.

MUCH LATER, COLONEL GEOFFREY Douglas opened the door to his cabin. Behind him, the sound of the ship's gong being struck four times filled the halls, signaling to the passengers that they were one hour from landing.

The woman may have escaped, but at least the murderer had not; Geoff had interrogated Dr. Lehmacher once the man woke from his chloroform-induced stupor and had confirmed nearly the same story that Captain Ramos had told him. Only a few rather inconsequential details were different. After the confession, he'd had the guards take the doctor to the brig, where he would wait until Geoff personally delivered him to the Grand Duke's gaol in Denver, to be tried for crimes against both society and nature.

Geoff sneered to himself. No matter what that infernal woman had said, he would be seeing the doctor hang for the full extent of his crimes.

Feeling bone weary, he took a moment to pour himself a brandy, which he set on top of the small safe he'd brought aboard. The now open, gaping, empty safe.

His predecessor might not have been terribly bright, but he'd left detailed enough reports for Geoff to piece together an idea of what sort of criminals he might be up against: smart ones, who believed all security chiefs were idiots. Idiots, for example, that would put valuable jewels in an easily moved and opened safe in an easily found room. Which was precisely why Geoff had brought just such a safe aboard, and placed a set of well-made fakes within it. A second set of fake jewels were hidden in his luggage, while a third set occupied the ship's safe. The real jewels were hidden in a crate of piano wire, stowed in the ship's tennis courts.

He'd made a terrible error underestimating the other half of his species. That lesson would be kept well in mind in the future, and better learned now rather than later.

And he was not the only one who had committed such an error this day.

Geoff sat on the bed and sipped his brandy, allowing himself just one moment of unbecoming smugness.

2
The Curious Case of
Miss Clementine Nimowitz
(And Her Exceedingly Tiny Dog)

IT WAS A PERFECTLY ordinary parlor, nicely decorated, pale lace doilies sitting atop furniture done in heavy brown and gold brocade. The general color scheme was maroon and brown, with enough pink and yellow accents to keep it all from seeming too heavy or dark. While many such parlors were given to clutter as the wealthy owners attempted to display both their taste and overflow of cash with countless bits of frilly golden bric-a-brac, this one was neat and carefully tended, enough empty space around objects to draw the eye and invite inspection without being overwhelming. It was austere and quietly dignified.

The careful effect of the decorating was, quite unfortunately, spoiled by the body majestically putrefying in the center of the rich carpet, a petite pistol with a mother-of-pearl grip still sitting in its lax hand. Even more disturbing to the serenity of the parlor was the shockingly tiny dog that stood next to the body, the white fur of its muzzle rusty with old blood. The little animal growled in what was presumably a threatening manner, though it sounded more like a teakettle burbling than anything else.

"You didn't expect this, did you, Captain?" asked Meriwether Octavian Simms, known by preference as simply "Simms" to friend and foe alike. He did his best to take only shallow breaths, one hand meditatively smoothing down his generous ginger muttonchops.

"There were many possibilities I considered for this particular break-in," Captain Marta Ramos replied in a thoughtful drawl. As they were in the city, she dressed as a common workman: dark, sober clothes with her masses of curly brown hair hidden under an utterly disreputable hat. Her normal, far more flamboyant, and classically piratical scarlet frock coat tended to draw too much attention from the Grand Duchy of Denver's police and security forces alike. "I am utterly unashamed to admit this was not one of them."

Simms cleared his throat. "Did the dog...?"

"Yes, so it would seem."

"Ah...well...hah. I suppose we can't blame the little fellow if it's been days and no one to feed him, can we?"

"Hm. Well. Yes, I concur."

"I would have thought if the old girl were planning to off herself, she might have sent her dog out for a walk." Well, it could have been worse. If she hadn't been kind enough to shoot herself in the head, they would have been confronting a much different scene with a much different source of growling. The tiny dog would have been eaten rather than eater after Infection had seen to the resurrection of its mistress, mindless and ravenous.

Ugh, what a thought *that* was. Simms sometimes wished his imagination weren't so finely tuned.

"Mmm." Captain Ramos rasped at her chin with fingers covered in rough leather. "Well, might as well carry on. We needn't even be quiet now." She gave the dog a long, assessing look, as if gauging just how much damage its small teeth, driven by an obviously outsized ego, would be able to cause. Then she gave Simms a long, equally assessing look. A faint shrug of one shoulder and she dug around in her pockets to disgorge a twist of string, a bird's nest of a fake beard, and then a packet of jerky wrapped in newspaper.

The burbling growl abruptly stopped, the tiny plumed tail beginning to wag with canine hope.

Captain Ramos snorted, untying the twine that held the packet closed. "Mercenary little thing, isn't it?"

"From what I've seen, most of 'em are," Simms observed mournfully. And indeed, the little animal fell eagerly on the leathery strips of venison the Captain tossed onto the carpet nearby, completely forgetting their presence in the bliss of chewing.

"All right." Captain Ramos nodded, folded the half-full packet neatly, and tucked it back into her pocket. "I'll unlock the wall safe. See to the unfortunate Miss Nimowitz, Simms. There's a good chap."

He eyed the body doubtfully. "Are you certain that's who it is?" Clementine Nimowitz was a somewhat eccentric but still highly respected lady of great society, the owner of the well-appointed townhouse, and the intended victim of their robbery. Simms knew that much. Or perhaps *had been* would be a more accurate way to consider all of those qualities. "She doesn't have much of a face left." He grimaced. "Or much of a throat."

"I almost hope she isn't. My life would be so much more interesting then."

"I vote for boring, if it's all the same to you." Simms sighed. Somehow, the moment the dank and earthy scent of decay had hit his nose, he'd known he'd end up dealing with the body. Unfortunately, as he lacked the Captain's skill with safes, he could hardly argue that they should trade jobs. He looked down sadly at his gloves. "I only just got these."

"You can have a pair of Miss Nimowitz's to replace them," Captain Ramos suggested in an overly sweet tone, before heading for the safe.

Simms scowled at her, which was no doubt precisely what she wanted, and moved toward the remains. While the unfortunate Miss Clementine Nimowitz might have been a grand lady of impeccable taste in life, death had done her no favors. In the darker, more proletarian depths of Simms's heart, he found that obliquely comforting.

Her dress, heavy blue silk with cream lace, was curiously undisturbed by blood but for the areas—neck, face, forearms, calves—that the dog had felt free to nibble. Simms cautiously moved his hands over the fabric, trying to breathe shallowly through his mouth. A crackle caught his attention at her breast. He dug for it gingerly, face turned away, and came out with a sheaf of messily folded papers, one corner stiff and gluey with a stray red rivulet.

Something tugged at his trouser leg. He glanced down to see the tiny dog. At his attention, it tugged again, tail wagging.

"Captain?"

"Hm?"

"Toss the jerky over here, if you please." He caught the packet, tucked the papers under his arm so he could open it, and pulled out a few more bits of dried meat. The dog gleefully snatched up the venison, which had the side benefit of forcing it to release his trouser cuff. It was probably a good sign it preferred that to a fresh round of human flesh.

The unpleasant task of rifling a corpse's pockets was thankfully abbreviated by the fact that Miss Nimowitz, as a refined, nearly cloistered lady, didn't have any. Simms took from her a bracelet, black with dried blood; a cloisonné pin; and a set of earrings. Feeling strangely guilty, he picked a series of gold hairpins from her blood-stiffened coiffure, finishing the destruction that bullet and dog had begun. He nearly discarded her fan, but the ribs and guard sticks seemed to be made of delicately carved ivory even if the cloth sail was ruined.

He retreated from the dizzying stink of the corpse and laid out the few items on a nearby end table, next to a small china tea set. At first he thought the teapot, single cup, and tray upon which they sat were a display piece, but when he tapped the side of the pot it proved to not be empty. Simms peered under the lid to find the pot half-full of brown liquid. "Huh. Guess she had a cuppa before shooting herself. Civilized, I suppose." Bemused, he turned his attention to the papers he'd retrieved.

"Captain?" he asked after a moment, "I seem to have found Miss Nimowitz's... er... last will and testament. Shall I put it back?"

"Curious, Simms, since I seem to have found it too."

He eyed the document with a new sort of dubiousness. "Right."

"Let me have a look." Captain Ramos walked over and tossed him an empty jewelry box lined with black velvet. "See if the spaces in this match the jewelry you removed from her. That box is for the most expensive pieces of her collection, so I can only hope she was wearing those pieces at the time of her death. Going out in style and all that."

Simms handed over the stained sheaf of papers, and then cracked open the box. The earrings did indeed fit perfectly, as did the bracelet, but the box still had more space, another neat slot. The pin definitely wasn't part of the set. "Should there be a necklace?"

"Hm? Wasn't there one on her?" Captain Ramos glanced up from the papers in her hands.

"Not that I saw. But…" Simms grimaced. "I'll have another look." Wincing all the while, despite the fact the lady was long beyond all pain or caring, he drew out his pocket knife and began to poke around the blackened mess that marked all that was left of her neck.

"Simms, the will you found on Miss Nimowitz is two and a half weeks old, which puts it as relatively new at the time of her departure from the mortal coil. And approximately one year newer than the one I found in the safe." There was a pause, the sound of papers shuffling. "They're nearly identical, but for the fact that Miss Nimowitz is now legally leaving the bulk of her estate to a fellow by the name of Mister Morris Emmett Nimowitz, rather than…" Another crackle of paper. "Deliah, of the same last name."

"Hm." All the digging had unearthed nothing. "Not really our problem, is it?"

"Hm."

"Hm?" Oh, he didn't like the sound of her tone at all.

"Well, not our problem, yes. But concern..."

"No," he said firmly. "Not our concern either. Unless we're named in the bloody will—and you already said we're not, which I'm actually quite glad for since I don't think I want to live in a world where suicidal elderly ladies are gifted with precognition—then the disposition of her estate isn't our concern at all, except for the more portable bits." Frustrated, he prodded the corpse's head aside and spotted a delicate metallic glitter, amidst a sea of not quite dry enough blood.

"It could be interesting, Simms."

"The affairs of the rich are ghastly and boring to anyone but themselves," he said stiffly as he bent to pry the bit of metal from the carpet.

"Your delight in boredom is something I will never understand, Simms. And—"

"—Captain, is this..." He interrupted the all-too-familiar speech by straightening, the metal bit in his fingers.

She leaned forward and eyed it. "The clasp of a necklace? Yes."

"Broken off, then." Simms frowned. "But how..."

As one, they turned to look at the tiny dog and its bloody muzzle, which had no doubt all too recently been in the vicinity of Miss Clementine Nimowitz's neck.

"...oh," Simms finished in a faint tone.

The dog, canine instincts addressing what to do precisely in this situation, wagged its tail, and lifted one little paw adorably, asking for a shake.

WHAT PULLED BOTH MARTA and Simms from their reverie was the dog emitting a high-pitched yip, presumably in protest that the two humans weren't complying with its reasonable request for attention.

"Well," Marta said, considering the problem of an expensive diamond and pearl necklace versus the digestive tract of a small dog and its many twistings and turnings, "the answer seems simple enough." She pulled a small pistol from the inner pocket of her workman's coat and pointed it squarely at the little animal, which only cocked its head in a curious fashion, ears flopping.

"You can't be serious!" Simms, without so much as a by-your-leave, yanked the pistol from her hand.

Marta shook her smarting fingers and gave him a narrow-eyed look. "That was quite unnecessary."

"You are not," Simms said, biting off each word, "going to shoot a tiny dog in front of me."

She couldn't help but give him a wolfish smile. He was so fun to prod at times. "You could turn your back, if you like."

"Dolly has a stuffed toy that looks just like that. I swear."

"Really, with the blood and everything?"

Simms threw up his hands in exasperation. "You know what I mean!"

She shrugged, one eyebrow arching up delicately. "You're the one who seemed so eager to see us out of here quickly, Simms. The Roost is hardly an appropriate place for an animal of this sort." Many would say that Devil's Roost, their regular home and hideout, built into the depths of an abandoned silver mine, wasn't really suitable for any type of inhabitant. But really, she found the quiet but constant hum of the ventilation fans and the mechanical tick of the doors rather restful.

"Shooting it isn't…isn't…*appropriate* either."

Idly, she wondered if this time she might push him into a full apoplectic fit. Who would have known that a little white dog would be what took Simms down in the end? But now, he seemed to have gotten his rather dangerous huffing down to a more manageable level, one hand stroking at his muttonchops. "Have it your way, then. We shall have to remain down here until the necklace has passed. Though it may well get tangled up in the dog's intestines, you realize, in which case shooting it would be a mercy of the highest order."

"Fine," he ground out. "But only then."

Marta waved the two copies of Clementine Nimowitz's will in one hand. "Since we'll be down here and at loose ends anyway, we may as well do something with our time. I don't really want to stay closeted with a moldering corpse, if it's all the same to you."

Simms took the revelation that he'd just fallen into a trap of his own making with more grace than Marta had come to expect from a grown man; he cast her a dire glare, nostrils flaring as he huffed out an exasperated and long-suffering sigh. He jerked a rolled-up satchel from his pocket so he could fill it with the fruits of the morning's labor.

Rather than poke the metaphorical bear with a stick one more time, Marta took a quick circuit around the room, looking for anything else that might be of interest. A quick pop up to the lady's bedroom yielded a prettily jeweled headband, really more suitable for a younger woman, but nothing else worth the trouble. There were a few pictures arrayed around the room, mostly well-done daguerreotypes of people whose clothing style marked them as decades old. The two newest pictures proved to be anthotypes with delicate lacings of color, one of a young man with a weak chin and a thin mustache in full cricket whites, the other of a striking young woman posing primly next to a globe—though, despite the pose, she also seemed to be about to wink at the photographer. The two anthotypes were as widely separated across the various bits of furniture as possible, as if the images might somehow come to blows if in proximity.

More interesting were the late Clementine's bookshelves: while there were the standard penny dreadfuls and slim volumes of absurdly turgid poetry, horticulture volumes occupied several of the shelves. Upon inspection, Marta recognized a few of the titles, scientific volumes that she owned herself and had found quite useful in the past, including one slim book on natural poisons: *A Compendium of Psychoactive, Medicinal, and Toxic Plants of the Continents of North and South America and Their Myriad Uses, Second Edition* by George L. F. Kensington. Odd that she had such a collection of books and no plants to go with them, not even the orchid that was ubiquitous to the bedroom of a lady.

"Unexpected," she murmured, pulling the book out and idly flipping through, pausing to look at lightly penciled notes—minor corrections for the most part—written in three distinct hands, two neat copperplate and the third shaky to the point of incoherence. Bemused, Marta added the book to her satchel. No doubt an odd choice for an ordinary thief, but she imagined whoever finally found Miss Nimowitz's body would be more concerned with the theft of valuables than the removal of one peculiarly specialized book.

Back in the parlor, Marta spied a curved white shape under one of the little tables, thanks to the new angle of perspective. Curious, she bent to retrieve what turned out to be a china teacup, mate to the one Simms had found on the end table, a brown stain dried on its bottom and side. Marta took a curious sniff, only to detect something bitter, hinting of almonds. "Oh my."

"I'm still not going to let you shoot the dog," Simms grumbled.

Marta crouched down, looking from table to corpse. It was too far for the cup to have rolled there on its own unless Miss Nimowitz had flung it in some final seizure, and that seemed unlikely since a few drops of tea had remained within. But perhaps it had been prodded by an unwary foot and sent skittering aside. More importantly, she somehow doubted that Miss Nimowitz would have prepared tea with two cups if it was just a final drink for herself.

Interesting, that.

"I'm less inclined to shoot it now," Marta said, rising back to her feet. "The dog is a witness to murder."

Simms gave her one of those looks at which he seemed to excel, his expression caught somewhere between disbelief and resignation. "Did you really just say that with a straight face?"

"I've rarely been more serious in my life." Marta waggled the teacup at him. "Miss Nimowitz was poisoned."

"And shot."

"Tough old bird." Marta smiled. She checked the teapot on the end table, but could detect no hint of poison in the liquid still within. "Unless our little friend there has developed opposable thumbs, she had outside help with at least one of those activities."

"Murdered twice and then robbed. Not a good week for her," Simms commented, but his expression had become markedly less grudging. While the man wasn't averse to firefights and throwing the occasional security guard off a train, his feelings about murder were generally in line with Marta's—it was the sort of thing that gave honest criminals a bad name.

Particularly when someone had tried so very hard to make it look like suicide. The murderer had even gone to the trouble of locking the house up after, presumably, since Marta had been forced to pick their way in. "We'll have to go a bit more high society for this one, I should think." She held out a hand toward Simms. He obligingly tossed her the half-full satchel. She tucked the teacup inside after wrapping it carefully in a handkerchief. Excavating a set of goggles equipped with extensive loupes of magnifying lenses and filters, she dropped to her knees on the carpet. "This is certainly the neatest murder scene I've ever come across. I'll have a quick look around and see if there's anything else of interest to find. Why don't you ask our little friend his name?"

THE LITTLE DOG TURNED out to be male and named, at least according to the tag on his rather fine collar, "Chippy." He also turned out to be amenable to being picked up, to the point that he attempted to lick Simms's face, his tongue heralded by a blast of breath that could have knocked a black fly from the air at twelve paces. Chippy was notably less amenable to being hauled to the kitchen and having his muzzle wiped free of blood, squirming and yelping as if he were about to be murdered himself the whole while.

Captain Ramos gave Simms and his new best friend a raised eyebrow upon their return to the parlor, but then nodded at the sight of the wet dog and only slightly less damp man. Good—Simms hadn't thought she'd want to explain to anyone on the street why her ladyship's pet looked like a site of carnage. "Find anything interesting?" Simms asked. "Such as this little fellow's lead?"

Captain Ramos tossed a fine leather strap to him. It was dyed a shade of royal purple to match Chippy's collar. "I found more ammunition for the pistol and a bill of sale; it seems to have belonged to Miss Nimowitz for the last two weeks. There's a bit of dirt about, a hair here and there. I've picked it all up, but it seems to me her parlor hasn't had a good clean in a few weeks so it's all a bit muddled. Though upon careful examination, I am led to believe she was shot by someone else, perhaps unsurprisingly. The angle's not quite right." Captain Ramos held up the pistol and demonstrated. "If she'd held the gun entirely by herself, I would have expected it square under the chin, or in the mouth, or even the temple. Right between the eyes is rather unusual and—while possible—rather awkward." She tucked the pistol away in the satchel. "Though I will say, this is definitely the best angle to make absolutely certain post-mortem Infection won't set in."

"Hm. Seems like someone was looking out for you, little fellow." Chippy the dog squirmed in his arms; Simms set the little animal down and hastily clipped the lead to his collar. The dog immediately began to bound back and forth over the short range offered by the lead, yipping excitedly. Hastily, Simms picked him back up. The yipping ceased, but the squirming resumed as if the noise were fighting to escape. "Enough of that, I say."

Captain Ramos stared meditatively at the fluffy white handful—Chippy, whatever his ego might say, certainly didn't qualify as an *armful*—and then smirked. "Remind me, Simms. Who among our crew has annoyed me recently?"

His eyebrows went up at that. "Pardon?"

"There's a bit of information gathering we must do, I think. Definitely a talk must be had with both Deliah and Morris Nimowitz. Bringing little Mister Chippy along wouldn't be all that advantageous right now. There can't be that many dogs like him about." Her expression became particularly sardonic. "Or at least I certainly hope not."

"They do tend to run in litters, you realize," Simms observed dryly. He quickly held up a hand. "But I think it's a marvelous idea. In fact, I was about to volunteer to look after him, myself." Given the option, he'd much rather walk a hyperactive fluff ball in the park than have an uncomfortable afternoon tea with the objects of Captain Ramos's interest while she constantly trod on his foot to remind him to not say out of character things. He wished Captain Ramos would acquire a real husband so he'd no longer have to play the part for her, but he couldn't begin to imagine what sort of neurotic genius with shins of iron and nerves of titanium alloy would be required to deal with her regularly in that capacity, let alone where such a man could be found. And as far as he could tell, neither could the Captain.

Captain Ramos laughed, *nice try there, Simms*, in the angle of her grin. "Oh no. Both Morris Emmett and Deliah Nimowitz must be questioned to see if they had any part in this. And then there's the interesting matter of this lady's maid, as she's more than well off enough to have one of *those* full time, and I find the absence rather suspicious. There's a lot of ground to be covered and I will require your help on this. You're not nearly as hopeless as the rest of the crew, you know."

Simms sighed. He should have guessed he wouldn't squirm his way out of the Captain's favorite hobby so easily. And it was true, even his limited skills at theater were miles ahead of anyone on the rest of the crew. He'd pretend he didn't feel proud about that, though. "Fine. If you give it a moment's thought, I'm sure Mister Masterson will present himself to you as the most likely candidate."

Not entirely true—Gregory Kinzer was probably higher on the Captain's bad list than Elijah Masterson, thanks to the incident with the lemonade in Berthoud. But Elijah had recently managed to blow out a piston in one of the smaller railcars through sheer drunken negligence, something that seemed to set the Captain's nerves completely on edge. And, more to the point for Simms, during that same escapade the man had ruined his best pair of boots by vomiting into the left one and then throwing it off a bridge.

Simms had been quite the drunken scoundrel at Elijah's tender age. But he'd always limited himself to normal things, such as brawls. And more brawls. And brawls of the sort that gave his nose its rather unique shape. He'd never done anything that determinately, stupidly *creative*.

"Ah yes," Captain Ramos said, looking for all the world like a cat that had just spotted a small and unfortunate rodent. "Mister Masterson. I have gotten the impression he needs extra employment for all that spare energy of his. Let us summon him via telegram. While we wait for him, we can acquire suitable clothes for our investigations." She eyed Chippy in a speculative way that had Simms fighting the urge to cradle the little dog a bit closer to his chest. "And a laxative for the little beast, I think."

Suddenly, Simms was glad that little Mister Chippy was about to become someone else's problem.

THEY MET ELIJAH AMONG the warehouses not too far from Union Station. He'd brought one of the more innocent looking railcars down from the mountains and thus was able to berth it along the public tracks. Elijah Masterson was a man of medium height and untidy habits, though today he seemed particularly untidy, perhaps because he'd been called down so abruptly. His brown hair stuck out in untamed curls and a shadow of stubble decorated his chin. He wore a rumpled brown-checked shirt, one sleeve half rolled-up, and a vest he hadn't bothered to button, no jacket in sight.

Or, Simms thought upon a closer look at the younger man's rather red eyes, today he wasn't so much untidy as quite hung over. This really only served to affirm Simms's decision to give him this task. It'd certainly keep him out of trouble.

Elijah still offered the Captain a snappy salute, after first glancing around to confirm that they were alone. "Sir, I was told you had an important task for me."

Captain Ramos waved a hand dismissively. "Oh indeed, Mister Masterson. Simms?"

Obligingly, he held Chippy out toward Elijah. The tiny dog began to squirm, yipping excitedly at the prospect of making a new friend. "Here you go."

"Sir?" As was all too often the case when an item, no matter how strange, was offered to a person, Elijah took the little dog without thought, and *then* stared at the Captain. This was a habit Simms had broken in himself long ago, realizing if he would be spending much time around Captain Ramos, more concern for his own physical health and sanity was necessary.

"His name is Chippy," Captain Ramos said in her most helpful tone, which wasn't helpful at all. More...amused.

"You'll be minding the dog while we see to things in the city," Simms supplied in his own, almost equally helpful, tone. "There's a nice bit of park not far from the station. You ought to walk him there. And pay careful attention if he...ah...hm."

"If he feels the call of nature," Captain Ramos finished. "Which he ought to, quite often, as we've had to give the poor thing a bit of croton oil."

Elijah's expression became one of horror as he stared at them. Chippy, still in his outstretched hands, squirmed into position to place his paws—which as luck would have it were quite muddy, thanks to a puddle they'd found on the way to the station—on Elijah's chest so he could give the man's be-stubbled chin an enthusiastic washing. "But...but *why?*"

It was probably a kindness to refrain from telling him what had been in the dog's mouth recently. "And when that happens," Simms continued, reveling in Elijah's befuddlement, "you must carefully check the results for evidence of a rather nice pearl and diamond necklace. We need it." Observing the dawning horror in Elijah's eyes, he was forced to wonder if Captain Ramos felt like this *all the time* and perhaps this was why she seemed so determined to mess with his mind at every turn.

"Do give it a thorough clean." Captain Ramos smiled. Perhaps observing Elijah's rather slack look, she drew a stained handkerchief from the top of her boot and tucked it into his breast pocket, giving it a little pat at the end. "There's a good fellow."

"Buck up, Elijah," Simms added. "There may be some ladies at the park. Ladies have a weakness for such tiny dogs, I've been told." Though presumably not when they were in the midst of explosive diarrhea.

Chippy still held out at arm's length, Elijah said weakly, "Oh, is that so?"

"If anything of interest emerges, Mister Masterson, any of my regular runners will know how to find one of us." Captain Ramos waved airily. "Have fun with your new friend."

"But!" Finally, Elijah set the dog down. All that prevented a well-timed escape by Chippy was Elijah's hasty grab for his leash. "I don't know anything about dogs! Mum never let us have any pets. Will he need water? What does he eat?"

Simms smiled sardonically as they turned to leave. "Nearly anything, it seems."

CHIPPY THUS MADE INTO someone else's problem for the time being, Marta saw to the suitable outfitting of herself and Simms for their errands, using carefully selected clothing from a bolt-hole she had constructed not far from Union Station. She'd done this by covertly bricking off bits of the storerooms of two adjoining shops and knocking down the wall between them. As one of the shops was a bakery, it guaranteed that everything smelled nicely of freshly baked bread, even if the heat of the ovens made the room incredibly stuffy in any season but winter.

Padded out to hide her proportions and properly dressed in a comfortable but stylish maroon tea dress and jacket, Marta selected an appropriate parasol to go with her ridiculously small hat and slipped out into the cheerfully sunny day. Simms followed along behind her, looking particularly hangdog in his plum-colored jacket and freshly-starched white shirt.

The will of the late Miss Nimowitz had, upon closer examination, yielded the addresses of both Deliah and Morris Emmett Nimowitz and clarified the relationships as grandaunt to niece and nephew respectively. In the street outside the station, Marta hailed a steam-powered taxi that didn't appear overly rugged and spent the cross-city ride mentally establishing the cover story for her and Simms as the granddaughter and grandson-in-law of one of Miss Nimowitz's school chums. There'd been more than enough keepsakes and reminders of younger glory days in the deceased lady's bedroom to provide the necessary veneer of detail.

The address for Morris ended up being a rather grand house not far from City Park, though the house showed subtle signs of not being cared for as well as it needed. The paint wanted to be refreshed, and some of the shutters had been damaged, probably during the last great storm of the recent winter. The interior of the house showed the same subtle shabbiness, the carpets a bit drab, the paintings a bit too spaced out as if there had once been more. Through sheer luck, it was an at-home day for Morris Emmett Nimowitz and his wife.

Marta surreptitiously kicked Simms in the ankle when she caught him fiddling with the starched shirt collar as they waited for the maid to convey their card—carefully sorted from her cabinet of stock as bearing one of the most common family names—inside. She answered his glare with a murmured, "If you'd only stand up straighter, it wouldn't worry you so."

"If I stand up any straighter, I'll run my head into the door frame."

"If only architects had taken into account the return of the Titans," Marta said dryly. She quickly smiled as the maid returned to see them in.

As Marta had expected, Morris Emmett Nimowitz was the male half of the two anthotypes, a perfect match from the cheekbones up. His chin was hidden conspicuously under a well-groomed goatee. Coupled with the rust-colored brocade day coat he wore, he looked rather like a circus ringmaster, one who was attempting—but failing—to be just to the titillating side of sinister.

He was dressed well enough, though to Marta's keen eye, there were tell-tale signs of financial trouble in his wardrobe. His day coat, while natty, was of a fabric that had been popular several seasons ago, likely an older garment that had been delicately readjusted to look more current. Covert glances around as they were shown to the sitting room revealed several decorations that were carefully plated pot metal; Marta had learned early on in her career of thievery how to discern at least cheap fakes with a glance. She'd wager anything the originals had been pawned or sold. Interesting, that.

Introductions were made and bows exchanged. From the look on Morris's face, this time around "Mister Smythe" had managed to keep his handshake below bone-crushing strength, and his bow was passable enough. Polite conversation was then had, the familiar and heartily boring routine of socializing. Marta carefully followed the motions until the last tiny cucumber sandwich had been consumed before remarking, "How is your grandaunt, by the way? Grandmama asked us to stop by her house while we were in the city, but she doesn't seem to be in. I'd like to be able to take some news back to the Duchy of Charlotte even if it's not from the grand lady's mouth."

Morris and Adelaide exchanged a glance that was likely intended to be unreadable, but it certainly howled of some kind of disturbance and nervousness. "Grandaunt Clementine doesn't travel around much at all these days," Missus Adelaide Nimowitz said, her tone just a little too bright. She was a slim, nervous woman with premature threads of white in her mahogany-colored hair. Her deep blue dress wasn't the most flattering shade for her and showed the same signs of reuse and alteration that her husband's coat did. "I'm afraid she'd have little news for you even if she was in."

"Oh, but surely a bit of tea talk..."

"Doesn't go out much for tea either," Morris drawled. "Her health, you know." A sharp look from Adelaide and he added, "Good health for a lady of her age, that is, but...of her age, you see. She doesn't take many visitors."

"Oh dear. She hadn't mentioned anything at all to Grandmama." Marta rearranged her expression into one of rather vacant concern.

"Well, you know. Stiff upper lip, wouldn't want to be a complainer." Morris shrugged.

"Well, at least she is surrounded by her loving family in her twilight years," Marta burbled happily, just to see what sort of reaction it might provoke.

Morris's expression went stony. "Adelaide and I do try to keep her entertained. I'll be certain to mention your visit when I next see her." His voice held a firm note of finality.

Marta sipped her cup of tea. "I thought I might visit your cousin Deliah, perhaps tomorrow. I've heard lovely things about her from Grandmama." She watched Morris's face with interest, trying to place where she'd last seen a color quite like the one his cheeks had gone. Somewhere between an eggplant and the top of a rutabaga, really. Adelaide was trying to catch her eye as well, making little sharp shakes with her head.

Still, Morris managed to keep his temper enough to only sputter and not actually degenerate into cursing in front of his guests. "Deliah," he ground out, "is no one you should waste any time on at all."

Marta pretended to be both shocked and contrite, taking out her fan for the sole purpose of fluttering nervously. "Oh dear, I have put my foot in it, haven't I? But she sounds so nice, and I have so few lady friends at home…"

"Deliah is very good at seeming nice when she thinks it politic to do so," Adelaide said primly. "I hate to speak ill of our own family, Missus Smythe, but she is…is…a consummate con artist, if I'm to be brutally honest. Do be careful if she asks you for anything."

"Oh my. That sounds frightful."

Morris cleared his throat as if trying to dislodge a chunk of bile. "Forgive my display of temper. It's been very trying, recently, with cousin Deliah worming her way into Grandaunt Clementine's affections for something so base as money." Marta began to wonder if the addition of the goatee hadn't been so much a fashion choice on Morris's part as an attempt to remove all family resemblance between himself and his female cousin.

"Morris is her heir, you know," Adelaide added. "Rightfully by law."

Only, Marta knew, since there was just a fortune involved and no actual title, the law would bend to whichever of the wills in her possession turned up. The fact that Morris had a few extra bits stashed in his trousers didn't really matter in the fact of the deceased Miss Nimowitz's wishes.

Whatever those had been. What a delightfully murky question.

"WHAT DID YOU MAKE of that?" Simms asked after they were a safe distance from Morris and Adelaide's little townhouse.

"I think their cook ought to be fired. The paté was a ghastly concoction of gristle."

He rolled his eyes. "You know what I mean."

"I do." Marta rubbed her chin meditatively. "And I don't quite know yet. We've only just begun to stir the pot, after all. But cousin Deliah sounds quite interesting, I think. Morris most certainly has motivation; if he doesn't have a gambling problem, I will eat my hat, including all of the pins. People will murder each other cheerfully over baubles and who got the bigger potato from the midden. I have little doubt that the money involved is suitable motivation for murder."

"So now what?"

"We talk with Deliah, of course. Or perhaps, *I* should. There was no husband mentioned in the will, so it's a safe assumption that she's a spinster. A woman to woman chat might be a bit more revealing." And if she truly was a con artist as Morris had claimed, presenting her with a single and obviously idiotic target might draw her out. "Perhaps Morris is trying to play us, but if so it wasn't a very subtle move on his part." A challenge, Marta liked a challenge.

"What should I be doing then, while you're off having crumpets with the Queen of Darkness?" Simms asked.

"Why don't you look into the disappearance of Miss Nimowitz's maid? That seems a piquant question all its own, and no doubt important." Marta gave him an exasperated look. "And it means you can take off the shirt collar before you ruin it with all your scrabbling."

DELIAH NIMOWITZ LIVED IN one of the nicer areas of the city that served as the Grand Duchy of Denver's rather rank heart, not too far from the Platte River. Her apartments were in a terraced house, which was situated to provide a nice view of the mountains when they weren't obscured by the brown fog of smoke. The house was painted a delicate robin's egg blue, with its trim and embellishments a much more emphatic purplish shade, similar to the juice of a blackberry. Pots, window boxes, and hanging baskets of flowers provided a minor riot of color for the front.

A crisply uniformed maid answered the door and took her calling card into the recesses of the house, her hand moving to turn down one of its corners as she did so. Marta cooled her heels in the dove-gray front hall, inspecting the umbrella stand, which contained nothing but ladies' parasols. There were several plants in the entry hall as well, mostly common houseplants such as grape ivy. On a small end table, Marta spotted a small potted plant with sprays of delicate white fluted flowers. Closer inspection confirmed it was a very well-cared-for Zacatechichi, notably far from its home environment of the Third Mexican Empire.

And, as a source of an interesting hallucinogen, not at all the sort of plant she'd expect to find in the possession of a well-bred young lady. Suddenly, she found herself all the more eager to meet Deliah Nimowitz.

Thankfully, the younger Miss Nimowitz did not disappoint, or she would have had to come up with a far more creative solution. The maid reappeared and gave Marta—or as she intended to be known for the purposes of this interview, Abigale Smythe—a friendly smile. "Miss Nimowitz would be pleased if you would join her for tea in the parlor, Missus Smythe."

Marta gave the maid her most fatuous smile. "I would be delighted! I've looked forward to meeting her ever so much."

The drawing room wasn't quite what she'd been expecting. For the most part, it was tastefully furnished but also very cluttered. Every available surface where a keepsake could be displayed held something, ranging from enameled eggs to interesting fossils to a few wooden and porcelain figures that looked shockingly cheap when put up against everything else. Marta took in as much of the clutter as she could with a single sweep of her gaze; if the selection were of personally acquired souvenirs, the younger Miss Nimowitz was exceedingly well-traveled. There were items there from each of the continents but Antarctica.

A single glance was all she could spare the room in her current persona, however. Abigale Smythe was supposed to be social in aim and buoyant in personality–and not terribly observant. She didn't want to put one of the main suspects for the late Miss Nimowitz on the defensive. Marta smiled broadly at the living and much younger Miss Nimowitz, who rose to her feet for a proper greeting.

Deliah Nimowitz proved to be the woman from the anthotype in Clementine's room. The light hints of coloration had not done justice to the rich tone of her skin or the long fall of slightly wavy black hair. A deep blue tea dress complimented her coloring perfectly. Her features were graceful, her lips curved slightly as if she'd thought of a joke but wasn't about to share it with anyone else. She had tawny eyes; the color alone was enough to put Marta in mind of a mountain lion, but there was a secretive, amused quality to her gaze that was even more distinctly cat-like.

More interesting to Marta, however, was the spark of bright, calculating intelligence she thought she caught in the woman's eyes, as calculating and considering as her own. The look disappeared a split second later, obscured by Deliah's lace fan and perhaps carefully packed away.

Or more reasonably, a figment of Marta's imagination. She'd never been one to believe in such fuzzy emotional ideas as reading someone's spirit in their eyes.

"Missus Smythe, welcome to the Grand Duchy of Denver. I hope travel has treated you well..." Deliah's voice was low and well-modulated.

"Oh indeed. And thank you ever so much, Miss Nimowitz, for such hospitality and on such short notice." Marta pitched her own voice higher, layering onto it an accent that would place her neatly in the borders of the Duchy of Charlotte. That duchy was still most tightly tied to the Caribbean kingdoms and Britannia; its few minor aristocratic families weren't so well known in the rest of the American duchies.

The maid returned to serve them tea, an array of delicate sandwiches, and biscuits. As was socially expected, they made polite conversation regarding the state of the weather, any news of a non-exciting nature from their respective home duchies, and did a bit of cooing over the announcement that the Grand Duke of Denver's daughter was pregnant and certain to produce a strapping grandson for him. Only after all those topics had been covered did the conversation circle back onto interesting territory.

"Now, Missus Smythe, I must say this has been a pleasant surprise, as we've obviously not been introduced before. If you don't mind me asking, what has brought you to our fair duchy?"

"I don't mind you asking at all!" Marta said, smiling brightly. "My husband has come here on a business trip. He's looking to expand his shipping interests west, since we've been hearing of such expansion in both Denver and Salt Lake."

"Oh, how excellent for you. I do hope his trip is a success." With a delicate tilt of her eyebrows, Deliah seemed to be indicating an additional question that she was in fact far too polite to voice.

"We've been here for a few days, but I believe it's going well. He let me out to do a bit of shopping and make some social calls while he takes a look at the warehouse situation near the stations. And social calls are what brought me to your door. I don't know if you've heard her speak of it, but your grandaunt and my grandmother, Eloise Gordon-Smythe, were school chums at St. Elbert's. They've been corresponding ever since, and Grandmama did want me to say hello to Miss Nimowitz while I was here."

There was nothing in Deliah's expression but mild curiosity. Either she didn't know her grandaunt was dead, or she was very, very good. "Oh, I see. Would you like an introduction?"

"I've a letter of introduction from Grandmama, as you might expect. No, the reason I thought to pay you this call is that I've been by your grandaunt's house these last two days, and no one's so much as answered the door or responded to either of the notes I left. I don't suppose she's gone traveling?" A fairly absurd suggestion for a woman of Clementine's apparent perimortem age, but the real function was to offer Deliah a polite social out if she thought Clementine simply did not want to receive these visitors at all.

Instead, the woman's fine dark eyebrows arched up. "No, she hasn't traveled at all in the last, oh, five years? Her health has always been quite good of course, but she said she wanted to spend her golden years near her heir." She quickly continued on before Marta could inquire just who the heir might be. "That *is* puzzling. Grandaunt Clementine prefers to live simply within her means, but she does have a maid who lives in the house." She snapped open her fan, obscuring her mouth for a moment as her brows drew back down. "Well, I'm certain there's a simple enough explanation for this. If you please, leave me the details of your hotel and I shall let you know once I've spoken with her."

Marta bowed her head. "I do appreciate it. Grandmama would worry so if I left things just as they are."

"But of course. I'm sorry you've been so troubled."

She smiled over the rim of her teacup. "No trouble at all, Miss Nimowitz. Ah…while we're on the subject of your relatives and their travel schedule, I don't suppose your cousin Morris is in town, is he? Mister Smythe has been eager to meet him." It was no effort at all to lie and pretend she hadn't just been to see the man. From the way Morris had spoken, it wasn't as if he'd be telling his cousin he'd had visitors.

Deliah's eyebrows went up. There was a distinct hint of distaste to the set of her lips for a moment. "Really? Whatever for?"

"I think it's something to do with sport. Mister Smythe played cricket in university, and he never tires of going on about it." She smiled indulgently, rolling her eyes. "Ever."

Apparently mollified, Deliah nodded. "My cousin Morris seems to have the same affliction in regards to his glory days, whether it's sports or his time in the Grand Duchess Elisa's East Asian Expeditionary Force. As you can imagine, there's little we have in common in that regard." She took a small sip of tea. "But yes, he is in his house in town. He and his wife have put down their roots here quite firmly. Investments and the like, I hear."

"That isn't the case for you?"

Deliah laughed. "It always seemed best to me to stay light on my feet, at least until I've caught a proper husband."

Marta indicated the room with a wave of her hand. "But you've done a good deal of traveling, haven't you? Some of these little curiosities seem quite foreign..."

Thus led, Deliah demurely admitted to a bit of travel throughout the Americas and even in to Asia, particularly the Chinese Empire, which explained much of the décor. More polite and innocuous conversation was made, Marta subtly poking at various topics in the hope of garnering some sort of interesting reaction.

But from the opera to literature to subtle proddings at the much less innocuous topic of politics, Deliah Nimowitz was startlingly, determinately boring. She thought the new soprano at the opera was terrible, limited her reading to poetry and cerebral romance novels that Marta was fairly certain no one read but everyone claimed to have, and had no thoughts on politics beyond what a lovely fellow the Grand Duke was and didn't he seem to be doing a lovely job, how could anyone think he was anything but lovely and more lovely.

Marta Ramos had met people like that before. The aristocracy was full of them. Yet somehow, it all seemed a little suspicious. Quite possibly because Deliah Nimowitz was also the only unmarried woman over the age of thirty of any sort of wealth and station that Marta had ever conversed with for more than three minutes. Or perhaps it was because those tawny eyes seemed to be challenging her at every turn to ask just one untoward question that the brainless Missus Smythe wouldn't possibly ever think to ask.

Marta didn't rise to the bait. Instead, she simply enjoyed the excellent tea and a few more baked goods than she probably would have on her own—Missus Smythe, unlike Captain Ramos, was rather pleasingly plump, however—and allowed Deliah to walk her to the door. On the way, Marta indicated the Zacatechichi on the table. "By the by, Miss Nimowitz, I was wondering where you might have found this plant? It's quite cute, but I've never seen one like it."

Deliah smiled. "I'm afraid I don't know the proper name of it. My grandaunt gave it to me years ago, and I never can remember what she called it. But the little flowers look a bit like lace, don't you think?"

"Indeed. It's quite a fetching effect. I'll have to ask your grandaunt when I do meet her. I've a little window box that would look darling if occupied by a few of these, I think." Marta smiled. After a hand clasp and a curtsey and a few more pleasantries, she was on her way, mulling over what she had observed.

What she found most curious was why Deliah had lied about how long she'd had the plant. Upon earlier inspection, most of the plants on the hall table had been there long enough to make marks or even rings in the wood, caused by careless watering. There wasn't so much as a blemish associated with the Zacatechichi; the plant must have been very new.

It was far too early in the game to yet draw conclusions, but Marta had a great deal to mull over as she listened to the chuffing of the taxi. There was an unpleasant metallic whine hidden in the normally cheerful sound that indicated some of the gears in the drive were in need of re-machining. Marta wrote a note to that effect and tucked it between the seat cushions as an extra bit of tip when she arrived at the designated meeting point with Simms, a coffee shop only a few blocks from Brown Park.

Rather than the big man, a small, grubby child perched on the nearby garden wall. Catching sight of her, the little girl scampered over and held out a crumpled bit of paper. Marta dug past her revolver in her handbag to come up with a quarter for the girl, and then read the message: *Need you back at the warehouses at once. V. urgent. —EM*

Marta sighed and strode to the street to hail another taxi, her long skirts swirling around her ankles. Sometimes she felt as if the world did its level best to fall to pieces the moment her back was turned.

SIMMS HAD GREETED HIS change of costume with relief, finding himself far more comfortable in the clothes of a lower-class laborer than those of a gentleman. He felt nearly buoyant after ridding himself of the hated collar and turned his energy fully to the task of finding out more about Clementine Nimowitz's missing maid. Or as the Captain often put it, "Turning over all of the obvious and boring stones." This was fine with Simms; boring was his loudly proclaimed preference.

Though he could admit in the privacy of his own mind that the sort of boring he'd been subjected to before had partially led him down a path that ended at the bottom of a bottle of whiskey. Ultimately, his desire for boredom was similar to a wealthy man crying for the simplicity of poverty from the comfort of his sumptuous drawing room, and he knew it.

And he would have liked a bit less boredom when it came to the search for the housemaid. Simms had been around the Captain long enough to know that the best way to find some things out was to simply ask in a friendly manner. He'd also learned from the Captain that simple, easy to remember lies were the best sort. Thus he became Zebulon MacElroy, a shockingly honest cab driver who had conveyed the lady from Miss Nimowitz's house to an appointment across town last week and discovered, to his dismay, that she'd left her scarf behind. Finally he had a day off and just wished to return the item to the lady in question, only no one at the residence was answering the door, and if it please you sir or ma'am, he didn't just want to leave it waiting on the doorstep because you never knew who might happen by.

Thus armed, Simms took himself to the shops nearest the late Miss Nimowitz's house, since it was likely the maid would see to the more domestic shopping for the household on her mistress's account. His first few inquiries came up with nothing, but then he had the luck of running across the mailman, a bluff and red-faced fellow with sparse curly hair and a generous mustache. "Oh, the maid? Yeah, name's Elizabeth Strickland. No one's answering, eh?"

"No one at all. Maybe the lady's out for a constitutional or some such."

"Miss Nimowitz? Don't think so. Used to see the sweet old lady out all the time, mucking about in the garden. Caused such a scandal back a few years ago, you wouldn't believe. But lately, she's not been out much. Lizzie—Miss Strickland to you, mate—runs all the errands." The man smoothed down his mustache, fingers lingering on the waxed tips. "Come to think of it, I ain't seen Lizzie in a couple of days."

"That so? Think she took ill?" Simms prompted, wishing he had the Captain's deft touch for this sort of thing. Then again, the mailman seemed like the kind who loved a good gossip, leaning in with a conspiratorial nod even for more mundane topics.

"Looked fine when I saw her. Though it was a funny thing. She came out to get the mail all wrapped up and ready to leave, right? Then when I was working around to the other side of the street, I saw someone heading for the house. Thought it was her, out the corner of my eye, maybe back for something she forgot, but she was with a gentleman. Tall, dark fellow, sporting a goatee. Looked a bit like a circus ringmaster, if you ask me, only Miss Nimowitz wouldn't hang out with that sort."

That description gave Simms pause, considering Morris's slightly sinister facial hair choice. Unfortunately, he couldn't ask more pointedly about it, since he had no reason to even know Morris Nimowitz existed. "'Course not, great lady like her. And she took him inside the house?"

"Right through the front door. Then Lizzie came out a few minutes later and went on her way. Had this big envelope tucked under her arm too. I offered to take it but she said it weren't for the mail." He shrugged as if to indicate *no accounting for some people.* "But she left the gentleman in there with Miss Nimowitz. Well, you know, at her age I guess the fine people don't bother with chaperones no more. Not that I'll hear a word against the great lady, not in my neighborhood. If Lizzie took him in, there weren't any nonsense going on."

Simms nodded, carefully trying to not think on the fact that "nonsense" had very obviously gone on, and was currently putting an extensive stain on an otherwise lovely floor.

The mailman didn't know anything else of use, though the name helped immeasurably. Simms headed back into the shops and thankfully had at least a vague direction in which to aim himself on the fifth try—*She comes from Bonnie Brae, bless her, my daughter did her laundry before she went into service.* Thus armed, Simms took himself to the neighborhood in question, feeling quite accomplished.

That smug sensation was quickly quashed as he observed row upon row of terraced houses, each no doubt divided into several apartments, each crossed and recrossed with new levels and temporary additions. So far from his normal stomping grounds, Simms had nearly managed to forget what a mess Bonnie Brae actually was. The neighborhood looked like a rabbit warren had been covered with brightly-painted gingerbreading, with the occasional stringy tree here and there for decoration. Here the steam-powered carts and cabs were far less frequent than hand and even horse-drawn carts, several of which he had to dodge to cross the street. The paving stones were a bit uneven and the drainage far less certain.

What would Captain Ramos do in his now unfortunately dampened shoes? Well, knowing her, she'd sniff the wind, pick a few leaves from the nearest tree, and declare that *obviously* Elizabeth Strickland lived in house number 415, as observation so clearly showed.

Simms slunk off to a bakery that he was able to locate by scent alone, catching the sweet, warm smell above the clinging sulfurous stink of coal smoke. He'd need a new story if he was going to go door to door looking for one woman in this mess. Without the Captain's seemingly natural facility for lies, he could only hope that coffee and a few pastries provided the necessary fuel. At the very least, it got him out of the noise and bustle of the street.

As Simms brooded into a rather scummy cup of coffee, two women entered the shop. One had a badly pockmarked face and was roundly pregnant; the other seemed to be along to help her manage her parcels and was quite a bit older. "—haven't seen her myself, but her sister said it's quite terrible. Poor thing's still laid up in hospital, not even awake," the pregnant woman said. "Anna's been with her, night and day."

"Wasn't Anna watching her boy already? And she's got children of her own, doesn't she?"

"Lizzie's boy's in grammar school, and Anna's two aren't even out of diapers yet. Though Missus Potts next door is watching over them, bless her."

"Bless, indeed. Should we pick up a bit of bread extra for her, you think? Can't be easy, with all those extra mouths to feed." The older woman smiled. "Bad enough, just trying to manage your own."

Simms carefully put down his coffee cup. It seemed a bit too lucky, this, but there was no harm at all in asking. Even if he made an ass of himself, he'd not be back to this area again anytime soon. "Excuse me, ladies," he said, rising to his feet. They both directed startled looks toward him, and he gave them a workmanlike bow. "I didn't mean to eavesdrop at all, but I can't help but wonder... are you speaking of Elizabeth Strickland?"

The older of the two women frowned, one hand reaching out to touch the other's arm. "Maybe, maybe not. What business is it of yours?"

Simms groped for another convenient lie. The cab driver one was a bit too fantastic, but he'd seen a milk delivery box at the house, hadn't he? That was common enough. "I drive the milk wagon, 'round where her employer lives. Last few days, no one's been picking up the milk out the box, right? So I thought maybe some trouble might be up with Missus Strickland, thought I better check up on her, what with her not havin' a proper man to pay her mind." He hastily pulled off his cap and held it nervously in his hands. The nervousness was sadly not feigned. He could feel his ears going red with the pressure of being so untruthful, but hopefully they'd think it the blush of a lovesick milkman.

The women gave him nearly identical searching looks, though their end results seemed to diverge. There was one vote of *proper enough* from the older woman and *no, not in the slightest* from the younger. Since the older woman seemed to have taken charge of the conversation, her vote was the one that counted in the end. "Yes, we are, I'm sorry to say."

"What happened to her?"

"Trolley accident, three days ago. Fell on the track, she did."

"Or was pushed," the pregnant woman added darkly. The very mention of it drew a cold line down Simms's spine.

"Oh you. Always such drama." The older woman shook her head. "She must have had the afternoon off, unexpected-like. Went downtown, to see a show I'd bet. She's in that great hospital down there, St. Joseph's. It was the closest one, so her poor sister has to go halfway across town to see her."

Simms nodded. He shouldn't be feeling so triumphant over the terrible maiming of a maid, though he reassured himself the feeling was more satisfaction that he'd found out such a compelling bit of information entirely on his own. "That's terrible news. I'll...I'll have to pay a visit. With some flowers."

"Hope she wakes up to see them, then," the pregnant woman said tartly.

He gave her a sickly smile. "Maybe it will tempt her back."

"Sorry to be the bearer of such bad news," the older woman said.

"No, no. It's better to know something for certain, even if it's dire." Simms sighed heavily. "Thank you both." He shook his head and added, "Her mistress must be worried sick."

"Can't be that worried," the older woman observed acerbically. "Anna said there ain't been a peep from her, for three days straight, not even to complain about her missing work. And to think, Lizzie always spoke so highly of her mistress. To hear her tell, you'd think she was a wise woman and a saint, rolled up together. If a bit forgetful."

"Couldn't really afford to not," the other woman remarked. "Never know who might be listening."

"Aye," Simms agreed. He had no allegiance to people of Miss Nimowitz's class, and he certainly couldn't afford to act as if he knew the reason behind her curious silence. "Can't really say either way, myself. Drinks her milk proper, that's all I can tell you." He cleared his throat. "Can't say as I feel like finishing my food after that. You ladies both have a good day."

"And you," the pregnant woman said. "I'll be sure to let Anna know you've been asking after her sister, Mister..."

"Sim…mons," Simms supplied, almost blurting out his own name in a moment of panic.

"Mister Simmons. She'll be glad to know her sister's missed, at least."

He put on his cap. "Her absence has been a cause of great concern, you can trust that." He made his escape from the shop as quickly as he could without seeming to literally run away. So the missing maid had fallen…or been *pushed*. He couldn't wait to pass that fascinating bit of news on to Captain Ramos.

As Simms retraced his steps, headed for the coffee shop where he was supposed to meet with the Captain, a small and rather dirty child of indeterminate gender scampered up, brandishing a bit of paper. He dug out a few coins from his pocket in exchange, used to these particular messengers by now.

The text on the grubby note was plain enough: *Need you back at the warehouses at once. V. urgent. —EM*

"Bollocks, Elijah. What have you done now?" Simms asked. The question earned him a sharp look from an elderly woman passing by but no other answer.

"I DON'T KNOW WHAT happened," Elijah said thickly.

Simms had no immediate answer for that assertion; he was a bit too busy looking Elijah over in horrified fascination. The young man's eyes were swollen nearly shut, his skin gone red and frighteningly blotchy.

"I picked him up and… I hadn't meant him to lick my face again, but then I started feeling so peculiar…"

"Right." Simms cleared his throat. "I think perhaps you'd better sit down."

Elijah did so on the nearby crates. Chippy, who had been spinning in circles in what seemed like a vain attempt to strangle himself with his own leash, immediately jumped into Elijah's lap and started licking his face again.

Hastily, Simms snatched up the little animal, who let out a squeaky yip. Immediately, Chippy turned on him and started trying to wash his muttonchops, and then Simms's hand when he tried to protect his pride and joy from the dog. "Perhaps a bit less dog slobber is in order as well."

This was the point when Captain Ramos showed up, turning the corner between two warehouses at a rapid clip, the heels of her shoes clicking boldly along the paving stones. "Mister Masterson, if you please—" She took in the tableau for a moment before delicately coughing into her hand. "Ah. Right. I see."

"I barely can," Elijah wailed.

"You never said you were allergic to dogs."

"How was I to know? We never had any when I was a boy!"

"Well then, Mister Masterson, it seems you've developed an allergy to dogs spontaneously, like the overachiever we all know you to be." Captain Ramos made a peculiar little cough. "And during his time with you, has Chippy achieved anything equally spectacular?"

"If you mean, has he shat," Elijah said bitterly, "I wouldn't recommend going anywhere near the park until we've had a good rain."

"And the jewelry?"

"None of that. Just…just mess. Everywhere. I think my shoes will never be the same."

"My heart *bleeds* for you," Simms said dryly.

Captain Ramos coughed again. "Right. Stubborn little thing that he is. I suppose in the interests of pretending I have some humanity left, I shall relieve you of this wee beastie and send you on your way before you have some sort of anaphylactic fit."

Elijah sagged back against the wall. "It itches so, sir," he said, one hand coming up to his eyes. Simms promptly slapped it away again.

"When you get back to the Roost, ask Cook for some oatmeal. I imagine she'll give it to you just to keep your face from scaring the yeast right out of her bread." Captain Ramos turned her attention to Simms. "Come along. You look like a cat that's eaten several small birds recently, all stuffed with feathers and proud. You must have found out something very interesting."

As they walked Chippy back toward the Captain's bolt-hole, Simms described everything he'd learned and listened to her description of her talk with Deliah. "Doesn't sound nearly so evil as Morris made her out to be."

Captain Ramos laughed. "If she's that good of a con artist, she wouldn't. But I don't take his statements on their face either. I need to go collect a bit of gossip, I think."

"All right, so you'll be sniffing about their respective neighborhoods, I take it?" They drew to a halt as Chippy suddenly developed an interest in a nearby post box. Simms averted his eyes as the dog proceeded to paint it down with a surprisingly robust stream of urine.

"Yes. And in the meanwhile, I want you to go back to Miss Nimowitz's neighborhood, since you've now a useful bit of gossip to share with the people there. See what sort of wild speculation springs up when you mention the possibility her poor maid might have been shoved from the platform."

"And what about him?" Simms tilted his chin toward Chippy, now regarding the humans with the ever hopeful look of a dog certain that treats will appear any moment now.

"He's with me. There is something thoroughly disarming about walking a dog. He'll provide excellent cover."

AND THAT CHIPPY DID, performing his part admirably by bouncing energetically around and sniffing endearingly at the shoes of everyone they encountered. Feeling as if she ought to offer him some reward despite the fact that he wasn't *working* per se, Marta fed him a bit more jerky on the sly as they moved between streets. Besides, hopefully the addition of more food into his digestive system would wash the necklace out since the croton oil had failed thus far.

People already charmed by the tiny dog seemed quite happy to stop and gossip a bit, of course only after covering the rapidly fraying subject of the weather. The talk from Morris's neighborhood revealed that the man did indeed have both a gambling habit and a love for stupidly risky business endeavors, as if one sink to his rapidly dwindling fortunes wasn't enough.

And in Deliah's neighborhood, what rumors Marta did pick up about the woman exceeded only in removing the middle ground, while leaving the extremes of innocent woman versus con artist completely untouched. Deliah was well-liked, generous with her neighbors, and apparently threw the most lovely parties every time she came back from a visit overseas so she could share all the stories of her travels and distribute small trinkets. She was either one of the most innocently generous people Marta had ever encountered, and she hadn't seemed quite wide-eyed enough for that, or she was very, very good at playing other human beings like a sophisticated musical instrument. If anything, it only piqued Marta's curiosity further. She already knew Deliah had lied to her once, and done so very well, in a way that never would have been caught without astute observation.

That really nudged her firmly toward the con artist camp. *Fascinating.* Any further thoughts she might have had on the subject were interrupted by Chippy, who suddenly began to bounce around like a demented rubber ball, wagging his tail so hard his entire body squirmed with uncontainable vibrations of happiness.

"Is that you, Missus Smythe?" A familiar voice asked.

Marta swallowed back the automatic, dry inquiry as to who else she might possibly be; that would definitely not be in character. And maintaining character was suddenly of the utmost importance, because the object of Chippy's excitement was none other than Deliah Nimowitz. Marta smiled at her. "Well, hello Miss Nimowitz. Oh Chester, do calm down," she admonished the dog in her most fatuous tones.

Chippy had no intention of doing any such thing, it seemed. Instead, he tugged on his lead with his pathetically small mass, somehow dragging Marta forward the few steps necessary so he could get to Deliah.

"Chester?" Deliah's eyebrows went up momentarily, suspicion lighting her eyes. The expression smoothed away almost instantly as she bent to let the frantically wriggling dog lap and nip at her lace-covered fingers. "You know, he's the spitting image of my Grandaunt's dog Chippy."

"I know. They were littermates," Marta supplied smoothly. Deliah glanced up to meet her eyes. *She doesn't believe me one bit,*

Marta realized. And yet Deliah did not protest further, simply held Marta's gaze longer than was at all polite, long enough to be rather captivating.

"Lucky you managed to get one of the litter, then," Deliah said. "They're very much in demand."

"There was quite a bit of squabbling over who would get him. All that decided the matter in the end was the will of the owner." She smiled slightly, wondering if Deliah cared to play that game.

"That's always the way, isn't it." Deliah straightened with a sigh, her eyes never leaving Marta's. "One hopes the owner got what he or she wanted in the end."

"I'd like to think so." Interesting indeed. "Have you been by your grandaunt's house yet?"

"I'll be on my way once I've finished my walk, as chance would have it. What do you think I shall find?"

"I haven't the foggiest, of course." Marta shrugged. "With luck, someone who will open the door for you."

Deliah laughed, the sound almost musical, completely at odds with the levelness of her gaze. "Of course."

"Oh, my husband and I happened to have tea with your cousin."

"Is that so?" Deliah smiled. "What did he have to say about me, I wonder?"

"Nothing but kind words."

Deliah took a step forward so they were nearly shoulder to shoulder. She smelled nicely floral, a corner of Marta's mind noted, but with a darker hint beneath, mixed and metallic, like a chemist. "Oh, you *are* good," she breathed.

Marta touched the brim of her delicate lady's hat with two fingers. "As are you."

"Whatever you're thinking...Missus Smythe, it's not nearly so simple as that."

Marta smiled, for a moment showing her teeth in a grin that had no business being on Missus Smythe's face. "I count on it. That is what makes life so very interesting."

Deliah's lips quirked slightly in response. "Good day. I shall let my grandaunt know you've inquired." She stepped past, paused, turned. "Oh, and you asked about that plant Grandaunt Clementine gave me, did you not?"

"I did indeed. It's quite pretty."

"Kensington's *Compendium* might provide the answer you seek. I never had much of a head for plants." A polite smile and duck of her head and Deliah continued on her way, Chippy straining on his leash to follow.

Marta absently ran one finger over her lips and watched her go, turning their conversation over in her mind and trying to decide which of that myriad of hints and cracks to pry at first.

"...AND I'VE WRITTEN IT all down here," Simms said, offering a tattered notebook to the Captain. "After a while, all the speculation got so wild I couldn't keep track of it all. There wasn't a single name that showed up on the list more than twice, I checked."

"Mmm."

Simms waggled the notebook at her, trying to draw attention away from her gently steaming coffee cup. They'd met up in one of the many coffee shops they routinely used for that purpose. Captain Ramos had entered with an exhausted, panting Chippy tucked under her arm like a purse and set him in her lap as soon as she'd sat. The little dog had proceeded to fall into boneless sleep, the Captain's hand idly tracing figures on his pale little forehead. It was all very odd, disquieting almost. In Simms's years of knowing her, Captain Ramos had never showed any sort of interest in animals, let alone affection—and hadn't she been all set to shoot the poor thing before?

Though far more disturbing was the fact that she didn't seem to be listening to him, in a real sense, rather than that studied nonchalance with which she normally took reports, indicating her mind was working furiously.

"Captain?"

"I heard you the first time, Simms," she said, tone rather grouchy. She snatched the notebook from his hand and thumped it down next to her cup, almost causing the coffee to slosh out. She did not, however, open it.

"Really? What was I telling you?"

She glared at him, the sort of liver-curdling look to which he'd by necessity become immune early on in their association. "Fine. Repeat yourself."

"It's all the notes. Look over them when you're in a better mood. The summation is, I don't think anyone's got a bleeding clue who might have wanted to off Miss Nimowitz's maid Elizabeth, let alone why. She was apparently one of those clean-living, universally well-liked sorts."

"Annoying," the Captain commented. "No hints of a dark secret life?"

"She stole a kiss from the butler across the street in broad daylight once."

"That sounds promising."

"She was also married to him at the time."

"Oh. What of her husband, then?"

"He ended up serving during the last expedition when we were still allies with the Duchy of Missoula, and that was the end of him."

Captain Ramos slumped slightly in her seat. "Right. No longer interesting. Heartily boring, really."

Simms directed a reproachful look toward her, but he already knew it would do no good. Captain Ramos seemed to only have two categories for classification when it came to the world—interesting and boring. In his opinion, for that particular scheme boring was very much preferable. "Did find out one interesting bit that kept coming up, though."

"Why did you wait this long to tell me?"

He had, and she hadn't been paying him any mind. Simms considered, and after a moment decided that was not an argument worth having right now. "Cousin Morris and the maid didn't get along at all well."

She sat up a bit straighter, almost ejecting Chippy from her lap. The dog let out a sleepy yelp of protest, and she settled him back down by resting her hand over him. "Now that is interesting. In what way?"

"It seems that on more than one occasion, Elizabeth wouldn't let him in to see Miss Nimowitz, saying her mistress was feeling poorly."

"And this, after we have been told time and again what a healthy, wealthy horse this lady was. Though on the other hand, she was poisoned…"

"Oh, but it gets better."

"Do tell." Captain Ramos rested her chin in her hand, for a moment looking disturbingly coquettish in the rich dress she currently wore. Except for her piercing gaze, which Simms was fairly certain would have sent any suitor in his right mind screaming from the room after he was made to feel like a beetle about to be dissected.

He continued on, "There was an occasion that was, and I quote, 'a few weeks ago' when Morris, his wife, and a—and again I quote—'man who looked like someone had stuffed a rat in a suit and put spectacles on 'im,' cut through Elizabeth's protests and bulled their way in to see Miss Nimowitz anyway." A few weeks ago—while the timing wasn't exact, the will naming Morris as the sole benefactor had been two and a half weeks old.

"Oh, now that *is* interesting."

"Thought you'd like it." Simms grinned.

"Anyone have a word to say about Deliah?"

"Not nearly so much. Most didn't mention her at all; anyone who did just thought she looked well enough and was unfailingly polite to the working class folks. Which you have to admit, are the bits that are going to stick in anyone's head." Simms shrugged. "So I'm still betting on Morris. You find out anything good?"

"Perhaps." Captain Ramos tapped her lips with one finger. Why did she look so pensive? "I ran across Deliah while I was in her neighborhood. She recognized Chippy."

Simms felt as if his eyebrows were attempting to climb from his forehead and invade his hair. "You still have him though."

"I know. That's the curious part. Well that and what she had to say." Captain Ramos sketched out the conversation, though Simms couldn't quite shake the feeling that she hadn't told him the whole of it.

Well, she often didn't. It was one of her more annoying habits, and he'd learned better than to argue. "So you think it's her, then?"

"I don't know what I think, yet. I won't be rushed to a conclusion. We're still in the weeds." She pursed her lips. "And Deliah seems rather too smart to off someone who intended to leave her inheritance to someone else."

"If she knew."

"If she knew," Captain Ramos agreed.

Simms glanced out the coffee shop window at the sun, which was about to slip past the peaks of the distant mountains, barely visible through the city haze. "We're not going home tonight, are we?"

"No, I think not. Chippy has still not produced our payoff." Captain Ramos tapped her lips again. "And Deliah claimed she was going over to Miss Nimowitz's house shortly. So we can presume the body will be discovered, and our little act of theft. That ought to stir up something interesting from the depths of the pot."

While Simms had hoped to return to the mountains tonight and get there in time to put his daughter to bed, even he had to admit this drama had gotten a bit arresting. He swallowed down his complaints, ready to summon them back up if she even hinted they might have to sleep in the damned engine or worse, some flea-bitten hostel. "Hotel?"

"Hotel. The Smythes are still in town, after all." She flashed him a grin. "Who knows, we may get to be part of the interesting thing that happens."

MARTA SENT SIMMS AHEAD to the hotel with the luggage, a temporarily exhausted Chippy tucked limply under his arm like a child's toy and visually lost against the expanse of his jacket. After checking in, he was to take the trolley to the station where the maid, Elizabeth, had her near fatal accident—or non-accident—

and see if anyone there had been around during that time. It was a long shot, but there were those who used the trolley every day for work or hung about the platform regularly to beg, so there might be a witness around to be had.

For her part, she was more curious just what might be happening at Clementine Nimowitz's house. She stopped to quickly change her clothes and add a bit of makeup to make her appearance something far more innocuous—day laborer was always a safe bet; no one ever looked at them—and returned to the scene of the crime.

Which had become another sort of scene altogether in her absence.

She perched on a low, decorative wall just down the street and covertly observed the hearse, drawn by matched black horses, that was parked in front of the house. A horse-drawn cab waited near it, and a steam-driven town car not far off, which both the horses eyed a bit nervously as it let out the occasional steamy exhalation. Mentally, she pinned the cab on Deliah, the town car on Morris, and was gratified to see those two parties burst from the front door a few minutes later and head to their respective vehicles, still shouting at each other.

Well, Morris was shouting. Deliah seemed to be very quiet, which only served to make him angrier. She said something Marta could not hear, which Morris answered with an enraged yowl. "I know damn well what you've been telling them! Trying to build support among her friends, eh? Well it won't help you!"

Oho, was he referring to the boring and innocent Smythes, perchance? If only she'd been around for the beginning of this conversation, no doubt started over the accusingly empty safe.

Another quiet remark from Deliah, and Morris shouted, "I know you took the will you...you *haybag*!"

Deliah's next comment, Marta could fill in just by knowing her well enough—"And little good it would do me, Morris you utter fat head, since if this goes to the courts you'll win." Well, the "fat head" comment was really Marta's own mental embellishment.

"What are you implying?" he demanded.

"She's very subtly implying," Marta murmured to herself, "that *you* are the one who did this. That there must have been another will you didn't want to have come to light." Add that to the column of "Deliah didn't know about the most recent will" evidence.

"Think he's gonna hit her?"

The skin on the back of Marta's neck did a good impression of trying to crawl from her body; she'd been so arrested by the argument she hadn't noticed a kitchen maid slipping out of the great house behind to stand next to her. She gave the girl, who wore the hungry expression of someone who didn't often get to have her full allotment of fun and gossip, a conspiratorial look. "I should hope he's not foolish enough to do so in public."

"Never know," the maid said wisely. "He's awful mad. Heard about him, I have. He's got a nasty temper." An interesting fact to know, but not something that really aligned with the patient care of a poisoner.

"You know bloody well she wanted her fortune to go to me! To Adelaide and me!" Morris shouted.

Deliah finally raised her voice, the tone nothing short of glacial. "I know no such thing. You barely even spoke to her except to tell her to stop tarnishing our good family name. Well, other than to demand more money for your so-called investments."

With an outraged shout, Morris launched himself at Deliah. Not quite conscious of the gesture, Marta rose to her feet. Deliah's hand moved quick as a striking snake, drawing her fan of all things, and suddenly the innocuous item was firmly pressed not-so-innocuously against Morris's throat.

"Oh, good show," Marta murmured, her normal detachment carefully set aside for a moment. It was a lovely sight indeed. Next to her, the kitchen maid quietly clapped her hands, bouncing up and down on the balls of her feet.

Morris hastily backed away after that, face gone purple with rage. A few more shouted imprecations and he flung himself into the town car, jerking the machine into drive with a grind of gears that made Marta wince, and accelerated down the street.

Deliah tucked her fan away, smoothed one hand down the front of her coat, squared her shoulders, and stalked back inside. Marta watched her go with interest that felt a little more intense than normal, reviewing in her mind the way the woman's hand had moved with such smooth, practiced ease to turn a fan into what seemed to be a weapon.

"Better than a play, that was," the kitchen maid commented. After a moment, she added, "Oi. So are them trousers comfortable?"

Marta watched the door of the row house close, and shot the maid a grin. "You ought to try them some time."

Tartly, the maid answered, "Cook says women who wear trousers are no better than they ought to be."

Her grin took on a wicked edge. "Then we ought to be very good indeed."

MARTA STAYED ON THE wall, as patient as the stone from which it was made, until she'd seen the hearse bear away Miss Nimowitz's body and Deliah leave not long after. By then the gas lamps had lit up and down the street with a sputtering hiss, and the kitchen maid had snuck out once to bring her a cup of hot tea and ask if anything else "fun" had happened.

Thinking of Deliah's odd mention of Kensington's *Compendium* led Marta to pause at the telegraph office and send a few inquiries to scholars who might know more about the book before returning to the hotel. Simms had made himself into a great lump on one of the beds, boots off and be-socked feet giving the room a slightly unpleasant odor, a cup of cool tea at his elbow. A copy of the *Post* lay spread across his bed and half the floor in drifts of newsprint. A sudden yip from under the pile of papers indicated the location of Chippy, and he burst forth a moment later for a paroxysm of enthused greeting.

Simms glanced up over the top of the paper and directed a look of long suffering at her. "He only just went to sleep."

"A bit like children, I've heard."

"Dolly was never that loud."

Marta picked up the coiled lead from the desk and tossed it to Simms. "Take him for a walk to tire him out, then."

"You take him for a walk."

"*I*," she said, looking down her nose at him, "have handwriting analysis to do."

Simms covered his face with the paper for a moment and muttered something unintelligible.

"Hm?"

"I said I think you make this nonsense up half the time to get out of doing your half of the muck jobs," Simms said. But he swung his feet over the edge of the bed and began to put on his boots.

"From your lack of enthusiasm, I presume nothing interesting came up at the trolley platform?"

Simms grunted. "There were actually quite a few people about who had been there at the time. It's a busy platform where several lines cross. Or at the least they claimed to have been around. You know how people are. But—" he extracted a scrap of paper from his pocket "—there were nine votes for *fell*, eight votes for *pushed*—but none of them could agree who might have pushed her and no one mentioned a villainous fellow with a goatee—and twenty-one votes for *gosh Mister Simmons, you have a cute little doggy, does he know any tricks*. I did discover that Chippy can shake a paw and roll over, by the way. I figure the crowd liked it better than his more specialized trick of eating an old lady's face and then her jewelry."

"Crass, Simms."

Simms flipped a hand in her direction and stood, groaning theatrically. "Anything interesting on your end?"

"A bit of light entertainment." She painted the witnessed fight in broad strokes for him. "It strikes me, Simms, that both of us have become lost in the bickering of the living, and thus all but forgotten the most important person in this equation." She sat at the desk and began to go through the satchel she'd filled in Miss Nimowitz's home, extracting the two wills and the *Compendium*. The valuables had already been sent back to the Roost with Elijah; all that remained in the limp sack now was the poisoned teacup. Marta spread out the papers on the room's desk, its top scarred with water rings, and began paging through the book. "To wit: what did Miss Clementine Nimowitz actually *want*?"

Simms shrugged. "Best I can say is she probably didn't want to get poisoned and then shot in the face. And then have a couple of rude buggers steal all of her jewelry."

Marta snorted. "Did you give Chippy another dose of oil?"

"Two. For all that he's cute and fluffy, he's got the digestive fortitude of a cockroach."

Marta snorted. "We may be taking him in for surgery soon."

Simms hesitated, Chippy running in dizzying circles at his feet, jumping at the lead held loosely in the big man's hands. "Gotten fond of the little fellow, you know."

"I assumed so." Chippy might have the intestines of a cockroach, but Simms had the heart of a forty-year-old matron with a penchant for misty watercolors involving kittens. "Have a lovely walk." She didn't look up as a moment later the door opened and shut, the sound of thumping boots, skittering claws, and excited yips fading rapidly down the hall.

Marta unfolded the wills and looked them over first but found nothing amiss with either; both were done by a typewriter, the only handwritten portions the signatures. Miss Nimowitz's signature wasn't significantly different between the two, but the handwriting was quite wobbly. She turned her attention to the *Compendium* and its three different sets of handwriting. She easily recognized the hand of the shaky notes peppered throughout as Clementine's. Some of the comments, while difficult to read, were quite insightful. Others had been scratched out and replaced by one set of the neater handwriting, which offered coherent commentary where there had been only confusion before. The second of the neat hands was a mystery, its notes never corrected, but always quite intelligent.

Marta followed the notes all the way to the end and discovered a slip of folded paper glued to the inside cover of the book. "Hm." She unhooked one of the folds and shook out a slim key, obviously mass-produced and milled on a standard sort of machine. She encountered keys like it all the time, and they could go to any number of locks. None of the locks she'd encountered in Miss Nimowitz's house had been for this sort of key, however.

Curious, that.

Out of idle habit, Marta retrieved a thin square mold she kept as part of her regular kit and made an impression of the key. She set the key down on the desktop and began another go through of the *Compendium*, searching for any hint of the key's origin or intended purpose.

In the middle of her third go through, as she'd begun to recopy some of the notes in their varied handwritings to see if there were similarities in wording, a breath of air stirred one of the pages.

That was her only warning as a black-booted foot, at the end of a leg concealed in flowing black trousers, swung in from the side at her head.

Marta shoved away from the desk, tipping the chair over and continuing to roll backwards. A person covered head to toe in black, eyes cunningly obscured with a thin piece of black gauze, paused to sweep an arm across the desk, swooping up one of the wills.

Marta regained her feet and lunged at her attacker, going for a double-fisted attack. Always more of a brawler when it came to fisticuffs, she wasn't quite prepared for the lightning fast block and counterattack. A hand straight as a knife blade slammed into her ribs. Marta gasped, but bulled forward, using the natural momentum to slam her elbow into her attacked arm, and then drive her other fist into his—her?—solar plexus.

The attacker made another clean, graceful block, hand snapping sideways and up. Marta tried to block the blow and only succeeded in bouncing it a bit higher so it hit her in the nose instead of the throat. While that might have been a good thing for her vital state, the stunning, cracking pain didn't help her efforts at fighting. Blood poured from her nose.

Marta gasped and retaliated, this time more carefully keeping her fists up. She exchanged a series of blows with her assailant, catching him a decent blow across the chin. The black-clad figure reeled to the side, half-landing on the discarded chair. Marta hurried to press her advantage, only to be caught as her attacker snatched up the chair and smashed it into her side.

Momentarily stunned, Marta stumbled back to catch herself on the bedpost, only a firm grip saving her from a fall. The attacker took a quick glance around the room and snatched up the satchel, all but forgotten under the desk. Marta grabbed the item closest at hand—a cheap and ugly vase, what passed for decoration at this hotel—and flung it toward him, her hand steady despite the hits she'd taken. In a lightning fast movement, the attacker kicked the vase back at her—that felt somehow *very* unfair—and then dove out the window as Marta dodged her own projectile.

Marta flung herself at the window, sticking her head out just in time to see the feet of her attacker yank out of view, accompanied by the whining hiss of gears rapidly reeling up a rope. She grinned with blood-painted lips and jumped through the window and sprinted up the rickety fire escape.

The roof was deserted by the time she made it up and cast around. All of the nearby buildings were close enough that any could have been an escape route. Marta took another good look around, considering this new wrinkle. She was quite good when it came to fighting, thus it had been a while since she'd been that thoroughly put on the ropes. However, reviewing what had happened, much of it had been because of the factor of surprise, of being faced with an utterly foreign style.

Also interesting was the fact that the person she'd faced had been a bit shorter than her own natural height. Which was right about the size for Deliah—or Morris. Though she couldn't help but recall the lithe movement of Deliah's hand as she drew her fan as if it were a blade rather than a bit of decoration. That, versus Morris's apparently legendary temper.

"This just got a bit more interesting," she murmured to herself as she climbed back to her room. Only then did she note that the person had taken the key as well as one of the sheaves of paper. Even more interesting was which will had been taken: the more recent one, naming Morris as the sole heir.

ONCE HE WAS OUT of the hotel, Simms decided to make his walk a long one. The night air was pleasantly cool, and the parks in this section of the city were quite well maintained. It was nice to, for once, be able to take a stroll on a level path and without having to carry a machete as a precaution besides. The streetlights had come on and the streets were beginning to surge with people headed to supper appointments as he finally turned back toward the hotel, Chippy still eagerly bouncing ahead of him.

"Mister Smythe, a moment if you please?"

Simms managed to keep from jumping, but it was a near thing. Firmly reminding himself that he was Mister Smythe and there was absolutely nothing at all amiss in his lovely world of tea parties, he turned to face the source of that request—Morris Nimowitz. "Ah, Mister Nimowitz. It is jolly good to see you, if a bit...unexpected." Simms cast a quick glance at Chippy, hoping for a growl or some canine indication of *yes him, he's the one wot did it,* but the dog's attention seemed wholly fixed on nosing a patch of verge.

Morris waved a hand. Whatever coat he'd worn tonight, the yellow light of the streetlamps rendered it a rather sinister black, his face above it shadowy. "I come by here often, just for a bit of time to myself." Sweat glittered on his brow; if he'd been walking, he must have been doing so at a furious pace.

Simms would have had to be blind to miss that several of the man's knuckles were split. "Been in a spot of bother?" he asked, nodding.

"What? Oh." Morris shook his head. "I... had a small fit of temper this afternoon, I'm ashamed to admit. I thought it best to burn it off athletically." He fell into brooding silence.

"Did—"

At which point, Morris burst out with, "It's that impossible harridan, Deliah. She always does try to twist my buttons."

Simms blinked owlishly, but decided to take a tack that had proven successful in the past. "Well, women tend to be like that."

"She's no woman. She's a jackal that's been trained to walk on its hind legs."

"I say, Morris..."

Morris shook his head. "I'm sorry. We barely know each other, and I'm dragging you into the family muck. But your wife seems quite taken with her, and I'd worry about that, were I you."

"Oh?"

"Unnatural ideas," Morris said. "They're like a disease, and the weaker sex does tend to fall prey to them."

"Ah…" Simms nodded, hoping he looked suitably wise as he did so. "Does that mean your Grandaunt…?"

"She was always a bit funny, I'll admit. Had some odd ideas, but everyone's got one of those in the family. You just do your best to ignore them at Christmas. But when, well… I took a bit of a beating on some investments, she was willing to help us out with a bit of cash."

Recalling what the Captain had said about the state of Morris's dress and his house, Simms was forced to wonder if he was still making these bad investments. Or if "bad investments" was wealthy twit speak for "compulsive gambling." "Oh?"

"And then Deliah showed up from one of those extended trips of hers and put some sort of poison in Grandaunt's ear. Oh, she was still friendly enough, but then she turned tight with her money." Morris snorted. "She said she wanted to set up a scholarship fund for girls, or some sort of greenhouse, or… Well, it changed all the time. But it always had something to do with plants, the woman could never leave the sodding things alone. And she'd do it all through Deliah, you see, with her guidance. Grandaunt said she couldn't keep the details straight in her own head any longer."

"Seems like a good cause."

"Help the huddled masses and leave your own blood to be eaten alive by creditors?"

That actually sounded just fine to Simms as well, but he firmly reminded himself that Mister Smythe had different priorities than Mister Simms. "Right. When you put it like that…ghastly." At his feet, Chippy, who had been sniffing around, paused at Morris's shoe and made an odd little noise.

"She would have been far better off letting me invest her money, and she'd *wanted* to. But after Deliah showed up, she changed her mind so suddenly. I can't imagine what sort of nonsense my cousin poured into her ear."

Simms nodded, hoping he'd managed to screw his face into something approximately sympathetic. "Ladies don't seem to have a head for money, I'll admit."

"Indeed. But oh no, it was Deliah, Deliah, Deliah…" Morris looked down, sniffing and frowning.

Simms sniffed as well. There was suddenly a very particular and unpleasant sort of aroma in the air.

Morris looked up, mouth snapping shut in a look of rage for a moment. "Mister Smythe, I say!"

Simms looked down, just in time to see Chippy finish making a rather large, mushy, and redolent deposit on Morris's shoe. So much for the dog not having an opinion of the man, he thought in near hysteria. Simms carefully cleared his throat, fighting to not smile. "Oh, I am sorry, Mister Nimowitz. I think the little chap must have eaten something naughty, to make a mess like that."

Morris took a hasty step back. Simms caught a slight glitter, perhaps the hint of something slithering within the mess. Hastily he patted his pocket and offered Morris his handkerchief, which the man stared at in horror. "Your dog," Morris ground out, "ruined my shoe!"

Simms stepped forward, carefully skirting the mess. His eyes watered from the smell, but that allowed him to hide the worst of it from view. "Frightfully sorry. You've no idea. Please, wipe it off as best you can and send the details of your size and the like to me at the hotel. I'll buy you a new pair. I couldn't possibly expect you to wear these again."

Morris seemed to calm at that suggestion, perhaps at the prospect of having a brand new pair of—no doubt expensive, and Simms wagered, with the price further inflated—shoes he didn't have to buy for himself. He snatched the handkerchief from Simms's hand. "Not after the leather has been so...so *traumatized*." Breathing pointedly through his mouth rather than his nose, he bent to mop at his shoe, and then tried to hand the handkerchief back to a horrified Simms before discarding it on the ground. "Good evening, Mister Smythe."

Relieved, Simms nodded. "Good evening, Mister Nimowitz." He resisted the urge to shoo the man away with his hands. Morris left quickly enough, walking awkwardly as if he was afraid to put any weight on the shoe.

Simms looked down at Chippy, who gave him a canine grin, tongue lolling. "And you, Mister Chippy. I don't know if I ought to give you more of that jerky or set your bum on fire. How you produced something that massive, I can't imagine. Not to mention the *stench*." He carefully poked the discarded handkerchief over the worst of the mess with a bit of a stick from nearby. No, a stick was not going to cut it. Off they went in search of the nearest groundskeeping shed. Simms liberated a bucket and trowel, and returned to the site to dig for gold.

Simms had the bucket in one hand, another handkerchief covering its top in an ineffectual effort to hold in the smell.

Chippy trotted happily alongside, looking disturbingly pleased with himself. Then again, Simms supposed, it was as if a great weight had left—or ejected—from the little animal. The lobby of the hotel was mercifully empty, though the clerk at the front desk jerked his head up in Simms's wake, one hand covering his nose. He made it to the elevator before the man called for his attention, the words cut off by the doors closing.

As he held his breath for the next four floors, he was forced to wonder if this was perhaps not the wisest decision he could have made. Perhaps the stairs next time.

Oh, heaven forbid there'd be a next time.

Simms opened the door to the hotel room and paused, bucket and stench momentarily forgotten as he took in the overturned chair, the shattered vase, and Captain Ramos, a bloody handkerchief clutched to her nose, sitting in the middle of it all.

She turned toward him, grinning around the limp crimson cloth. "Ah, Simms," she said. "I hope you had an interesting walk."

"Not by your standards, I'd guess." He held out the bucket toward her. Her eyebrows went up, presumably as the stink penetrated even her thoroughly abused nose. "But I got you some jewelry," he said, deadpan. "Though I'm afraid you'll have to take it as-is."

MARTA VENTURED OUT TO hide the jewelry in one of their drop boxes before any other discussion was had, taking the most twisting and circuitous route she could find. Remembering her attacker's frantic snatch for the satchel, she had little doubt the missing jewelry had been the aim as the most valuable things that she and Simms had liberated.

A thoughtful Simms greeted her upon her return. He'd at least swept all the debris out of the way and cleaned the blood from the floor before returning to his newspaper. Chippy lay sprawled across his lap, snoring gently. "Didn't get to tell you before you ran off, but I saw Morris just now," he said over the top of his paper.

Marta paused. "Is that so?"

"Yeah. He was a bit out of breath when we started talking, too." Another glance. "Coincidence, that."

Marta picked up the *Compendium* and retreated to her own bed to sit. "Sometimes a coincidence is just that."

"Also had some freshly split knuckles."

She grimaced, lightly touching her nose with one finger. It was going to take a lot of makeup to conceal the worst of the damage. "I'll admit, Simms, the prospect of having had my nose broken by Morris Nimowitz is not one I relish."

"The man *is* a twit."

"For now, while we still have two operating hypotheses, let us leave it be."

Simms grinned evilly at her. "You're the boss. Oh, and two telegrams came. I tucked them into the book."

She hurried to open the little volume, only to have Simms say, "She wrote it, apparently."

"Wrote what?"

"The first telegram says that Clementine Nimowitz is George L. F. Kensington. Or rather he was her beard, I suppose."

"Ah." That, she had expected; it wasn't exactly uncommon for a woman to publish under a man's name in such circumstances. And that added some sense to the notes, to be certain; they were the changes to be made for the next edition of the book, presumably. Which would—

"And the second says that the pages for the third edition were turned in last week."

—which would then make it the final project completed by Clementine Nimowitz before her death. "Oh my…" Marta breathed, ideas swirling through her mind as she connected this idea, of one last scholarly work completed, to the handwriting, the odd throw-away statements that had been made about Clementine. And why would a dedicated horticulturist be in a house without plants? Might she have given them all away first, wanting to see them well-looked-after? It added up to an interesting but still incomplete picture, the solid beginnings of *why*, ready to branch out into *how* and *why now*.

"Hm?"

"You said Miss Nimowitz's maid was at Saint Joseph's, correct?"

"Yes, but they said she was unconscious last they heard."

"It'd be helpful if she was awake, but not necessary." Marta shut the book. "We'll be at the hospital as soon as the doors open for visiting hours."

"Fine with me. Means I get to sleep in for once." Simms stretched out his arms. "Dolly does like to get me up early."

It was Marta's turn to grin evilly. "Little Mister Chippy may have something to say about that."

AND INDEED HE DID, twice during the night. But it was Marta who took him out for both walks. She had no idea how Dolly managed to wake her father as he claimed, considering he snored cheerfully on through whining and yelping and scratching at the door. She'd heard him once described as sleeping like the dead, though she'd never known a corpse to be so noisy.

When Simms finally did deign to crack an eyelid open, they had a strangely leisurely breakfast, coffee and soft-boiled eggs and shockingly nice steaks, to which Marta added a bowl of chili, much to Simms's dismay. Leisurely or no, she dragged them promptly from the hotel in time to catch the trolley that would take them to St. Joseph's. Chippy spent most of the journey in Simms's arms, cheerfully covering his brown jacket with fine white hair and panting hotly against his ear.

The matron for the third floor took them to see Elizabeth Strickland with a murmured, "So good of you to visit. Poor lamb, I think she can hear you even now."

That answered all Marta could have asked about the woman's condition—still unhelpfully unconscious. And she did look a mess when they were shown into her section of the room, divided off by a series of curtains. Elizabeth Strickland had probably been a woman made pretty by animation; still and pale, she became wholly unremarkable, wisps of brown hair poking from under the bandages swaddling her head. Marta sincerely doubted the poor lady would ever hear anything again.

Simms doffed his hat, looking down at her. Chippy squirmed out of his hiding place in Simms's coat and refused to hold still until set on the bed. There he snuffled at her fingers, nosing them disconsolately. "I'm sorry, little man," Simms said, his voice gone rather hoarse. "I don't think she'll be waking up."

Marta bent to peer at her. "I'm afraid I must agree. Nasty business. Simms. Keep watch at the door if you please."

Without further ado, she retrieved a locked wooden chest from under the bed—the possessions Elizabeth had with her at the time of the accident. She made quick work of the flimsy lock with her picks and examined the contents. No clothes—those had likely been far too bloody to be worth keeping. A few bits of surprisingly high quality jewelry—those were in keeping with what she'd seen in Clementine's home, so either the maid had been a thief, or her employer had believed in generous gifts. No sign of the envelope that Simms's mailman had mentioned, suspiciously enough. Marta picked up the little leather handbag, noting a small bloodstain on one corner, and upended it onto the bed. A small mirror, cracked pocket watch, pen, paper, and key ring fell out. Marta gave the bag another little shake and one more key slithered onto the light blue hospital blanket, this one attached to a leather cord.

Marta picked it up, frowning. It was an unremarkable key, cheap and mass produced...just like the one she'd found in the *Compendium*. She retrieved the mold of the other key from her pocket and confirmed that, yes, they were the same.

"This," Marta said, waggling the bit of metal in her fingers. "Quite literally the *key*. How frightful."

"Someone has a sense of humor."

"A terribly literal one." She returned the rest of the items to the chest and re-locked it, and then stuffed it back under the bed. "What time is it, Simms?"

Obligingly, he checked his pocket watch. "Just gone half past nine."

"There are rather a lot of banks in this area, I saw as we came in. Banks offering safe deposit boxes." She turned the key in her fingers. There were many possibilities for such a key, but that one certainly fit the location. "The banks all ought to be open by now." And for half an hour—they might already be too late.

"Whoever attacked me last evening took an exact copy of that key from me, and has no doubt put it to use already or will soon. We'd best hurry."

Only hurry was quite difficult, when one didn't know where to aim hastened footsteps. Chippy trotted gamely along, fluffy tail high like a flag, as they crossed and re-crossed the broad square.

They found the correct bank on the fourth try, one reputable enough to trust but still small-time enough to warrant cheap keys and slightly shoddy locks. Confronted by the bank of safe deposit boxes within the vault, Marta referred to the *Compendium*. There were no numbers in the notes, but... Marta turned to the page of the Zacetachichi and snorted, a little shock running through her. "Oh, you rude thing," she murmured. Yet that was a sense of humor she could certainly appreciate.

"Captain?"

Marta waved a hand to shush him. "Box 202, Simms." The key proved to be a perfect fit for that lock, confirming what she now knew, the details sliding into place in her mind. Deliah must be quite good at disguise, to have gone about masquerading as Morris. And she was quite good at other things as well, Marta thought ruefully, lightly touching her still-aching nose.

"No envelope," Simms said. "Just this." He handed her a folded note.

In neat copperplate handwriting now familiar from the notes in the *Compendium*, the note read:

Dearest "Mrs. Smythe:"

I'd like to thank you for retrieving my key. Breaking in to a bank vault is a messy proposition in the best of times, and I've a timetable.

If you would be so kind, I'd like my dog back now. I helped Grandaunt pick him out. Oh and I'd like my jewelry back as well. It's part of my rightful inheritance, you know.

Sincerely,

Deliah

PS: I'll be waiting at the little coffee shop across the square for the next hour. I'll be ever so disappointed if I don't see you.

Marta laughed, folding the note back up in her hands. "Rude indeed. Wonderfully rude."

"What?"

"Fancy a spot of coffee, Simms? I've a few questions left I'd like answered."

As promised, Deliah Nimowitz waited in the back corner of the coffee shop across the square. She took out her fan and waved it coquettishly at Marta and Simms as they approached. As soon as they were within sight, Chippy began tugging madly at his lead. After a hand wave from Marta, Simms shrugged and let him go; the little dog raced to cover the last bit of distance, the leash whipping and snapping behind him. He immediately squirmed into Deliah's lap.

There was something satisfying to Marta, to see Deliah's black mourning skirts get coated with dog fluff just as Simms's jacket had. It made her look slightly less collected and smug. Deliah's face was partially obscured by a black lace veil, though Marta could sense amusement crackling around her like an electric halo.

"Hello, little darling," Deliah murmured to Chippy, and patiently allowed him to wash her chin. "Please do sit...well, come now, you might as well tell me your real names."

"You haven't figured that out yet?" Marta asked. "I'm a bit disappointed."

"I have been a bit busy," Deliah said tartly. "Though if the two of you are married, I'll eat my fan."

Simms snorted. "Do I look mad to you?"

Marta was fairly certain that was supposed to be her line. But amusing enough, normally their bickering seemed to render their occasional role as a married couple more believable. "Captain Marta Ramos, at your service." She swept Deliah a bow, doffing a hat she wasn't actually wearing, and sat. "And my associate, whom I haven't enough breath to name, and he'd rather you just call him Simms anyway."

Deliah's fan snapped open and fluttered, perhaps obscuring a smile. "Oh, I *am* honored," she said.

Simms had remained standing; he glanced between the two women warily. "So *she* murdered Clementine Nimowitz?" His eyebrows went up as if to ask *and we're going to have coffee with her?*

"Do sit down, Simms." Marta patted the chair next to her. She turned her attention to Deliah, meeting those remarkable tawny eyes again. The veil was no impediment at all. "Miss Clementine Nimowitz killed herself. Correct, Deliah?" With a bit of post-mortem assistance, obviously. But the intentional nature of it seemed clear: sending the maid away on an errand, giving away all of her no-doubt beloved plants, finishing the book that had been her life's work first.

Deliah nodded. Something tightened in her expression as if in pain, though Marta now knew better than to take any such tells at face value. "I was simply there to make certain it wouldn't get... ugly... after."

"It was plenty ugly when we saw it," Simms muttered.

But they all knew it could have been immeasurably worse, all three glancing at Chippy.

"Also, the intention was to give it the appearance of a murder, since she didn't want to…*shame*…the family with a suicide. Always the bloody family and the reputation. And now you'll ask why, I suppose," Deliah said, sighing. "That's rather personal…"

"I know why already." Marta leaned forward, elbows on the table. "She'd become senile, hadn't she?"

Deliah drew back a bit. Marta took oblique satisfaction in that. "How did you guess? The entire family had conspired to keep it quiet. One of the few things upon which we could agree."

"I don't *guess*," Marta said. "I might have ignored the comments here and there about her having gone a bit forgetful or odd, since that's the sort of thing people often say behind the backs of the elderly. But the corrections written in the *Compendium* were inescapable. She'd only partially updated the book before she began to lose herself, hadn't she?"

Deliah's voice was a bit hollow when she answered. "Just control of her hands, at first. I helped her with the last of it, taking dictation when she could focus. She knew she was struggling, but she wanted it finished." Her delicate features thinned out with sorrow. "She was so frustrated. Such an intellect, and then…"

That was a specter Marta hoped would never haunt her, though she did also wish to live to a ripe old age. While not normally given to sympathy, it still struck home, though not enough to put her off her line of reasoning. "And knowing her weakness, the less scrupulous members of your family sought to control her."

"Yes." The word was a venomous hiss.

"But not you yourself?" Marta raised an eyebrow.

"You took the evidence yourself. The will that named me as heir, which Morris so vilely attempted to replace, was signed before any symptoms began to intrude upon her life."

Which they had only Deliah's word for, not that Marta felt a compelling urge to make herself magistrate over this familial squabble. The questions were being answered, and that was her primary concern. Next to her, she could all but feel Simms radiating discomfort at the implication. "I can only presume that Elizabeth Strickland's final errand was to take a new copy of the will to the safe deposit box, then."

"Ah, Elizabeth," Deliah sighed. "That was unfortunate. She was a good woman, and to be felled by random chance…" She stroked Chippy's head. "That was why Chippy was left in the house, you see. She was supposed to have been back, perhaps an hour after the deed was done, to find her mistress murdered. But when she didn't return, well…I could hardly be the one to find her just on my own. Morris had already been such an ass about me visiting Grandaunt that I had to start creeping about disguised as him to do so."

Marta snorted. "I don't think you *had* to make him your disguise."

Despite the grim topic, Deliah laughed lightly. "Well, true. It was just a bit more fun that way."

"Why, then, take his now-invalid will?"

There was something very predatory about Deliah's smile. "So I could tuck it away in Grandaunt's house where he would find it. I want to see the look on his face when his hopes are thoroughly dashed at the magistrate's bench."

Ah, family. The source of such warm feelings. "And just what are you, Deliah?"

The smile turned secretive. "A spy, dear Captain."

"For whom?" Oh, but that was *fun*.

"For whoever can afford me." Deliah retrieved a small filigree watch from an inner pocket of her jacket, checking the time before snapping it shut. "And with that, I'm afraid I must go. I've an appointment with Grandaunt's solicitor. You took longer than I expected." But rather than rise immediately, she leaned forward, Chippy momentarily hidden by her bosom. "But I'll take my jewelry back now. That set was Grandaunt's favorite."

Marta spread her hands, this time her smile taking on a smug air. "I no longer have it, I'm afraid. I've sent it to a safe place, but you know how this goes. Sometimes things simply get lost."

Anger flashed hotly in Deliah's eyes for a moment, and then she laughed, sitting back again. "I should have made my request before telling you of my profession, shouldn't I?"

"Wouldn't have made a bit of difference, I'm afraid. You've already made quite an impression on me." Marta resisted the urge to touch her nose.

Deliah set Chippy down on the ground and rose to her feet. Automatically, Marta rose as well. Deliah stepped around the table, putting them in closer proximity than was probably necessary. A stray corner of Marta's mind noted, again, that Deliah smelled quite lovely. "Well, then. As a personal favor to me, would you mind looking for it?"

"Well, we don't normally take jobs…" Marta drawled. "We're pirates. We tend to take rather than return. But…"

"I take personal favors rather seriously." Deliah reached out as if to pick a bit of fluff from the bodice of Marta's dress, but instead leaned in more closely.

"I—"

Deliah proceeded to cut off the conversational riposte Marta had prepared by kissing her, a technique no one had ever dared try before.

A moment later, Marta caught Deliah's wrist, pulling her hand away from the pocket sewn on the inside of her jacket. "Naughty, naughty," she said.

"Well, I did have to try."

"I don't—"

Deliah gave her a particularly wicked smile and kissed her again.

As gambits went, Marta decided after a moment, she could get to like this one, particularly when it involved such soft lips and— *oh my*—a very clever tongue, nearly so clever as the exceedingly attractive mind behind it all.

After a long moment in which Marta heard nothing but the thud of her own heart and the sound of her breath rushing, Deliah pulled back. Delicately, she reached up to touch a finger just to the side of Marta's nose. "More makeup, dear Captain. You're still looking a bit squashed. I'd offer to kiss it better, but I think your man Simms might have an apoplectic fit." She turned to go, Marta's hand falling away—when, exactly, had she gripped the edge of Deliah's sleeve like that?—and said over her shoulder in a thoroughly amused tone, "I look forward to hearing from you."

For once robbed entirely of words, Marta watched her go silently. Deliah did not glance back, her skirts swishing gracefully as she walked away, though Chippy did cast a few little looks toward Simms before bounding happily along in her wake. Only when Deliah had left the shop, her departure announced by the tinkling of the bell, did Marta murmur, "Oh, you wicked creature."

Simms looked rather like someone had hit him in the back of the head with a brick. At some point he'd risen to his feet—oh, the dear man, had he thought Deliah was going to attack her?—but now his legs seemed to no longer be prepared to hold him, and he thumped back down into his seat. "Well," he said after a long moment, his tone shocked and affronted. Had he been an elderly society maven, Marta would have expected him to be clutching at his pearls. "Well, now I have seen *everything*."

"Oh, I hardly think that, Simms. I've gotten the impression there's quite a bit more to it." Marta sank back down to her own chair, carefully licking her lips. A thoughtful smile turned up the corners of her mouth as she considered the jewelry, the opportunities, the chance to work both with and against someone of that caliber—someone of that caliber with such gorgeous eyes and clever lips. "I'm certainly looking forward to finding out."

3
The Jade Tiger

"YOU DO REALIZE I'M not a hired gun," Captain Marta Ramos said, staring over the rim of her pint glass. "I don't...take jobs." She was a brown, handsome woman who wore trousers and boots by preference, since both were easier to fight in.

"We really don't," Meriwether Octavian Simms—known by preference as "Simms"—agreed. He was a lanky man with a face made overly serious by muttonchops, his vest and coat of buttery buckskin.

"It is not a job." The woman shook her head. She looked old, though to Marta's keen eye it was old before her time, worry lines creasing her face and her black hair gone stringy and shocked with gray. She was dressed like the other women of Silver Cliff, work boots and a canvas apron singed from the furnaces, but her high cheekbones and almond-shaped eyes were unusual in this part of the duchy.

Marta set down her glass delicately. "Well, then, please speak your mind."

There was a certain level of *infamy* that Captain Ramos possessed, and Simms was fairly convinced that she reveled in it. While she never went into the large cities of the Grand Duchy of Denver without some sort of horrifying disguise, in the smaller mining towns (where infamy transformed to fame) she insisted on wearing her scarlet frock coat. It meant that they were constantly approached by those hoping to hire them (always unsuccessful), sell them information (occasionally useful), or pick a fight with Captain Ramos over the fact that she happened to be female (often good for a laugh).

"May I...?" The woman tilted her head toward the empty chair at the table.

"As if it's been waiting for your arrival." Simms gave it a push with the toe of one boot.

The woman sat with a sigh that spoke of long hours on her feet. "My name is Jun Xing. I was formerly employed in the house of Lord Pike."

"I take it that your parting was not on good terms," Marta said.

"I was blacklisted."

"So this is about revenge."

"No," Jun said firmly. "It's about justice."

Marta shrugged. "I already told you. I'm a pirate."

Jun's hands were squeezed so tightly in her lap that her knuckles were white. "I merely have information. Perhaps you will find it useful. If you do not, telling you has cost me nothing."

"And what information could be so worthwhile?"

"Lord Pike is coming to Denver from the Grand Duchy of Salt Lake. Within the week. And when he comes, he will have a gift for the Grand Duke." Jun's smile was brittle. "They did not part on very good terms either."

"What manner of gift?"

"A large box of treated calcite lenses. Perfect ones, I have been told."

"That's quite interesting," Marta still sounded quite bored. The way she steepled her fingers in front of her lips spoke volumes to the contrary; to Simms, it was a warning bell indicating that his life, through no fault of his own, was about to become complicated. "I'll be certain to consider what you've told us."

Jun opened her mouth to speak again, but shook her head and stood, her chair scraping across the floor. "I'm sorry I wasted your time."

As she turned to go, Marta asked sharply, "What did Lord Pike take from you?"

Jun looked over her shoulder, one hand coming up to her throat. "A gold and jade pendant of a tiger. The greatest treasure of my family."

"I see. Good day to you, Mistress Xing."

Simms waited in silence until the saloon doors had swung shut. "That was a bit cruel even for you, sir."

Marta snorted and picked up her beer. "She's directing us to a trap, Simms. It's obvious."

"If it's a trap, we're not going."

"We most certainly are. If there's even a hint of truth, it's too valuable to pass up. I need to replace the lenses in my microscope, and you've been wanting a new set of goggles."

"Or you could just, I don't know, finally take a look at Lord Mastern's house, the one with the safe just sitting in the front room? The one I told you about weeks ago? Then we could buy all the lenses you'd ever want."

Marta laughed, leaning back in her chair. "I could, it's true. But where would the fun be in that?"

Jun's story was easily confirmed with a few discreet inquiries around the nicer tea parlors in Denver, accomplished by Captain Ramos disguised in a hideous magenta dress, her back kinked in a way most unnatural to make her appear nearly a foot shorter. Lord Pike's return was the talk of society, good for juicy gossip about just what bit of crockery he'd thrown at the Grand Duke during their last, explosive dinner.

Messages sent by telegraph had to be obtuse by necessity, but within two days, they knew that Lord Pike had chartered a private train and supplied it with a small private security force. Even more important, they were given details of the train's departure time by the secretary to the Station Master in Salt Lake, whose dignity had been affronted by the notoriously rapacious Lord's demands.

Thus, Simms came to be driving the smallest of their rail cars through the Rocky Mountains at an uncomfortable speed, with no headlamps. Captain Ramos, who had told him only to wake her three hours beyond the continental divide, was asleep with her feet propped on a corner of the control panel. Her expression was so peaceful that Simms felt an unbearable urge to grab a handful of her curly hair and shake her head back and forth until she was awake and just as tense as him.

It was—sadly—an urge he'd long since learned to ignore.

Three hours after beginning the descent from the continental divide, his hands white-knuckled on the controls and his fingers beginning to ache with fatigue, the little wind-up timer he'd set let out a quiet ding. With no small amount of glee he peeled his fingers from the brake lever—all but useless at these grades anyway—and shoved the Captain's feet off the control panel.

Only she was already awake, eyes glittering faintly in the backlights of the dials. "Really, Simms, was that necessary?"

He clutched the brake lever again, to comfort himself. "Next time, say something."

She dismissed the complaint with a flick of her fingers. "We haven't yet passed through the canyon, have we?"

"I haven't been in a hurry."

There was a rustle as the Captain pulled a bit of paper from her pocket. "What's our average speed been?" She consulted the paper after Simms answered. "In twenty-five minutes, we ought to be by Dotsero. Do you remember the switch there?"

"The track's terrible and the road's worse."

"Still. It will get us to the top of the canyon. There's a bridge that I've a date with."

THE BRIDGE IN QUESTION was a rickety affair of wood and not nearly enough iron bolts; it had once been a railroad bridge before being cannibalized of its useful parts. It was still stable enough to bear the weight of cattle, as attested to by the bits of dung strewn across the weathered boards.

Simms gave the bridge a dubious glance. "How long before our train passes by?"

Captain Ramos checked her pocket watch. "Twelve hours if there aren't any delays."

"Except there are always delays."

"Of course. You'll have plenty of time for those sandwiches you packed after you get back up to the divide. The train shouldn't be that far until well after dark"

"At least they'll be running with headlamps," Simms muttered.

She waved him off. "A little danger is good for the spirit. I left that anatomy text I picked up last week under the seat if you fancy some reading."

"I don't think I've ever been that bored."

Marta busied herself rigging the bridge for a safe descent onto the tracks fifty feet below. A few fitful catnaps on the wind-swayed boards followed in the warm afternoon, though she woke instantly as the rumbling of a train echoed through the canyon.

The train, a short one with only seven cars, came around the curve slowly; the narrow, winding canyon made for relatively safe speeds for jumping a train. Unhurried, Marta pulled on her leather gloves. As the engine, belching soft clouds of steam and smoke, slid under the bridge, she kicked the rope over the side.

With economy of motion, she slid down the rope, letting her gloves bear the brunt of the friction. Less than a foot above the top of the moving cars, she stopped, took a deep breath for timing, and then let go.

Even at low speeds, the impact was unpleasant. She threw herself into a controlled roll to keep from tumbling backwards, bruising her shoulder in the process. The thick leather gloves squeaked against metal as she flattened herself to the roof and clung.

Letting out a breath she hadn't been conscious of holding, Marta crawled to the escape hatch built into the roof. She pried up the hatch using a metal wedge and dropped into the car. It was filled with crates, part of Lord Pike's household packed up for transport to Denver. Marta paused to pull a small mirrored lamp from the satchel hidden under her coat, folding the contraption together and lighting it before she closed the hatch.

"Well," she informed the crate she crouched on, "I've several hours before the passengers sleep, so I suppose I might as well have a look around." She didn't think Lord Pike the sort to keep something so valuable in with his luggage—he was far too grasping for that—but one never knew.

AFTER A FRUITLESS SEARCH, she made her way back up to the first freight car. The sky had grown quite dark in the meantime, though she hunkered down to wait for another hour for safety's sake.

The first two passenger cars were plainly for the household members and guards, retained against a general attack. She froze once to sleepy murmurs as she opened a door, but after just a little stirring of the curtain across the berth, the sound subsided.

There was a guard in the third car, standing at something approximating attention.

He opened his mouth to shout; she sprinted down the short length of the hallway, feet silent on the rich carpeting, and drove her fist into his throat. That stopped any sound and he toppled. She snatched the lapels of his coat before he could crash to the floor and dragged him to the lavatory. There she dosed him with a bit of chloroform, just to be certain he wouldn't wake at an inconvenient moment. "Thank you for marking the room I want, by the way." She gave his face a light pat.

Opening the unlocked door a crack allowed a fascinating array of horrible snores into the hall. Marta listened for a few moments to find their rhythm, and then let herself into the room. The snoring gentleman was no doubt Lord Pike, a man with coal-black hair and a mustache that made him sneer even in sleep. Marta freshened her handkerchief with more chloroform and dangled it near his face.

An array of drinks glasses, their insides thinly coated with the remnants of sticky liqueurs, covered the top of the safe. Marta rested her ear against the front of the safe, eyes half closed as she felt her way through the lock.

The safe contained an array of rather overdone jewelry and a wooden box filled with the treated calcite lenses, each wrapped in a scrap of silk. She stowed that in her satchel, and then as an afterthought added a pearl necklace, the nicest piece of the bunch. A little nod toward money would make Simms happy, since he was always concerned about such practical things.

Behind her, the door opened.

Marta spun, drawing her pistol. Down the blacked-out barrel, she found herself looking at a teenaged girl. The girl did not look wholly Asian, but there was a fineness to her features that Marta found familiar; an instant later she caught sight of the necklace she wore, a pendant of jade and gold shaped like a tiger.

She quirked one eyebrow at the girl, who had covered her mouth with white-gloved hands as if holding in a scream. "You're Mistress Xing's daughter?"

Hands still covering her mouth, the girl nodded, eyes flicking toward Lord Pike.

"He shan't wake up for a few minutes." Marta lowered the pistol. The girl was fully dressed despite the late hour, a small satchel in a heap at her feet. "You've been in contact with your mother, I take it?"

The girl nodded again.

"And what horrid thing is your father intending to do with you, which will no doubt tug at my heart strings?"

"I'm to be married," the girl whispered.

Marta ran a hand through her hair, an annoyed sound caught in her throat. Well of course, what other torment would await a young lady of a noble house? And of any option, it was the one most likely to catch the attention of Captain Ramos, known for her peculiar ideas about women. While no one had any idea what horrors filled her past—not even Simms—Marta had strong feelings on the subject. "Well played, Mistress Xing," she murmured.

"I'm sorry?"

Marta shook her head. "I suppose you'll be coming with me?"

"I'd very much like to."

She holstered her pistol. "Two conditions: you'll never tell anyone I did anything but kidnap you cruelly, and if you fall behind I will leave you."

"I promise, Captain Ramos."

"And what is your name?"

"Fei." The girl smiled. "Fei Xing."

"Fly away. Appropriate. Come along." Marta shut the safe, and then led the girl to the freight cars.

Fei's face was pale as Marta boosted her up onto the roof, but she bit her lip and remained silent. She hugged the roof fiercely as Marta climbed out and shut the hatch.

"You needn't fear, the train's not going to buck like a horse and throw you off. Though I'd recommend you remove your shoes." Marta paused while the girl did so. "Just walk along the roof as it was a bridge." She led the girl to the end of the train, taking care to help her across the gaps between the cars.

"Do we jump?" Fei asked, staring at the darkness with horrified fascination.

"Not quite yet." Marta removed a flare gun from her satchel and fired. Yellow-orange light threw the rough terrain—and more importantly, the shape on the tracks a few hundred feet behind them—into relief for a brief moment. "There's my lieutenant, Simms. He'll be picking us up."

Fei clutched her arms around herself, shivering. "How?"

"We'll jump." Marta caught the horrified look the girl gave her. "It's perfectly safe so long as you jump straight. He'll be going the same speed as the train. It's simple physics."

Fei's expression said that she had little faith in physics.

Simms pulled the rail car up close to the train—on an uphill grade, the speed was predictable. A steady stream of steam flowed from the car's steel stack. A moment later, a platform padded with a few thin cushions slid forward from the roof of the car.

"Go on then," Marta said. She grasped Fei's arm, but the girl leaned back, setting her heels against the roof.

"I don't think I can."

"Of course you can." For a moment, Marta considered reminding her of the second condition she'd agreed to, but knew it would do nothing to assuage the girl's fear. Instead, she leaned down and whispered: "The first time I did this, I was only your age. And it was terrifying, yes, but also exhilarating. That's how freedom is. If you're not prepared for that, it might be best for you to stay put and let your father make your decisions."

Fei shoved her hands off with a narrow-eyed glare. "He blacklisted my mother when she told me who she was. I want nothing to do with him!"

"Then I think you've made your choice."

Fei made a sound suspiciously like a snarl. An instant later, her feet made a hollow *thump thump* on the roof of the car and she jumped the short distance with an undignified scream.

Marta grinned. While she'd never admit it, the first time she'd jumped off a moving train, she'd screamed far louder.

JUN WAITED FOR THEM at the small rail depot in Silver Cliff, huddled under a shawl against the cold.

Fei tried to run to the woman. Marta caught her arm, ignoring the girl's startled yelp. "Mistress Xing, I must thank you for your information. Or rather, my microscope will thank you once I've installed the new lenses."

Jun's eyes never left her daughter's face. "I'm only glad I could be of assistance, Captain."

Marta hooked one finger under the pendant Fei wore around her neck. "And I stole something else, as you can see. I'll be keeping this, but you're welcome to the bit that tagged along."

"Mother!"

"Give her your pendant, Fei." Jun smiled. "If you're too greedy about pretty things, you'll turn into your father."

Fei couldn't pull the pendant off quickly enough. Marta released her arm, the bit of jewelry dangling from her fingers as daughter and mother embraced. When Jun looked up again, Marta gave her a mocking bow, her face set in dispassionate lines. "Well played, Mistress."

"It wasn't a game."

"It's always a game." Marta tucked the pendant into her pocket. "But in this one, I think we can both count ourselves the winner."

4
The Ugly Tin Orrery

THE LANTERN WOBBLED FAINTLY, caught by the low thrum of the engine, boilers banked and waiting. The lantern was also at an odd angle relative to the ceiling.

This was due to the fact that the Engine, fondly called Diabola, currently sat at a severe twelve percent grade. The commonly used tracks through the Rocky Mountains rose much more gently; such steep grades were limited to hidden ramps cut into the side of the mountain.

It wasn't the most comfortable of angles for a person to work at, let alone rest, but Marta Ramos managed it with the ease of long practice. She watched the lantern through slitted eyes, her feet, clad in black leather cavalry boots, propped on a weapons locker. Thanks to the boilers, the air inside was close and heavy. She had her linen sleeves rolled up, revealing slim brown forearms pocked with shiny pink-white scars. Her normally wild, curly brown hair was pulled tightly into a braid that had been coiled into a bun and secured with several pins far thicker and sharper than those traditionally seen in a lady's hair.

"Captain?"

"Hm?" She glanced up at the tall man framed in the doorway, head ducked and shoulders hunched to keep from bumping the ceiling. In silhouette his face looked strange, thanks to his carefully tended gingery muttonchops.

Meriwether Octavian Simms—known by preference as simply "Simms" to friend and foe alike—stepped fully through the doorway and poked at her feet until she dropped them from the locker. "Lights sighted on the ridge. They should be heading up the incline in about five minutes or so."

"Excellent." Marta stood, adjusting to the strange tilt of the floor with ease, and pulled on her coat. Scarlet velvet, the frock coat was both her signature and her one bit of flash. If she was to commit acts of robbery across the Rocky Mountains, she wanted her marks to know that they'd been seen to by a true pirate. "Do you have the new calculations from Masterson?" She took the slip of paper he offered and read it over quickly. Elijah Masterson had taken over the more annoying duties of engineer from her, thankfully freeing her up for the more interesting work of the actual raid.

"Don't know why you don't just do them yourself."

"We won't be a one ship operation forever." She nodded and returned the slip. "No math errors this time. We'll hit the rails properly."

"You're certain?"

"When have I ever led you wrong?" She flashed him a grin and popped open the weapons locker. Saber, machete, three pistols, were briefly checked and soon all arrayed on her person.

"I seem to recall an occasion near the Duchy of Missoula that involved jumping entirely over the rails…"

She waved a hand. "Technicality. No one had bothered to tell me we were running seven tonnes light. I'll not be held responsible for that. My calculations were perfectly sound."

"Took two years off my life and an inch off my height."

"The height you can afford. You're a monstrosity. Don't tempt me to do it more often." Captain Ramos was quite tall for a woman, enough so that it made most men uncomfortable. Simms topped her by a few inches; some found that comforting before it was made abundantly clear that he was *her* lieutenant, not the other way around.

She handed Simms his own set of weapons, snapping her fingers at him when he tried to wave off the machete. "Required, Simms. Do stop complaining. It doesn't suit a man of your years." She sincerely doubted that any Infected would be encountered on a train, but stranger things had happened in her lifetime. She preferred to not be surprised, all told, and she'd found that it was always best to have a diverse array of tools, whether for engineering a solution or fighting off a ravening horde of Infected.

"My advanced years, yes, not much more advanced than yours." He hung the heavy, thick blade from his belt.

"Always advancing, never in retreat."

"Lights even with our position, sir!" the lookout, Gregory Kinzer, called back.

"Excellent, Mister Kinzer." Captain Ramos took up her hat and slapped it onto her head. "Mister Cavendesh, sound the general alarm!"

"Aye, sir!" Amelia Cavendesh caroled back from the front of the engine. She had once confided in Marta that her original goal had been to gain acclaim as an opera singer. While she had never been entirely clear what had scuttled that ambition, she was still quite dedicated to the cause of keeping her voice in training.

A moment later the lights dimmed, power rerouting entirely to the engine itself as the generators labored, spinning up the automated coal conveyers and bringing the boilers back to full roar. The brass alarm bells pealed down the length of the engine, alerting the crew to secure themselves immediately.

Simms slammed the weapons locker shut, secured it, and hurried to the front, Marta hot on his heels. In the short hall between aft rooms and the cab, the rest of the crew had secured themselves to walls with leather harnesses there for that purpose. Marta and Simms slipped into the last two open spots, hurriedly buckling themselves in place.

"All secure?" Amelia called back.

"All secure, Mister Cavendesh! You may proceed when ready." Marta grinned wolfishly as those around her clung more tightly to their straps.

The rumble of the generators rose to a fever pitch. "On my mark," Amelia said, her voice now at a more normal volume as she spoke with the navigator. "Three... Two... One... Mark."

An unholy squall and rumble ran down the hallway as Amelia released the brakes and threw the engine into full drive. lurched, the violence of the movement drawing protesting shouts from several of the men, and then careened down the ramp. It wasn't the most well-maintained of staging places, a holdover from times more ancient, and the engine bounced and jerked over the terrain, throwing the raiding party tight against their harnesses and shaking them fit to rattle teeth.

One of the men across from Marta seemed to be mumbling a prayer, eyes closed tightly and face gone white, though no sound could be heard over the clamor. He was new. He'd get over it, or find another line of work.

Alarm bells rang. Next to her, Simms drew in a breath and held it. She had little doubt that he had the same image in his mind as she, that of Elijah Masterson, long-fingered hand clutching one of the bronzed levers of the control panel, eyes focused on the stopwatch in his other hand, counting down seconds and milliseconds with precision and then, at the right instant, yanking the lever down.

With the tormented whine of overworked machinery, jumped into the air, propelled by a series of massive steam pistons. A loud clank sounded almost simultaneously, the road wheels snapping up into the engine's undercarriage to give the rail wheels clearance. It was only a split second, though it felt longer, a full exhalation, all rattles and bangs going silent.

Crash.

The engine hit the rails. Metal screamed, and one of the men whooped as the hallway tilted crazily for a moment. The leather straps cut into Marta's chest. Another smaller crash and they were fully on the rails. Only the barest amount of acceleration lost as they began the uphill climb in pursuit of their freight engine target.

She had begun to unbuckle her harness, as had Simms and a few other veterans, when the bells rang a third time, the unnecessary all clear. Had they missed the rails or only clipped them, well, life would have been far more interesting, and quite likely, brief. "Well done, Mister Masterson, Mister Cavendesh, full pursuit if you please."

She stepped into the doorway, inspecting the view through the rather scratched glass. The tail lamps of the train ahead of them were pleasingly close. Amelia and Elijah were still strapped firmly in their seats, Elijah with a map spread out in front of him, stopwatch in hand. The control panel spread out before the two of them was a maze of dials, buttons and levers, Amelia's pale hands wandering over them with the sort of grace normally reserved for concert pianists.

"Already there, sir," Amelia said. She shot Captain Ramos a grin, her short-cropped blond curls lying in wisps around her face. "If you care to man the grapple, we'll be right on their tail in a moment."

Simms had the men scrambling to their own stations, shouting in tones that would have done a sergeant of the militia proud. Calmly, Marta stepped to the ladder bolted to the wall and ascended, unlocking the hatch that let her onto 's roof and the largest of the mounted guns, already fitted and prepped with a wicked hook, its claws set for firing with charged pistons, the chain it would carry loose and ready. Next to it was mounted a Gatling gun that had been liberated from an arms train nearly a year before. Stinging cold wind whipped past her face. Marta loosed the moorings that secured the gun and swung it with practiced ease to take aim at the jittering lights of the train before them.

She stomped on the roof twice to let those below know that she was firing, and then jammed her foot on the pedal that acted as the large gun's trigger. The gun jerked in her hands, sulfurous smoke rolling over her, and a much more distant metallic bang sounded a moment later as the grapple hit.

"Secure, Mister Cavendesh, reel us—" The sharp crack of gunfire split the night and Marta ducked, flattening herself to the roof. "Getting quicker these days, aren't they?" she remarked to herself.

"All prepared for boarding, sir."

Marta slid along the roof and dropped hastily back down, followed by another volley of fire. "It seems they are as well."

Amelia grinned as a muffled bang reverberated through the wall—one of the secondary grapples being fired. "Sure they are. But we've got the bigger guns."

BOARDING WAS ALWAYS A messy, confused affair, even when boiled down to a science by a mind as keen as Marta's. The enemy was kept from firing on the boarding crew with well-timed bursts of bullets from the Gatling gun. But once on board the other train, there was still by necessity the car-to-car fighting against an increasingly desperate force. One of the men had to be sent back to in a safety harness, his right arm dangling uselessly from a bullet wound. He was, thankfully, the only major casualty on Marta's side.

This ultimately lead to Captain Ramos, as was her habit, patiently explaining to the conductor of the train why it was really in his best interest to make this transaction as painless as possible. "You see, it would be very inconvenient for all of us if you insisted on forcing me to shoot you," she informed the man, casually fingering one of the pistols slung on her hips. "You would be dead, I'd be out a bullet, and then I'd have to waste a few extra minutes locating the safe and unlocking it—and trust me, I *will* unlock it—before sheer annoyance forced me to derail this train in a fit of aggravated pique."

"You wouldn't dare." The conductor, a fit man in a crisp blue uniform now unfortunately stained with sweat and powder thanks to his insistence on resisting rather more athletically than had been necessary, gave her a wide-eyed look. Recognition and horror dawned in his eyes as he took in her scarlet coat. There was only one pirate who had that particular quirk of dress, after all. Perhaps he'd missed the memo explaining that the infamous Captain Ramos was female.

Marta smiled at him. It was an expression she had, quite literally, practiced in front of a mirror for years to perfect. In her role as pirate captain, that smile was calculated to state, *why yes I am quite mad and have a fraction of concern for human life so small, you might as well save your time and round it to zero.* "Pirate, Mister—" she peered at his little name badge "—Lewis. I'm a pirate. Is there anything my ilk does not dare?"

Mostly a bluff, that. Captain Ramos was not one to slaughter droves of innocent civilians, though she had in fact shot a conductor once because he'd gone after her with a paring knife from a nearby fruit bowl. It had been an embarrassing incident for all involved— terminally so for the conductor in question—but Marta had made good use of it nonetheless in the cause of convincing other potentially brave souls that she really was that mad.

"You're a madwoman."

"If I must keep repeating myself, this conversation will become intensely dull." But she examined him carefully, taking in the signs of distress and mentally calculating which way he would crack if just a bit more pressure were applied. She drew her pistol and pointed it squarely in his face.

The man's eyes went wide, and he tried to jerk his hands up defensively, only to be stopped by the firm hands of one Lucius Lamburt. Lucius played his part beautifully by growling into the man's ear, "Now then, sonny, you don' want ta give us no trouble." Lucius also played the part beautifully of having been born, as far as anyone could tell, as some sort of gorilla who was subsequently partially shaved and outfitted with the surprisingly well-tailored clothes of a man.

Though knowing Lucius, Marta reflected, he was quite likely serious. The man was unhinged in all of the most useful ways. "If you please, Mister Lewis. I wouldn't want to overexcite our Mister Lamburt with the sight of blood."

Lucius laughed into the conductor's ear, the sound accompanied by a fine spray of saliva. That, at least, was more obviously an act. Lucius had a bit of a thing about bodily fluids.

The conductor was quick to lead her into the third freight car then and rip up the floor paneling that hid the safe. While the main point of the raid had been the train's cargo—a shipment of steel bars and some much-needed, delicately machined replacement parts for their various engines—there was really no reason to leave the store of gold and silver on the train behind. It was just good business.

"Captain, this ought to be the last of the crates," Simms called from behind them.

Marta glanced up to see the tall man walking down the narrow hallway toward her. He held one end of a wooden crate that had been painted a rather odd shade of green. "Are you certain, Simms? That doesn't look like the rest."

"The maker's stamp—" Whatever Simms might have been about to point out was lost when the door to the car crashed open and a man with a shock of wild yellow curls flung himself through. His dove-gray jacket was torn and his tie in complete disarray, one glove missing as well, the other stained with ink or possibly grease. It was difficult to tell from this distance.

With wild desperation he flung himself at Simms, arms flailing. "That is my trunk! Mine! You can't have it!"

The attack was sudden and ferocious enough, despite the almost comical size difference that was revealed when the short, slight man proceeded to cling to Simms like a monkey, that Simms dropped his end of the crate. It hit the floor with a crash and the man who had been holding the other side lost his grip as well, cursing as he did so. One side of the crate lost its integrity, boards splintering outward.

As Simms tried to pry the fingers of the much smaller man free, bearings cascaded from the splintered crate. Swearing, Simms stumbled and began to slip freely on them, arms windmilling and legs skating to and fro as the much smaller man pummeled him about the head and shoulders with one hand.

Marta, Lucius, and the conductor, momentarily forgetting he was a captive and this might have been the perfect opportunity to escape, openly stared.

"Ah…shouldn't someone help that man?" the conductor said after a moment.

"Naw, 'e's fine. Winning even, I'd say," Lucius answered.

The sad truth of it was, Marta wasn't entirely certain to whom they were referring.

The man who had been helping Simms with the crate rushed forward to try to help, slipped, and landed heavily on his back with an undignified scream. Captain Ramos eased forward, feet firmly on the floor to avoid the bearings that still streamed from the crate and flowed toward the downhill side of the car. She drew her pistol, waited for the precise moment of calculated vulnerability, and slammed the butt against the passenger's temple.

Mercifully, he went limp and dropped heavily to the floor. Simms snatched at air and caught Marta's offered hand, though he nearly jerked her arm from its socket in the process.

"What in heaven's name—" He sucked a scarlet thread of blood back into his nostril before it could begin to stain his mustache. Hastily he yanked a handkerchief from his pocket and covered his nose. With the other hand he helped his erstwhile companion back to his feet. The flow of bearings had, thankfully, ceased.

"One of your security men, Mister Lewis?" Marta inquired with poisonous sweetness as she turned her pistol in her hand.

The conductor quickly shook his head as Lucius leaned rather closer than he had any business being and breathed into his ear. "No, I swear it."

Simms nudged the unconscious man with one foot. Voice muffled by the handkerchief and made nasal with blood, he said, "Too short to be security, isn't he?"

Marta gave the unconscious man a measuring look. "For the Grand Duchy of Denver, at least." The Grand Duke had *standards*, which at times seemed far more aesthetic than anything else. "Simms, why did you take this crate? We don't need bearings."

"Manifest said it was engine parts like the rest."

Marta frowned. Obviously, then, the bearings would be to weigh down the crate. It wasn't the sort of thing one shipped like this. "Mister Lamburt, why don't you return Mister Lewis to the engine room and make certain the crew is moving back to ." She acknowledged his barked "sir!" with the wave of one hand as she drew her machete with the other. "And you two," she informed Simms and his erstwhile companion, "clear out the safe."

She pried the lid from the crate with the machete and frowned at the contents. Clothes and papers, mostly, nothing that looked like contraband but also nothing that looked like engine parts. Carefully she looked through the contents, pocketing a few bits—a very nice hand lens, a tiny but well-crafted pistol, and a small leather-bound book that would either be a volume of bad poetry or something interesting indeed—until she stirred up a tin orrery wrapped in a towel. As orreries went, it was quite ugly, battered and stained and more than a bit bent, very out of place among the finery in the crate.

She heard the shriek of Diabola's whistle outside, three long blasts, two short. They were approaching the Continental Divide.

There wasn't really time to consider the problem further on-site. Marta tucked the orrery away in her satchel. She spared one glance for the odd little man who had been so upset about his crate of contraband, noting a few odd scars on his gloveless hand, his fingers apparently smudged with newsprint, before the shrill call of Diabola's whistle drew her away.

She confirmed head count with Gregory before she locked her harness onto the grappling chains and wheeled herself across. As soon as she was aboard, the chains released and Diabola abruptly slowed.

"How much time, Mister Masterson?" she asked as she came in through the side door, where one of the secondary grappling chains had been fixed for convenience.

"Forty-four minutes before someone else will be on our stretch. More than enough time."

"Very good. Mister Cavendesh, take us home with all due haste." Marta headed back into the depths of Diabola's cargo area, wanting to check on the spoils gained. As she walked, she had to steady herself against one wall as the engine slowed, stopped, and then began its steady acceleration back down the hill.

Farther back in the rather tight troop space, she heard shouts of celebration, cheers for a job well done. Marta allowed herself a grin at that. First Sunday of the month and they were already well ahead of the game.

"FOUND ANYTHING INTERESTING, CAPTAIN?" Simms cautiously stuck his head just inside the doorway of the subterranean lab Marta had built for herself over the years. Caution was necessary, because one never knew what might be going on inside: noxious smells; objects being flung with deadly accuracy, fueled by a foul temper; the bright, sparking light of a welding torch; or even on one memorable occasion, the Captain dangling, half-naked, from an iron framework, whooping madly and deep in the grips of a peyote dream.

Nothing untoward today, however, just the statuesque form of Captain Ramos in her shirtsleeves hunched over her work, hair straggling around her shoulder as it attempted to escape the clip she'd put it in. A half-eaten bowl of congealed chili sat at her elbow, scraps of tortilla dangling from it.

"Captain?" Armed with the two newest newspapers from the Grand Duchies of Denver and Salt Lake taken from a dropbox in Silverthorn that very morning, he approached. He'd used newspapers as a shield often enough.

"We captured quite a few glorious little toys." Marta picked up the object from her worktable and held it up for Simms to see. It was a tin orrery, battered, smudged, and undeniably ugly in the focused electrical lights of her workspace. "And then there is this."

"Don't recall seeing that."

"I pulled it out of that trunk that gave you such fits. I thought… well, I thought it might be something interesting, the way it was so carefully hidden. And the way its owner was so obviously beside himself."

"But?"

"It isn't even accurate. The mechanism works all right, but if you were depending on it to tell you when to observe Venus, you'd be at least six weeks off." Marta shook her head. "And I could just go on from there. For all the obvious workmanship that's gone into the mechanism, it's quite the poorly thought-out device." She tilted it this way and that. "I'd think it a souvenir from the Nature Museum perhaps, but goodness it's a bit ugly for *that*."

"Bargain bin, perhaps." Simms bit back the suggestion that it had been created for function rather than form; knowing the function was off, that thought seemed far too stupid. "Going to play with it a bit more, then?"

Marta eyed the device, turning it in her hands. "Perhaps some other time. I'd thought with the fuss its owner kicked up, it would be something interesting, but I think his state had more to do with the codebook I lifted from that trunk. Do you think Dolly might like to play with an orrery? It seems nigh indestructible, and she ought to have something other than those frightful, simpering dolls you insist on giving her."

This was not a discussion Simms was willing to re-open with the Captain. "Think she might have a bit of fun with it. She knows the names of the planets and such-like. Amelia's been showing her things on that telescope of hers." Marta only seemed to take an interest in his daughter when it was a way to tweak at his whiskers or outrage someone who had managed to retain a few more social mores than even he had. Otherwise she tucked the children of Devil's Roost into a mental box labeled "loud, sticky, and annoying" and ignored them; unlike their city cousins, they wouldn't have any tidbits of information for her.

"Right then, here you go." Marta tossed the orrery to him. It made an odd, almost musical little *plink* as he caught it. "Simms."

Simms fiddled with the crank on the device; it made the little planets advance in their orbits. "Hm?"

"Are those my newspapers?"

"Oh yeah, these, right." He untucked the folded papers from under his arm and offered them over. "Still nice and crisp." He'd learned not to let anyone else have a look at the papers first. They tended to disorder the pages, and the Captain had strong opinions on that topic.

Captain Ramos snatched them from his hand and retreated to her desk, worryingly like a coyote that had just made off with a particularly nice haunch. Simms inspected his hand but yes, all of his fingers were still there, though with the addition of a few paper cuts. He brought his attention back to the little orrery, twiddling with another little switch that seemed to do nothing at all, and turned to go.

"Simms."

He knew that tone. He stopped, froze in place actually, and glanced over his shoulder.

"Tell me, does this man look familiar?" Captain Ramos turned toward him, holding up one of the papers. Half of it was a set of advertisements: a butcher shop headlining its fantastic sausages, three lawyers, a doctor claiming he could cure warts of all sorts, and a rather large and gaudy ad for an astrology society of all things. The other half of the page was far more interesting—*MAN FOUND MURDERED NEAR BUTCHER SHOP*—some irreverent part of Simms wondered if he'd been going for sausages—and a sketch of a vaguely familiar face.

An instant later, recognition hit. Right. He'd last seen that face as the little bastard scrabbled at his head, during the train robbery. Only for all the residual humiliation, Simms didn't particularly like the thought that he'd ended up dead quite that quickly. "It wasn't anything we did, was it? He took a pretty heavy fall..."

"Not unless he fell on a bullet." Captain Ramos glanced at the paper. "Oh, excuse me. Three of them." She shook her head. "Yet somehow, I find this juxtaposition of events rather...tantalizing. What might our flighty friend, one Levi Smith, have been up to, to get himself so spectacularly killed?"

Simms suppressed a groan. "Probably wouldn't give his wallet over to a thief."

"You have no imagination, Simms." She slapped the paper shut. "It might explain some of the odder things in that little notebook I took from his trunk. And who knows where that might lead us?"

He sighed, though that thought did stir a bit of interest; he wasn't an entirely incurious man. "Denver or Salt Lake?"

Captain Ramos held up the paper: *The Tribune.*

"That'll be half a day away—"

"Best get going now, then. We can take the small rail car." She waved him off. "Go give your daughter a kiss."

Simms gritted his teeth, hand tightening around the little tin orrery until it let out a warning *plink*. Well, perhaps Dolly would take it better if she got a toy out of the deal.

THERE WAS AN UNPLEASANT smell in the Grand Duchy of Salt Lake's main city: earthy, thick, and faintly fishy. Something to do with the gathering of cold weather and the proximity to the Great Salt Lake, Simms had been told. He only knew it made him wish he could invent an entirely new way of breathing that did not involve either smelling or tasting the air. Despite the brilliant, cloudless blue sky overhead, the world felt quite gray between the smell and the mostly unadorned concrete and stone buildings that lined the street.

Looking at the apartment building—five narrow stories squeezed between a set of offices and a rather questionable hotel—he also found himself wishing he hadn't turned his nose up at the church, either. Captain Ramos had given him the choice of looking through church records or hunting around for the dead man's apartment. He'd felt as if the massive square building of gray stone that housed the main temple of Salt Lake had been looking on him with severe disapproval, and the sensation had only been intensified by the rather stern angel that sat over the large but unadorned doors, holding his trumpet like a machete. This building, however, seemed to be giving him the eye as well, but it was far more calculating and seemed to want to know how much money he had in his wallet, and if he had any gold dental work besides.

Well, he had a pistol hidden in his buckskin jacket, a machete worn much more openly (he was presumed to be a frontiersman by most curious passersby), and knuckles crossed and recrossed with white scars from fights of all sorts. He shook off the oppressive atmosphere as best he could, hooked his thumbs in his belt, and strolled across the unusually wide street, so unlike those of Denver, to walk boldly up the steps.

Up another set of steps. And another. Once in the building, the wallpaper of the narrow wooden stairway was peeling and nearly as gray as the day outside. The smell also wasn't all that different from the heavy atmosphere outside, tobacco smoke and cabbage and something unpleasantly fishy all mixed together. Had it been possible to hold his breath for four flights of stairs, Simms would have. At each landing he checked the slip of paper from his pocket, but no, still not the proper flat.

The correct door, when finally reached, was not altogether promising. It was sagging, cracked, and the color of oatmeal, but far more worrying was all the noise emanating from behind it. The sound of shouting was quite clear through the paper-thin walls, only the words blurred out. Something smashed against a wall.

Simms, his hand raised to knock, winced and seriously considered leaving the way he'd come. Unfortunately the Captain would expect answers from this little foray. He waited for a lull in the shouting and quickly knocked.

Silence fell. A moment later the door was yanked open by a short, plump woman with straggly gray hair, dressed in a rather shapeless calico smock. Over her shoulder, Simms saw two young women in equally unflattering dresses, both brunette, one nursing a black eye and the other rubbing at her nose with the back of her hand.

He carefully pasted a polite smile on his face. "Good day, are you the mistress of this house?"

She inspected him through narrowed eyes and scraped a tangle of hair from her face with rough fingers. "I already paid my tithe this month. Tell Elder Jonas I ain't puttin' up with his double dippin' no more." She made to shut the door.

Simms hastily used one hand to keep the door open. "I'm not from the church." While the Grand Duchy of Salt Lake was sovereign territory like all the duchies, this one was a bit of a theocracy, the Grand Duke only enthroned by the good will of the Temple and its Bishops. That was all Simms knew of the matter, and all he wanted to know.

Another squinting look. "Then what d'ya want?"

"I'm looking for a friend of mine, actually, a gentleman—"

She yanked the door back open. "Oy, you're one of *his* friends? You tell that bastard he better get back here with a ring for Arabella or I'll hunt him down m'self, you see if I won't!" She jerked a thumb of her shoulder at the sniffling girl who, Simms realized, was a bit rounder in the belly than she probably should have been.

"I'm here because I don't know where he is!" Simms protested.

She grabbed him by the sleeve and yanked him forward. There was perhaps something to be said for the occasional quips Captain Ramos said about low centers of gravity, he thought grimly. "All you men are liars an' thieves. Or what, he owes you money?"

"I—"

"He owes us money!" the girl who wasn't Arabella shouted. "Stole all my washin' money when he left on Sunday, the bastard!"

"Liar!" Arabella shouted back. "You spent it yourself on them shoes!"

At which point the room once again erupted in loud quarreling. Simms grabbed the doorframe to keep the older woman—the mother, if heredity had anything to do with lung size—from dragging him fully into the apartment. Broken crockery crunched under his boot with the one step he was forced to take inside.

"Ladies!" he shouted as Arabella grabbed up a plate from the table, the woman whom Simms could only assume was her sister advancing on her threateningly. "Ladies! If you please!" The roar of a different voice caused them to pause, at least. "Sunday, you said?"

"Yeah, Sunday. He ran off when we were at church. Blasphemous, too," the older woman said.

Sunday made absolutely no sense as a time frame; Levi Smith had been on the train, getting robbed on Sunday evening—the train returning to the Grand Duchy of Salt Lake. Simms dug through his pocket, producing the sketch from the newspaper of the unfortunate Levi and holding it up. "This is the man I'm looking for."

The three women peered at it. "Oy," Arabella said, one hand smoothing over her belly. "Ain't that the man, got murdered over the other side of the valley?"

"He ain't never been here," the other girl said. "Even if Joseph deserves to get shot too."

Arabella's eyes narrowed, the expression so like that of the woman still holding Simms's sleeve that he took a step back, dragging her along. "You got that, you must know he's dead. What's this really about?"

What it was really about was, Simms decided, leaving as quickly as possible. He tried to yank his sleeve from the older woman's hand, and then pried her fingers away when that didn't work. "You ladies have been very helpful, now carry on."

"Oy, what's all this about?" the older woman shouted.

Simms ran. A plate crashed into the wall over his head as he clattered down the stairs, firmly holding onto his hat with one hand.

He met up with Captain Ramos outside the train station. In slightly less fraught territory than normal—and there to perform far less illegal acts than normal—the Captain had elected to get their railcar a berth in the city. The station was a grand but ugly building, half red brick and half concrete blocks probably reused from older buildings, with a large clock face hanging over the door of black unadorned iron. The only decoration was another angel standing over the doorway, trumpet in hand, though Simms found this one far less disapproving than the one guarding the Temple. The best color on the street was provided by passersby, the working class in bright calicoes, the finer sorts in various shades running from burgundy to hunter green. Red hunter jackets seemed to be in fashion for both men and ladies, judging by the numbers.

"Run into a bit of trouble, Simms?" the Captain asked.

"What—"

She reached up and plucked a chip of porcelain from off his hat. "Well that, and you've some interesting fresh scuffs on your boots and coat."

He snorted. "I checked the man's shipping address. It was home to a quarrelsome family, and definitely not one that knew him."

"Also one with bad aim, it would seem."

Simms frowned. "You don't sound at all surprised."

"I'm afraid not, Simms. You put yourself in harm's way for no reason at all, it seems. I talked my way into Temple records, and our man doesn't exist."

"Doesn't exist."

"Never was born, never died, had no parents or cousins," she said firmly. "Yet if memory serves, from the accent he had when he was shouting at you, he was either born here or has lived here since he learned to talk."

Simms let out a low whistle. "So we're chasing after a ghost that got himself murdered in front of a butcher shop. Something a bit twisted about that." Had they been anywhere else, that would mean very little; records, particularly for the working class, were normally quite sparse if they even existed at all. But the Grand Duchy of Salt Lake had a peculiar obsession with genealogy that Simms didn't quite understand, though he knew it had something to do with the theocratic side of the government. Which was precisely why he also did not *want* to know.

"And this is a duchy whose only ghosts are intentional," Captain Ramos said.

Which could mean only a few things, first of which was an agent of the Grand Duke or the Temple. Funny, the man hadn't felt so weighty when he'd been hanging on Simms's shoulders and screeching invective. Torn between excitement and resignation, he turned to head down the street.

"Where are you going, Mr. Simms?" the Captain inquired.

Simms looked over his shoulder at her. "You'll be wanting to go to the Grand Duchy of Denver next. Well and good, but I'm buying some sweets for Dolly first since I'll be missing another day with her." And the saltwater taffy was, in his opinion, no replacement for a father, but a worthy apology nonetheless.

THE GRAND DUCHY OF Denver proved more fruitful in providing a useful address for their ghost. The crate he'd shipped on the train had to come from somewhere, and had to be picked up by someone, since it seemed unlikely he'd just conjured it out of thin air. Simms bluffed their way into the offices of several shipping companies before they found the right one, pretending at different times to be an inspector, a hapless man trying to find where his vengeful wife had shipped his clothes to, and an angry merchant who wanted to know where his bloody merchandise was bloody well now *thank you very much*. All the while Captain Ramos remained demurely silent as his titular assistant, wearing a hunter green dress that had an unflatteringly high collar and a cut specifically chosen because it was two seasons old.

Then it was simply a matter of finding a record of a green crate, picked up on a particular day and delivered to the station. Simple being a relative term, in Simms's opinion, when it came with so many paper cuts.

That slip of paper led them to another rather shabby apartment building on the outer edge of one of the more industrialized areas of the city. Everything was coated with a fine layer of coal dust, the small puddles of water in the gutters covered with oily scum. Vendors selling tamales and pasties competed for the attention of the factory workers, the lucky ones allowed to shuffle out into the street for their short lunch breaks.

"Doesn't look much more promising than the last," Simms remarked, skeptically eying the gaps in the shingles that faced the building. "I would have thought being a ghost would pay a bit better."

"I'm sure it does," Captain Ramos said, lip curling. "But if you think the work's any more glamorous than what we do, you've been reading far too many trashy novels. They'll rot your brain, Simms." She glanced behind them. "Coffee?"

It was warmer here than it had been in the Grand Duchy of Salt Lake, but a warm drink would be welcome, as would—according to his stomach—something to eat. "Not taking care of this first?"

She shook her head, glancing down the street toward a sausage vendor with a merry little cart painted red. "I don't like the smell of that at all."

"Wrong bit of the city if you want sausages anyway," he muttered, her point taken. The vendor didn't look at all untoward to Simms, but he'd long since learned to trust the Captain's powers of observation. It meant less mess in the long run.

They went into the small cafe, which had wobbly tables and cracked plates, but the coffee didn't actively seem to be taking the enamel from his teeth, and their sandwich cake was just gooey enough to please Simms and utterly disgust the Captain. He ate his way cheerfully through two pieces, paging through the day's paper as the Captain stared at the window at the passersby. Red riding coats seemed to be quite the rage here, as well.

As he paged past a spectacularly yellow piece of journalism about the new ambassador from the Grand Duchy of New York, a large advertisement caught his eye—another black bordered monstrosity from the astrology society, very like the one he'd seen in the *Tribune*. "Is astrology making a comeback?" he asked.

The Captain snorted. "I don't think we've ever been fortunate enough for it to have gone away."

"Apparently Saturn is on the rise," he observed, and turned to the next page to read about a banking scandal of some sort. Not much of a scandal, in his opinion, if no one had ended up caught in an office in only their knickers.

"Utter nonsense," the Captain opined, though it felt more like form than anything. She continued to stare out the window, cup of coffee untouched at her elbow and, to Simms's eye, developing a disturbing skin of greasy scum.

Three pages from the end of the paper, the Captain demanded his attention by the simple expedient of yanking the newspaper from his hands and folding it up. Simms sighed but didn't protest otherwise. It could have been far worse. "Satisfied?"

"Very. The sausage vendor is definitely on the take. As is that gentleman pretending to sell pencils in front of the building. He's the most pathetic excuse for a blind man I've ever witnessed."

"Oh?"

"He does keep turning his head to watch the ladies go by." She stood.

"Right." Simms rose to his feet as well. "That's it, then?" He very well knew it wasn't.

"We'll go in from the side, I think."

Could be worse, he reflected quietly. The Captain had an affinity for sewers that he found utterly distressing.

They walked down a block together, Simms with his collar turned up against the cold, sticking with the steady flow of scarlet riding coats that headed toward the local train station. Just past a shop selling parasols and paper fans, they cut into an alleyway heavy with the cloying scent of urine and piles of refuse. Rather than continue on to the next true street, they turned up another alley that ran parallel, skirting a man with a large shaggy dog and an elderly person with a hunched back and no discernible gender pushing a wide cart filled with junk.

Nearly at the back of their target building, Simms stubbed his toe on what turned out to be someone's leg covered with newspapers.

"Oy!"

"Sorry," he apologized hastily, and dug out a handful of coins that he dropped in the vicinity of the man's lap. It proved a good enough distraction that he didn't protest further.

The Captain tried the rear door of the building, a heavy wooden affair covered with peeling gray paint. She rattled the knob, and subsequently wiped a dusting of rust off on her skirts. "Could try to pick it, I suppose, but I don't think the mechanism's been turned in the last decade."

Simms looked it over dubiously. "Breaking it down would make a good deal of noise."

"And some of the cracking might come from your shoulder. No, Simms, I think the fire escape is in order."

He looked up at the thin construction of rusted struts and grimaced. "Depends on what you mean by 'in order.'"

It shook alarmingly as they climbed, squealing and rattling in a way Simms hoped was entirely for show and masked by the noise of the street. A few bolts rained down onto the alley below.

At the fourth floor, Simms broke in the pane of a window with his elbow and in they climbed to what Captain Ramos insisted was the proper apartment. The curtains were drawn, letting in only a thin bit of yellowed light, but that was enough to reveal a scene of chaos. Furniture had been overturned, cabinets left open, plates and books strewn across tables, shelves and floor.

"Left in a hurry," Simms said.

"Yes..." Captain Ramos pulled on a pair of gloves and carefully sifted through the wreckage of a meal left moldering on a plate. "And then subsequently given a hasty search." She picked up a book from the floor, fanned through the pages, and looked at the cover.

"Oh?"

"Things lifted up and replaced a bit off, like this cup, moved off the ring it originally left on this book...so that then the book could be given a look through." She moved farther into the little apartment.

"So they were looking for papers?"

"Or a thin little book, like the one I took from the man's belongings. Though if that is a cipher book, it's one of the strangest I've ever seen."

Simms paused as paper crackled underfoot. He frowned, stepping back and lifting aside a carelessly thrown tea towel. "There's newspaper all scattered over the carpet here." The source was, he thought, probably the overturned wastepaper basket that had also hidden under the towel.

"And?" Captain Ramos didn't even glance up from where she bent over a pile of discarded clothing.

He stirred at the mess with his fingers. "It's a bit odd, this. All shredded into strips."

"Packing material, perhaps." The Captain straightened. "Grab a bit of it, though."

Simms had just gathered up a handful when a knock came at the door.

"Mr. Smith? Mr. Smith? Inspector's here, says he wants a word with you." The muffled voice belonged to a woman, perhaps the landlady.

Simms hastily shoved the newspaper into his jacket pocket and caught the Captain's eye. She jerked her head toward the window.

"I told you, he's not here," the woman said.

"Yes, I know that," a man answered, rather impatient. The voice made Captain Ramos's eyebrows jump up. "He's been murdered. Now open the door or I'll have it broken down."

"All right, all right, let me just…" Keys jangled.

Captain Ramos scrambled out of the window, Simms on her heels. The fire escape creaked a warning that haste might not be an option.

Simms hissed at the Captain and flattened himself against the rusty fire escape as he heard the door open. She immediately went still.

"Rather dark in here—"

Simms squeezed his eyes shut, as if that would somehow render him invisible, and then hastily opened his eyes again as he realized that he really ought to be watching what happened. The man who was undoubtedly the Inspector in question jerked the curtains open. "The window's broke— *You!*"

Simms looked up at a man with light brown hair and a neatly trimmed officer's mustache, one hand raised with a straight wooden cane in it. Captain Ramos gave the man an utterly horrifying grin right before she jumped up and down on the fire escape twice in quick succession.

With a metallic scream, the rusted bolts of the fire escape gave way, and it crumpled majestically away from the building, rather like a tall, thin woman collapsing into a faint.

Simms clutched the railings and didn't scream as gravity yanked them toward the alley, though it was a near thing. *Crash*—and he almost lost his footing as they struck the wall of the building next door, metal screeching as they dragged down the bricks, but it slowed their descent.

They stopped with a gentle bounce and another shrill creak, just above the first floor.

"Stop! By order of the Grand Duke!" the man shouted.

Captain Ramos dove over the railing; Simms launched himself after her without hesitation and broke into a run as soon as he landed, protesting knees or no. An outraged shout followed them down the alley.

"Someone you know?" Simms gasped out as they dodged around the elderly person with the cart again.

Captain Ramos laughed, the sound alone telling him more than he really wanted to know. "That was the Grand Duke's Chief of Security, Simms. Colonel Douglas."

Simms groaned, the effect ruined when he skidded on a bit of—oh he didn't want to think about that—and had to catch himself on a wall.

"If he's in on this, it's just become very interesting."

Simms didn't have the breath to groan again.

TWO DAYS LATER, 'INTERESTING' had failed to materialize, much to Simms's relief. The Captain had vanished into her work room once more, the scraps of newspaper Simms had scraped up off the carpet in the dead man's apartment firmly in hand.

Amelia caught him in one of the long hallways, formerly a main shaft for the mine but now lit with faintly buzzing electrical lights, spaced out a little too far for the comfort of anyone who felt at all paranoid about the dark. "Simms!"

"Yeah?"

"Elijah's been agitating to go out to the hot springs. Think we can do it?"

He rubbed the back of his neck. "You checked with the Captain?"

She suddenly seemed to find the air over his left shoulder very interesting. "She's been awful busy, hasn't she?"

"…worse than my daughter, the lot of you." He sighed. "I'll ask her. But I think there might be a train coming through tomorrow or day after. I doubt she'll want you gone that long." Actually, he knew that to be true. But he'd begun to cotton to the fact that in their bizarre little pseudo-family, Captain Ramos had somehow become "Dad" and he'd been stuck firmly in the role of "Mum." "Go into town for a bit instead? We still need to drop off the last cargo at the fences, at any rate."

Amelia looked a little glum, but nodded. "Be nice to get out even for that. Perhaps ask her when we could plan a trip? Elijah…"

Simms grinned at her. "Just Elijah wants it, right?"

She stuck her tongue out at him, and he went to locate Captain Ramos. As he'd suspected she was bent over her workbench, slips of paper strewn around her.

"Sir? We were thinking about going in to town for the evening. Thought you might like to come along."

She waved one hand at him lazily, an invitation to enter. "Which town?"

"Silverthorn, we were thinking. Can drop the last of the cargo off there, and then go for a bit of...ah...relaxation in the brewery."

The Captain paused for a moment, head tilting back. "What, not Berthoud? Oh, right. The lemonade incident."

"Right. We're not taking Gregory along, but I think they just sort of blamed...all of us."

"Burn down a few buildings..." She sighed, her breath sending strips of newspaper scattering. "Are you going to start up that tiresome line about fresh air, Simms? I can all but feel it radiating off of you."

"You have been down here since we got back."

"It hasn't been so long." She pulled her watch from her pocket. "Just a few hours."

"Two days, sir."

"Oh. More like fifty-one hours then." Captain Ramos sat back and sighed, stretching her arms out. "These bits of paper you found are a pretty problem, Simms, make no mistake. I doubt you noticed when you picked them up, but they've all had holes punched through them, quite precisely at that." She picked up the thin little book she'd brandished before, taken from the now-dead spy's trunk. "I'm certain it's something to do with this, but I haven't found a correlation to speak of yet."

Reluctant but curious, he moved forward to take up one of the little strips, turning it in his fingers. He caught the word *sausage* on it, only the *u*, *g*, and *e* had a pattern of pinpricks shot through them. "All right, I'll give you that. It's a bit odd."

"The question is how, and why. To what end?" A wave of her hand scattered more paper strips. He saw another curl up with the words *ascending Saturn* on it.

"It might have all come like that."

The look she gave him was a most eloquent one.

"You've been at it two days, sir. Come back to it in a bit with fresh eyes. We need to deliver the cargo to our man anyway."

"Eyes don't go bad like mangoes," she said acerbically as she leaned back and shook her head. "But you are right about the cargo. And the news stand in Silverthorn ought to have some of its old papers left over...perhaps finding out the dates on these will offer some insight." She slid off her stool and began to put on her coat. "Have Mister Cavendish start preparing Diabola. She's the one that put you up to this, right?"

"Couldn't say." Simms hid his little sigh of relief with a careful cough.

"It's NOT TOO LATE to go to the springs," Elijah Masterson said, for what had to be at least the tenth time as they moved out of the thinning trees and onto the main road, Silverthorn laid out before them.

Captain Ramos had parked on some supposedly abandoned track to the south of the town; while it meant they'd have to run if they needed to make a quick getaway, it was still better than risking the engine getting stuck at the station in case of some unfortunate event. They'd run and fought their way free over longer distances, and the woods near Silverthorn, while not surrounded by an electrical fence, were kept free of Infected by regular patrols. The few younger men they'd brought along had nearly sprinted from the engine, likely headed for the questionable delights of the town's one bordello. The cabin crew had hung back with the captain, taking the path at a less desperate pace.

Lucius Lamburt laughed, revealing a mouth full of teeth better left hidden. "We parked, sonny, ain't no goin' back 'til you're carryin' me."

"If you didn't want to come, why are you here?" Amelia shoved Elijah's arm.

He grinned at her. "Still better than being halfway under a mountain, right? Look at that lovely sky…somewhere behind all the smoke." The sound of an engine's whistle, three long blasts, was sharp even in the noticeably thick air.

Silverthorn was a tiny town of mining and basic industry, nestled in the mountains and criss-crossed with rail lines. It was the first stop for much of the ore that came from the mines deeper in the Rockies, and the first and last stop for much of its coal, keeping the smelting furnaces burning along and the smokestacks belching out thick gray clouds. Depending on the source of the coal, sometimes the air even stung with the smell of sulfur, a fact not lost on more superstitious city folk, who had dubbed the place (among other things) "Devil's Mouth."

Silverthorn, in Marta's opinion, was a much prettier but far less interesting name. She watched her crew bicker with the sort of benign amusement often seen in parents, quickly tuning out the words so she could instead watch the street. She knew the rhythms of the little town well, the general comings and goings of its be-aproned smelters and dust-grimed stevedores.

Something seemed off, but she couldn't quite put her finger on it. But different was, while not always good, at least interesting.

"If you're just going to be at the Rat's Tail, I'll go take care of the shopping," Simms offered.

"Quartermaster gave you your marching orders before we left, then?" Marta asked, tone idle. It was for form rather than function. Simms had two modes: teetotaler and rotted alcoholic, though he'd managed to maintain the former and avoid the latter since they'd rescued his daughter Dolly from a workhouse and brought her home to the mountains nearly two years ago. Simms had remained Marta's right-hand man even after the arrival of his daughter; Dolly was quiet and serious for a girl her age, and there were more than enough quasi-responsible adults about at the Roost to make certain she didn't get caught in the machinery when he was away. Stockton, the rotund and intimidating cook, had a particular fondness for the girl.

Normally Marta enjoyed having a good poke at Simms over his enmity with drink for the sheer pleasure of watching him squirm, but her attention was taken instead by a sudden influx of loaders heading away from the station instead of toward it. "Hm?"

"I said yes, Captain. Even if it's a shorter list than normal, Stockton'll have my ears for a necklace if I come back without any vanilla. And that's a direct quote. Something about not being able to flavor cakes with engine parts."

"How rude of us to not knock over the bakery train," she said dryly. "Go along. You know where to find us." Simms departed with a sardonic wave.

"Mister Simms gone along to run errands for mummy like a good boy?" Elijah asked a little mockingly once Simms was safely out of earshot.

Marta had a feeling he was trying to either impress her (unlikely, the men knew better by the time she let them near one of the engines) or Amelia. She raised an eyebrow. "Watch your tone, Mister Masterson. If word reaches the ears of the Quartermaster, you might not like what ends up in your rations."

"Is good advice, that," Lucius noted. "There's three women you should never anger, boy: your wife, your laundry woman, and your cook." He glanced at Marta. "Did I say three? I meant four. Shouldn't get on your captain's bad side neither, not if you ever want to see the right side of a sunset again."

"That's...that's not what I meant," Elijah said hastily.

Amelia giggled and patted him on the arm, which seemed to mollify him a bit.

"Please, Mister Masterson. Navigate us to the Rat's Tail so we can stop your mouth up with a pint before you say something else ill-considered."

The saloon was the same as always, wooden floor gone an uncertain sticky brown from years of drinking in spilled beer and even less noble spirits, chairs and tables nearly the same color and texture. Questionable looks aside, the saloon also brewed its own beer, and that more than made up for having to pry one's feet from the floor.

As the man who'd been foolish most recently, Elijah was sent up to get the first of what was guaranteed to be many rounds. Most of the other patrons were off-duty workers, tired and dirty and content to keep their eyes mostly on their own beers and own business. Captain Ramos's crew, while not quite an installation at the Rat's Tail, was well known and reasonably liked. Pit bosses might not like pirates all that much, but the common laborers were happy to turn a blind eye to those who tweaked the noses of the high and mighty.

It was Marta's practice to drink perhaps half a beer every other round. The others knew by now to not twit her about it. She leaned back in the slightly wobbly wooden chair, long legs stretched out in front of her, and simply listened to the background chatter with half an ear. As usual, rumblings about wages being too low, liquor prices too high, and which supervisors were the unfortunate union of a wild pig and one of the Infected out in the woods. More interesting, though, was the talk of overtime, complaints of exhaustion flavored with avarice at the extra wages, poor as those were. A large order for steel, it seemed, something in its own way far more precious than gold or silver, and all of it coming from the Grand Duke himself.

Interesting, that, though not terribly helpful. Trying to capture trains on the downhill slide from the divide to the grand duchy so far below was a tricky proposition and required extensive reward to justify the risk. But Marta liked to have her finger on the pulse of the duchy, and it beat out a fascinating rhythm indeed.

Oh, and there was the gratifying talk that someone's brother's cousin had been in the telegraph relay office, and there was news of a robbery—someone had made off with a safe worth of jewelry, some of which had belonged to the Dowager Duchess of Provo and what a delightful scandal *that* was. Oh yes, and the bastards had taken a bunch of steel and engine parts too, not the most glamorous sort of loot, wasn't that puzzling?

Marta smirked into her beer.

All thought of smugness fled as a clatter from the street reached such a pitch that it cut over the normal noise of the saloon. It was difficult to see more than shadow and light through the rather murky front windows, which had not been cleaned at any point in recent memory, but around the half-doors at the front Marta could see a small forest of highly polished boots and trousers of a particular bottle green. That color Marta knew well as the uniform for the Grand Duchy of Denver's army. The exodus of loaders from the station, she realized now, had been the sign of the army regiment's arrival, the workers fleeing ahead of potential trouble.

She stood abruptly, chair scraping over the floor. Amelia looked at her with wide eyes and Lucius managed a more-slurred-than-normal "Wha…?" as she turned, picked up her chair, and flung it at the most soggy of the tables within range. It knocked aside a card game, quite a few coins, and two beers, before striking a rather ugly man with a massive red beard in the face.

The forceful introduction of the chair to the alcohol-soaked chemistry of the taproom had the desired effect. The man rose to his feet with a roar, flipping the table up for effect, and charged at her. She grabbed up Elijah's half-finished pint and flung it over her shoulder toward another table before darting back. Lucius caught her intention quickly at least. He flung his own chair at another table with one hand and yanked Amelia to her feet with the other. Marta caught his eye, jerking her chin back toward the door that led to the brewery.

Marta dove under a punch, came up under another table, and shoved it over. That was the tipping point. Chaos spread from there with gratifying speed.

It was into that chaos the saloon doors were flung open, a man in a bottle green jacket to match his trousers, gold braid lining cuffs and collar, and an officer's mustache making his rank of captain clear enough, standing in the doorway. He roared to be heard over the din. "You will cease at once! Cease this at once! We are here to arrest Captain Ramos but I'll throw the lot of you into the Evergreens!"

The threat of such punishment—the Evergreens being the misleadingly picturesque name of the Grand Duke's most unpleasant prison and nothing so innocent as trees—cowed those nearest the guard captain.

Marta ignored the words, only taking a quick glance over her shoulder as she shoved through the chaos, adding a punch or kick when necessary as she worked her way toward the back. She caught sight of the captain craning his neck, of him recognizing the scarlet coat perhaps. He pointed right at her. "You! Stop!" He drew his pistol. "Halt now or I will shoot."

If he shot, he was an idiot, she thought grimly, dropping under another table. There were too many unrelated bodies in unpredictable trajectories, which had rather been the point.

Three things happened in quick succession. Marta rose up from the other side, and one of the saloon patrons actually lunged for her, arms wide as if to take her into a bear hug. From the corner of her eye, she saw a bulky man, his face streaked with old burns and distorted with rage, fling his own glass forward, toward the guard captain. A split second later, she heard it shatter, followed an instant later by the crack of a gunshot.

The man lunging for her went down, blood spraying from his shoulder.

The fight Marta had started with her chair was nothing compared to the chaos that erupted now. She dropped down again as more gunshots sounded.

This she had not intended, nor planned for. Annoying, how often stupidity reared its ugly head and made things infinitely worse. And hell, they'd probably give that captain a medal for bravery in the face of a slavering horde of drunks.

Someone stepped on her hand, another kicked her in the side and she rolled with it, fighting to regain her breath. They weren't after her, any more; it had gone to a place without reason. She scrambled to her feet and got shoved back toward the wall for her trouble. That she was more than willing to comply with, catching herself up on the rough boards with a slap of her hands. Marta squeezed along the wall, glancing back and forth in the hopes of catching sight of any of her crew in the melee.

Her hands found the door that led back into the brewery. Locked, of course. She yanked her picks from her pocket as a heavy hand fell on her shoulder—only recognition of a rather particular burn scar on one of the fingers kept her from jamming the pick into the nearby flesh. Amelia. "Captain! Elijah!"

"Not now, Mister Cavendesh," she shouted to be heard over the din. "Get them both here, I'll have the door open if you stop distracting me!"

The hand—and Amelia—were gone an instant later and Marta concentrated on the door, the process complicated as people insisted on being shoved into her. Teeth clenched, she elbowed someone who smelled strongly of garlic back and gave the lock's mechanism one last desperate rake and twist, and felt it give way. She clawed the door open as more gunshots sounded. A moment later, Amelia squeezed through the doorway, and then Lucius barreled in, dragging Elijah with him.

Marta let the door slam shut and re-engaged the lock. The din of the fight retreated to a muffled roar, which revealed a far more unpleasant sound—panting, burbling breaths coming from Elijah.

"Captain, Captain, it's Elijah—"

"I know," she said curtly. "Mister Lamburt, get him laid down. Mister Cavendesh, go peep out into the back alley. If there's not a clear way through, bar the door and find something heavy to barricade it with."

"But Captain—"

"Do it!" she snapped. While Lucius dragged the unfortunate Elijah a bit deeper into the brewery, Marta located the bar for the door and slid that home. A nice workbench joined it as an impromptu barricade. Satisfied that would hold while the guard subdued the riot outside, she hurried to Lucius's side.

Things did not look good at all. Elijah was awake still, dark eyes rolling frantically. He weakly clutched a bloody rag against his chest. More scarlet dotted his lips, a long string trailing down from the corner of his mouth. Lucius cursed a streak so blue it was nearly visible to the naked eye. He tore his jacket off and folded it into a pillow that he could shove under Elijah's head.

Marta dropped to her knees on the dark wood floor, pulling her leather gloves from her pocket and yanked them on. "Let me see that, Mr. Masterson, there's a good fellow..." She pulled his hand away from the rag for a moment, yanking open his shirt to expose the wound better. Buttons sprayed onto the floor. There was a red wet hole in his chest, air burbling unhappily from it every time Elijah tried to draw breath. She pressed the rag firmly down again, ignoring his strangled sound of pain, and dragged his hand back over it. "Did it go through, Mister Lamburt?"

Lucius shook his head. "Bullet's still rattling around in there."

She looked down at the pale-faced man, throat working as he breathed raggedly. "All right. I'll stay here with him. You and Mister Cavendesh will go."

"Go where?" Amelia demanded with a tight voice. "I just barricaded the back door. They'll be knocking it in at any moment. I barely got the bar down before they reached it; workers ran out that way, I guess."

"Even so, can't say I like the idea of you stayin' neither, Captain," Lucius said, beetle brows drawn together.

"The Duke went to a lot of trouble to look for us specifically, and with an overwhelming force. I mean to know why." Marta's tone had gone dangerously quiet. And she knew that it had to be the Grand Duke himself behind this move and not just his Chief of Security, who was her normal opponent. As Chief of Security, Colonel Douglas was in charge of the police and special security forces, but normally had no power to dictate the movements of the uniformed soldiers. She would have been more inclined to flee and tweak the Grand Duke's tail had Elijah's blood not been slicking down the fingers of her gloves at this moment.

"And Elijah—" Amelia began.

"Mister Masterson will not make it even as far as the train." Marta began divesting herself of her weapons, sword and pistols and knives, followed by a few of her more eclectic and specialized belongings—the collapsible spy-glass, most of her lockpicks, everything else but the twists of string in her pockets. "Immediate medical attention is his only hope." She feared none would prove immediate enough, though she did not voice it. "I will not have him left alone now." She closed her hand over the hilt of her machete, an automatic gesture as if she thought to hand that, too, over to Lucius.

No. She let it go.

"And where will we go, Captain?" Amelia asked again, caught somewhere between defeated and defiant.

As if in answer, a well-hidden trapdoor popped open in the floor with a hollow boom. A moment later, the grinning face of Simms came into view. "Heard you were in a spot of bother, Captain—" His eyes widened. "Oh, hell."

"Smuggler's tunnels," Marta said. Sometimes she forgot that the others hadn't bothered to get to know the town as well as she and Simms. She also found it quite annoying that they would need to be told to make such explorations. "Go!"

A hollow boom sounded from the door at the front, followed by another from the back, as if to add emphasis to her command.

"Sir?" Simms asked as the other two headed toward him, protests cut off by that sound.

Marta glanced over her shoulder, lips curling in a smile despite the situation. "I'll be wanting a visit from my maiden aunt in prison, Simms."

He was still cursing as he retreated from view, Amelia and Lucius following him. The sound was only cut off by the trapdoor returning to its original place with a final thump.

With them safely gone, she turned her attention back to Elijah. He stared at her with wide, burning eyes. "Steady as you go, Mister Masterson. You should not have to wait long."

Perhaps too long. Logic dictated giving the others a head start by keeping the bulk of the force outside distracted by its efforts to get in. They had a better chance than poor Elijah anyway. Marta remained kneeling, silent and grim as the booming from both doors did not quite manage to mask the sound of increasingly labored breath. Elijah frantically clawed for her hand, and she let him, holding on tightly until his fingers went limp.

He stopped breathing.

She set his hand carefully down on the floor and counted the seconds roughly by the assault on the doors, having sent her pocket watch with Lucius. Two minutes later or close to it, Elijah's fingers began to twitch.

"I am sorry it had to come to this, Mister Masterson," Marta said. She drew her machete and rose to her feet.

The back door splintered. A resounding crack sounded from the front.

Marta raised the machete and brought it down unerringly on what had once been Elijah Masterson's neck. It sheered through flesh and sunk into his spine with a meaty thunk. A second precise blow as the workbench in front of the door fell over with a loud crash, and the machete went cleanly through, biting deeply into the wooden floor behind. Elijah's head rolled away from his body; his fingers twitched once more, spasmodically, and then went mercifully still.

"You! Hands up!"

Marta stopped trying to pry the machete from the floor and straightened, hands coming up. The idiotic captain who had turned the riot into a shooting fight strode into the room. "Marta Ramos, sometimes called Captain, you will stand for arrest."

"You certainly took your time," she said poisonously. On closer inspection, the man looked freshly promoted and far too young. The lines of his uniform were sharp enough to cut cheese, buttons bright even in the dim brewery, and his beard and mustache, while neat, still seemed to be coming in. Either troops had been sent in on special notice to come look for her—quite a long way for a potentially fruitless search—or the nearest garrison had changed commanders very recently.

His eyes widened at the sight of the headless corpse next to her. He did not, however, need to ask what happened. "And what of your other compatriots?" he demanded.

"Transformed into birds and flew away. I think all the pounding startled them." Marta smiled with sweet insolence. "Add sorcery to my list of charges."

The man's eyes narrowed, and he gestured two of his soldiers forward to drag her arms down and secure her at the wrists, rather more roughly than necessary. One of them, she noted with nasty pleasure, had a bloody nose. "The Grand Duke wants a personal word with you."

"Funny, that. I rather wanted to speak with him myself."

It was with no small amount of trepidation that Simms approached the ornate little row house, a gingerbread fantasy done in green and brown. He resisted the urge all the while to claw at his overly starched collar. He hated playing the role of the gentleman caller on a normal day, and hated it even more now, knowing the sort of viper's den into which he was about to walk. But the Captain had been very specific in her own way, and Simms also had to admit that he was in well over his head at this point. He'd never had a head for prison breaks; those were always the Captain's department.

An impeccable butler answered the door. While he followed social form politely enough, the way he eyed Simms indicated clearly that he thought the man had come to the entirely wrong entrance of the house. "Yes, sir?"

"I'd like to speak with the lady of the house," Simms said, taking his hat into his hands. "News about her jewelry."

The man's eyebrows moved almost imperceptibly. "Ah. Please, come in." He escorted Simms to a sitting room that had once been familiar, only now lacy doilies and intricate bits of statuary and enameled *objets d'art* cluttered every spare surface. Simms found he disliked it even more than when last he'd been in here, with a body putrefying majestically on the floor. He felt afraid to touch anything, let alone sit, as if a simple action might start a chain of chaos that would end with everything in the room broken and him in the middle of it like a guilty dog.

The butler opened the door a moment later for a woman dressed head to toe in black, her face obscured by lace veil. The fine line of her chin was still visible, the secretive curve of her lips. Deliah Nimowitz, unlike the room, hadn't changed in the slightest. In her arms was a tiny fuzzy white dog. At the sight of Simms, it began to squirm excitedly and yip until Deliah put him down. The dog scurried over to him and began sniffing at his shoes and pants cuffs with avid excitement.

The butler, very pointedly, shut the door behind her and left the two of them quite unacceptably alone.

"Mr. Simms, what a pleasure it is to see you again. Chippy is very excited too, as you can see."

"Miss Nimowitz." His mouth had gone very dry. For all the pleasant grace in her voice, the soft glitter of her tawny eyes from under that veil put him in mind of a lion watching an antelope from a thicket.

"I know this can't possibly be a social call, since you seem to have left your most delightfully social half elsewhere, unattended."

Simms swallowed hard and did his best to ignore that ridiculous jab. "I'm sorry to say that Captain Ramos has been arrested by the Grand Duke's men. Very trying, of course. She'd probably enjoy a visitor, if you have the time."

"How sloppy of her."

"It was a sloppy situation."

Deliah laughed softly, the lace in front of her mouth stirring with her breath. "I might, at that. Oh, and what of my jewelry? Any luck...finding it? I know you've been looking ever so hard."

Jewelry that had been stolen fair and square by Captain Ramos, and only belonged to Deliah thanks to the death of her wealthy Grandaunt Clementine. For all that Captain Ramos seemed to think it a lark, Simms still felt distinctly uncomfortable about the circumstances of the old lady's demise. It was one more reason to not trust Deliah in the slightest. He inspected his blunt fingernails carefully. "We may have turned up a piece or two. The Captain would know...perhaps you ought to ask her yourself." All of this lying—and Simms lied, Deliah lied, and they both damn well knew they were doing just that—made his skin crawl.

That just seemed to amuse Deliah all the more. "I suppose a favor calls for a favor." She offered him her hand.

Not liking this one bit, Simms took her lace-covered fingers and shook.

THE GRAND DUCHY'S CENTRAL gaol was like an old familiar friend to Marta, one she'd spent many a quiet stretch in while she waited for some bit of planning to fall into place. The predecessor of Colonel Douglas had, for some reason, always put her in the women's wing, where security was far more lax and the adventure of escape therefore proportionally less interesting.

Colonel Douglas apparently wanted to take no chances this time. She was escorted through the men's wing of the gaol, accompanied by a good deal of confused hooting since the inmates seemed divided over if she was man or woman. The gaolers tucked her into a cell meant for solitary confinement, its single high window far too small to make escape more than an insane fantasy.

This was fine with Marta; she had no intention of going anywhere until she'd had a word with Colonel Douglas if not his master, the Grand Duke of Denver. She lay down on the pallet in the corner that functioned as the cell's bed and composed her thoughts, charting potential courses and rolling the question over in her mind as to why the army had been sent looking for them, not just Colonel Douglas's security forces. Why the army was composed of green recruits. Why Silverthorn's furnaces roared into the night, smelting steel.

She did her best not to think of Elijah's fingers starting up their tell-tale post-death twitching.

The Colonel didn't keep her waiting long. That, she'd expected, since he'd always been a punctual man in their other encounters. No, what made the meeting surprising was that he did not come to her, to taunt her through the door of the gaol cell; rather, she was taken from her cell, put in shackles, and escorted into the courtyard where a wagon with thick bars and thicker walls waited, the guards showing the sort of wary caution normally reserved for mass murderers and the dangerously insane.

The guards stuffed her into their Black Maria, two of them sitting in the back with her, rifles at the ready, and they took a jolting ride through the more narrow winding streets of Denver. Her eyebrows jumped slightly as she recognized the heavy chocolate scent of a confectioner, the particular accents of the children shrieking and playing outside as they passed.

A few minutes later they paused to go through the gates of the Grand Duke's Palace. The Maria rattled around to the back to the shabbiest of the wings, and the guards hauled her out and marched her in through one of the side doors. Rather than upstairs to the office she'd been familiar with from many an information gathering trip, they took her along the ground floor to what had once been a briefing room and was now, it seemed, Colonel Douglas's office.

Or was, she had a feeling, only temporarily so. If she'd already made him this paranoid, she'd wager he wouldn't keep it in the same place once she'd escaped his clutches yet again.

The office was almost suffocatingly, overbearingly masculine, all dark woods and sternly patterned wallpaper, pictures of hunt scenes and generals on horses. It affirmed her assessment of the colonel as someone deeply invested in the social order—nothing new there. Far more interesting were the items artfully arranged around his desk blotter—pens and papers as usual, a cigar box and snifter, a desk lamp, and most interesting, a cheap little tin orrery, a halo of off-white dust surrounding it.

Marta took that all in with a quick glance, as well as the fact that every scrap of string and twist of metal that had been in her pockets was now laid out neatly on his blotter. She let no curiosity betray itself on her face, just smiled slyly at the man behind the desk and held up her hands to display the manacles. "Are these really necessary, Colonel Douglas?"

"Jewelry becomes a lady," he said dryly. "You do know why you're here. It's a long list and I'd rather not waste my breath."

"Acts of piracy and the like, I'm sure. Though that isn't the *true* reason you've gone to all this trouble, is it?"

He raised an eyebrow, gesturing for her to go on.

Marta tilted her head toward the corner of his desk that contained the orrery. "Lost a souvenir, and hoping some kind soul picked it up?"

"That? No, just a little gift from a friend. They sell them at the museum now for seventeen pence."

He was lying, Marta decided, looking at his eyes. And he wasn't even trying to disguise it. How interesting. "I'm glad to know it isn't at all valuable. You see, I saw one of those during the last robbery, and we just chucked it out the window to lighten the load." And he saw, she thought, just as clearly that she was lying. What was this about?

"You'll be hanged tomorrow," he informed her. "We're not bothering with trials for your sort anymore."

"I'm terribly sorry. I can't possibly fit you into my schedule until a week Wednesday at the earliest." She tilted her head; she felt the shape of the problem, far larger than what she'd bargained for, though that only made it more interesting. Something still seemed to be missing, some piece misaligned. "I hadn't realized you were in the habit of using the regular army to do your work these days. Short staffed?"

Colonel Douglas smiled tightly. "Not at all. They were just lucky enough to be in the area."

"I expect a reprimand on the record of the captain in charge. Last I saw, even this duchy hadn't descended so far into barbarism that we were quelling brawls with bullets."

"I heard."

She stared at him, the anger she'd swallowed down at the situation burning in her eyes for that moment. "You'll look into it."

"There are some matters to investigate in regards to the unfortunate workers who were injured on your account." There wasn't an ounce of anything but unsympathetic righteousness in his expression. "But perhaps men that take to a life of piracy ought to consider the danger of the company they keep." He made an abrupt gesture with one hand and the guards took her arms again, turning her.

Marta turned her head to keep an eye on him even as they dragged her from the room. "See to it, Colonel, or I bloody well will!"

The guards stuffed her back into the Maria and they rattled their way to the gaol, Marta caught between fuming anger and the whirling possibility of just what could be going on. It was all that damned little tin toy, but she'd looked it over before.

Perhaps she hadn't looked it over *enough*. Perhaps she should have taken the little thing to pieces.

At the gaol, rather than taking her directly to the cell, they turned a corner and headed toward the front of the building. "Dinner time?" she asked with false cheer.

"You've a visitor." They deposited her in a small bare room, its single chair already occupied.

Marta smiled at the sight of that visitor. Simms worked swiftly these days, it seemed. Deliah had dressed herself in an unflattering shade of puce, hair and makeup done so that she looked thirty years older than her own modest age. She rose to her feet, leaning heavily on an ivory-headed cane, and spoke with a well-done tremulous air. "Oh, my dear girl. I always told your father you'd come to a bad end."

"Yes, Auntie. Terribly sorry about that." Marta suppressed a grin, clasping the hand Deliah held out to her. As expected, Deliah used that moment to slip a bit of metal into Marta's sleeve, the sleight of hand delicate and subtle.

"Your uncle's urn would be spinning like a top just thinking of the hair-curling mischief you've been up to."

"I imagine so. I'm a very naughty girl, I know, and I've shamed the family name. If only poor Uncle Edgar hadn't let me read so many books when I was young." She did a terrible impression of contrite and was rewarded by seeing a sparkle of amusement in Deliah's tawny eyes as she peered at her over the top of her spectacles.

"If only your Uncle Edgar hadn't read so many terrible books, he might have had a good clean life and would still be singing terribly in the church choir."

Somehow, she kept a straight face. "And how is your garden, dear Auntie? Does the hemlock grow?"

"Cheeky girl! You'll be the death of me. But the weather has been lovely, though as always we could use more rain..." They made polite conversation about the weather, and played a game where they made up horrendous fictitious relatives for the purpose of then making up even more horrendous gossip. Neither of them cracked a smile, which made this round a tie, though Marta thought there might have been a bit of cheating on Deliah's part, concealing a snort behind a lace handkerchief when she feigned a coughing fit.

After twenty minutes, one of the guards returned. "Visiting hours are over, ma'am," he said, back stiff.

"I'll see you again tomorrow, my dear girl," Deliah called, waving as the guards led Marta away. "And I'll bring Father Crispin with me this time!"

Marta caught the subtle movement of her fingers. Ten minutes, then.

They hadn't even gotten her back to her cell when the smell of smoke burst in through the windows, accompanied by shouts of "Fire!" While the guards were distracted, Marta took the chance to open the locks of her manacles, though she left them carefully in place. "Come on, look lively!" The guards chivvied her along and put her into the cell without any inspection at all before rushing off to help with the fire. Or perhaps gawk—that seemed nearly as possible.

They didn't notice that she'd put the bit of wire to good second use, jamming the mechanism of the door so it didn't shut all the way. Two minutes later, she walked confidently through the temporarily emptied halls, into the kitchen, and climbed cheerfully out the garbage chute. She resisted the urge to hum a merry tune as she did so; they were old friends, she and the municipal jail, and it never ceased to amaze her how the most charming security holes never saw their way to getting patched up—or when they did, she made it her business to create new ones. Out in the street, she broke into a trot, moving away from the crowd to an alley.

Rather than Simms waiting for her the normal three streets over, Marta was surprised to find Deliah leaning against a brick wall, idly turning her now-decorative cane in her hand. She was somewhat less surprised when the markedly shorter woman took her by the shoulders and shoved her against the wall.

And by that point not surprised at all when Deliah pressed their lips together in a kiss that involved far more tongue than was strictly polite. Marta returned the favor with equal fervor and obligingly ruined the woman's carefully crafted hairstyle by combing her fingers through it until Deliah took a step back.

"Powder, really?" Marta held up her white-dusted hands. She might have been breathing a bit harder than when she started, but had no intention of admitting to any cause but her flight from the gaol.

"Why bother with the effort when it isn't needed?" Deliah smirked, pointedly licking her lips. "Your man Simms says you may have a word or two about my jewelry."

Well, that certainly explained Deliah's surprisingly swift appearance. "I may have found one of the earrings."

"Just one? That's not terribly useful. But I'll expect it in the mail, nonetheless." Deliah laughed. "You can't hold that over my head forever, dearest Captain. I'll tire of playing."

"Then one of us had better think of a new game."

Deliah leaned in for another much lighter kiss. Marta parted her lips invitingly, hand coming up to play with her hair again, but then Deliah took a careful step back. With a wicked smile, she opened her mouth to let out a blood-curdling scream, "Here! Escaped prisoner! Escaped prisoner! Oh help! Murder!"

Marta laughed. "Oh, you wicked creature." As Deliah started up another round of screaming, Marta turned on her heel and pelted down the street, sprinting for the nearest alley.

"Here it is, Captain." Simms offered the Captain the ugly little orrery, having bought it back from Dolly with a toy dog.

She snatched it from his hand and turned it over and over, examining the mechanism with new enthusiasm. "Aha... Simms, trim me a strip of that newspaper there. A full line of text."

Bemused, he did as he was told, carefully cutting through an article in the *Post* and offering it to her.

"How I missed this before... I must be going blind." She took the newspaper and fed it into what had seemed to be a natural seam in the base of the orrery. But when she turned the mechanism to make the planets move, the paper disappeared inside and then fed back out. She held it up. "Ah, look...all those little pinpricks again." Shake of the orrery and a powdering of off-white dust drifted from it. "So that answers that. But to what end?"

Simms watched her cautiously as she froze a moment, and then let out a victorious cry. She shoved the device into his hands again and came up with the thin little book she'd also taken from the now-dead spy. "These aren't codes listed here. These are configurations for the planets of the orrery, so it might decipher the codes in the newspapers."

"Awful lot of stuff in the newspaper. All the articles alone..."

"But it wouldn't be articles, you see, not unless every reporter in these rags is suspect. Possible, but better to have something they can control the text of start to finish, not something that would have to be built into an article about some high society fluff-brain's dog vomiting on a general's trousers—"

"The advertisements!" Simms interrupted her. "Has to be all those advertisements, doesn't it?" He scrabbled through one of the newspapers until he came to a page with the large ads again, butcher shop and astrology society once again paired side by side. "Oh, it's got to be the astrology, right?" It was stupidly, glaringly obvious now.

The Captain burst out laughing. "Clever boys. Certainly easy to work in patterns of planets there, to set the cipher. Start cutting, Simms."

He handed her the orrery again and took up a pair of shears. It took far more care than he liked to cut up the newspaper and not rip it, to keep the lines straight. Particularly when he was so infected with the Captain's enthusiasm—he wanted to know just as much as she what this was about.

It was a torturous hour of snipping from the shears and muffled plinking from the orrery, Captain Ramos laying out strips of newspaper in ordered care. Simms set the shears down eagerly when he finished, shaking out cramped fingers as he leaned over the strips of paper barely daring to breathe. What he saw spelled out didn't make much more sense to him, seemingly random combinations of letters and numbers, nary a whole word in sight. "Think we might have done that wrong, Captain."

She shook her head, smiling wolfishly. "Oh, not in the slightest, Simms, not in the slightest. You took this one from the *Post*, correct?"

"Right."

"Let's have a look at one from the *Tribune*."

Simms was markedly less enthusiastic in the hand-cramping process, but complied nonetheless. Otherwise, she'd never tell him anything.

Captain Ramos lined up the new set of strips and stared at them moodily. "Oh my," she said after a moment, "they *have* been busy."

"With what?"

She tapped one set of the strips with a finger. "These are troop movements, Simms. The advertisement in the *Post* is a record of the troop movements and map coordinates for the army of the Grand Duchy of Salt Lake. And the advertisement in the *Tribune* is instructions for the spies who have collected all of that glorious data. Spies of the Grand Duchy of Denver, no doubt." She sat back, a wave of her hand scattering the papers. "We're looking at a war, Simms. Or the lead-up for one, with the Grand Duchy of Denver readying to invade its neighbor. That certainly explains the sudden influx of green troops, the shifts in rank, the Duke's building up his army, and working the smelters in Silverthorn and no doubt every other mining town over time to supply all these starry-eyed young warriors with pistols and sabers. No wonder our dear little ghost in Salt Lake paid for this with his life. Had he gotten this into the hands of his superiors, he would have scuttled the whole matter."

Simms let out a low whistle. "Explains why the Chief of Security was so eager to get it back."

"Does it now," the Captain murmured, idly turning the little mechanism again. "Though it doesn't explain at all why he *wanted* me to know that very fact."

She'd told him about the odd meeting. Simms still had no idea what to make of it himself. "Could have just made a mistake."

"Colonel Douglas does make mistakes on occasion, true. But none so blatant as that. No, he bloody well knew I'd have this knot unraveled sooner rather than later with the stink of his involvement all over it. But he not only wanted sooner, he wanted it to be understood from nearly the moment I escaped."

"Seems to me that if he wants anything in particular, best not to give it to him, right?" Simms still hadn't forgiven the man for his prank with the jewelry upon his arrival in the duchy. "So what do we do about it?" This was too big, duchies and politics and war.

"I'm inclined toward nothing," Captain Ramos said. "Considering where Elijah's blood sits, if I were inclined to help anyone at all it would be the Grand Duke of Salt Lake, and I'd rather eat nails than do anything to benefit that fatuous, god-bothering git. Now that I have the answer, I don't really care if the two Grand Dukes want to annihilate each other."

"Well, I care."

Simms and Captain Ramos both turned toward the sound of the voice; it was Amelia. Her eyes were dark and hollow, nose red, hair uncombed.

"Mister Cavendesh. You should have knocked."

"You seemed to be having a bit too much *fun*." Amelia shrugged, the jerk of one shoulder. "Elijah is dead because of that *thing*."

"Amelia, I'm sorry—" Simms started. It was Captain Ramos that stopped him, one hand on his arm.

"And what would you have us do about that, Mister Cavendesh?"

"Every time the Grand Dukes play, people like Elijah end up dying for it. People like us. People better than us. I don't want anything to do with territory and politics." Amelia's lips compressed in a thin, angry line. "That's why I left the duchies. I want you to make them stop."

"I don't know if I can do that," the Captain said. "That's quite the tall order."

"Maybe not always. But make them stop this time."

Her words felt like a punch in the gut to Simms. Looking at the Captain's face, he wasn't certain how she felt at all. Appeals to her humanity tended to fall flat, from what he'd seen in the past. She was rational before anything, always weighing risk and cost.

"Well, the current arrangement is rather advantageous to us, and even if the ensuing chaos might be put to some use, I do not think the end result of one duchy expanding its borders so widely will be of much good." She smiled sharply, the sort of smile Simms found himself very glad wasn't directed at him. "Because you asked, Mister Cavendesh. I've a few ideas."

Colonel Geoffrey Douglas was a habitually early riser, and thus he was dressed and just in the process of knotting his tie when the knock came at his door. He glanced at the window— still determinately dark outside—and went to open the door himself.

Outside waited a young man in blue and white uniform, wrists and collar edged with the red braid of the palace guard. Geoff's eyebrows went up. "Something the matter?"

"His Royal Highness wishes to see you," the young soldier said. He didn't sound particularly happy to be out in the city on the wrong side of dawn.

"His Royal Highness is up a bit early, isn't he?" Geoff commented dryly, even as his stomach seemed about to tie itself in knots.

"You don't know the half of it, sir."

Geoff stepped over the paper that had been delivered at his doorstep—the maid would pick it up shortly, he was certain—and followed the guard to the carriage. A silent, tense ride later, he was escorted to the private rooms of the Grand Duke, though mercifully he didn't have to venture farther in than the outer parlor.

Thus far in his career, he'd only once seen the Grand Duke in such a fury that he'd been brought to attend him in his bedroom. Geoff hoped to never experience that again. The outer parlor was more than grand enough, sumptuous furniture done in reds and golds, and at this hour of the morning a rather shocking breakfast spread already laid out, including a silver coffee post etched with a design of elk.

The Grand Duke of Denver was a surprisingly short man with square, broad shoulders that gave him a bullish appearance, imposing even in a dressing gown and slippers as he wore now. He'd served in the military at the behest of his father and had, to all reports, done well, though often such things had to be taken with a large grain of salt when people were afraid ill-considered words would reach the wrong ears. But the most intimidating part of the Grand Duke was not the carefully trimmed black goatee and neat hair that gave him a purposefully villainous air, but his dark eyes, sharp and sparking with intelligence.

Geoff had learned this the moment he'd met the man: he may have inherited his throne, but he kept it through a mixture of cunning, sheer intellect, and intimidation that bordered on fear.

And all of that was currently directed at him. Geoffrey Douglas had not blanched during his service on the Canadian Front when faced with the Infected hordes, and he certainly wasn't the sort to be intimidated by his employer or turn so much as a hair when confronted with angry nobility. He also was not, as it happened, stupid. He kept a respectful distance, leaning on his cane perhaps a bit more than was necessary as he styled a bow. "You sent for me, Your Grace?"

The Grand Duke wheeled to face him, one hand slapping down on the breakfast table and coming up with a newspaper—

the *Post*. He sliced it through the air crisply, as if it were a blade. "Do you know what this is?" he demanded

"Today's paper?"

The Grand Duke made a disgusted sound and threw it at Geoff, who caught it with one hand before the pages had begun to scatter too badly. "Something in it you don't like?" With a sinking feeling, he contemplated arresting a reporter. They were rather scummy creatures, in his opinion, but that didn't mean he quite had the stomach for throwing one into the gaol, or worse. And that, not even considering what sort of brightly yellow things his compatriots would end up writing about him in retaliation. Geoff greatly preferred to remain beneath the notice of the press.

"Page thirteen."

He flipped through as instructed until he came upon a full-page advertisement for...

For...

For *Professor Elijah Masterson's Ciphering Solar System.*

Geoff pretended to look over the text and drawings, though he knew perfectly well already what they were: a precise description on the use and construction of their little enigma-making device. Oh, and how kind of Captain Ramos, an offer for copies of a "book of codes and ciphers, fun for all ages" if just five pence were sent to an address Geoff was willing to bet did not actually exist.

"Well," he said after a moment.

The Grand Duke's eyes blazed. "Well?"

Geoff swallowed hard, raising his eyes carefully as he stood at attention. "Well, there's no stopping it, sir. Papers have already been delivered." He cleared his throat. "And I'd lay even money there's a similar advertisement in today's *Tribune*."

"And would you care to explain to me how this came to happen?"

"It's all in my report, sir. But..." He proceeded to explain the unfortunate events around the escape of Captain Ramos, the fact that she'd claimed to have thrown the orrery away, and certainly hadn't had it with her. That it hadn't seemed worth further action, since she was to be executed anyway.

The Grand Duke was still for a moment after in a way that made Geoff's mouth go dry and his stomach cramp. "And just like that," he said quietly, "we've lost our advantage."

Geoff nodded. "Afraid so, sir. You'll have to consult with the generals, but last I heard, we still weren't in a good position to proceed...militarily."

"We shall see about that. General del Toro will arrive within the hour. I'm certain he'll find this all *very* fascinating."

Geoff cleared his throat. "I'll go make up another copy of my report for him now, then. With your permission, sir?"

The Grand Duke waved a hand to dismiss him, though as Geoff turned to go he commented, voice soft and musing, "A relief to you though, isn't it, Colonel Douglas? You were opposed to this plan from the start."

And for so many reasons, Geoff thought: the loss of life, the breaching of perimeters, the threat to the safety of a grand duchy that had enough problems without fighting a war to take territory that they only really wanted for a greater slice of the shipping pie, the young soldiers demanding something more glorious than campaigns against the Infected when they had no idea that in the end, blood was blood. Del Toro was a mad old fool who hated Salt Lake's theocracy, and the Grand Duke was an ambitious man whose grasp sometimes exceeded even his formidable intellect.

He choked out, "I am your Chief of Security, sir. I advise. I do not decide."

"Just so. I will send for you again when the general arrives."

Geoff took the dismissal and left the room, though he kept his pace unhurried, that of a man chastened rather than cowed. He limped up the two flights of stairs to his office, newly moved from the one the self-styled "Captain" Ramos had seen, and dropped into his chair as if his knees wouldn't hold him up any longer.

Not far from the truth, that.

He fumbled for the bell to ring for the footman. Tea sounded like just the thing to steady his nerves. A scrap of paper fluttered out from under the bell to land on the floor next to his shoe.

A new sort of dread settling on his shoulders, Geoff bent to pick it up. The spiky scrawl was unfamiliar to him, but the contents of the message made it clear enough who had sent it: *Poor Colonel Douglas. It seems that you owe me a favor now. Don't worry, I shan't hold it over your head forever.*

And was it not favor enough to let that mad harridan play the hero and avert a war? He had a terrible feeling that argument would hold no water. Geoff twisted the note into a tiny screw, which he flung into the fireplace.

Feeling a thousand years old, he rang for tea. Rather than cream, he doctored his first cup with a generous dollop of whiskey. It seemed just the right drink for celebrating a deal with the devil. Lives, he reminded himself. Blood. The security of a peaceful duchy was far easier to see to than that of one at war. Even if, he reflected grimly, it wasn't anywhere as secure as it should be.

And would, unfortunately, remain that way for the foreseeable future.

5
The Flying Turk

S ANNOUNCEMENTS WENT, THIS one had been greeted with the level of enthusiasm one might expect from a cure for Infection or the discovery of a mystical golden fountain that produced endless quantities of hot chocolate: Her Grace's Airship *Titania*'s gilded bridge was to be given completely over to the calculated and imperturbable precision of clockwork. It was an end of an era, the daily papers trumpeted—the end of human error!

They would, Captain Ramos had noted dryly, indulge in such terrible puns, wouldn't they? Such a possibility was enough to make even the only slightly mechanically inclined weak at the knees. The very thought caused many a dry mouth among the well-heeled hobbyists who seemed to populate the upper ranks of society, legions of would-be inventors and renaissance men created by a surfeit of money and leisure time.

And tickets to this momentous event, if it was to be believed, were there for the taking if one was well-moneyed, well-connected, or at the very least well-liked by the Grand Duchess of New York. A brilliant move on her part, to auction off every bit of space not crammed with her friends and hangers-on.

The tickets were, of course, sought-after by droves of the would-be engineers, all of them at least mentally clutching at their wrenches and spanners and more sophisticated tools that their dear wives insisted upon dismissing as "fiddly bits." But the tickets were even more desired by those very same dear wives, saddled with marriageable daughters to distribute. This mechanical installation was cause for more plotting than went into most assassinations, a deadly combination of intricate diplomacy and vicious backstabbing. It promised to be the social event of the season—of a decade's worth of seasons—a chance to rub elbows with the truly first-class royalty and then brag about it for years to come.

Unsurprisingly the minor nobility, whether they had marriageable daughters or desperately craved bragging rights, were discretely clawing each other to ribbons over this chance. Metaphorical and, on at least one occasion gleefully recorded in the *Tribune*, literal blood was spilled in gouts that would draw the approval of even the most spoiled and battle thirsty Caesar of old from his opulent perch in the Coliseum.

The tickets were like diamonds—no, that was too common— like golden eggs laid at random by scattered bad-tempered geese, mythical and sought after by those who were more interested in shiny things than their own self-preservation.

Which perhaps offered an explanation as to *why* Captain Marta Ramos, pirate, inventor, and gleefully self-proclaimed thorn in the side of many a Grand Duke and Duchess, had against all odds contrived to receive two tickets for this most hallowed of voyages. It said absolutely nothing as to the *how* the feat had been accomplished.

Meriwether Octavian Simms—known by preference as simply Simms for obvious reasons—had long since learned to never ask certain questions around Captain Ramos on the off chance that she might actually answer and thus place him at risk for spraining something deep and irreparable within the confines of his skull. But this was one of those moments he was sorely tempted, because the circumstances were such a tricky combination of ridiculous and impossible. And perhaps also because the stiff, overly starched collar the captain had insisted was a required part of his costume had partially cut off the blood flow to his brain.

"You didn't kill anyone, did you?" he muttered at her from the side of his mouth. He trusted his beloved and well-groomed muttonchops—normally a gingery color that served as sure a warning as the coloration of the Monarch butterfly but now colored a disturbing near black thanks to a bottle of evil-smelling dye—to hide both the sound of his voice and the movement of his lips and keep the inquiry confined to the captain.

Captain Ramos trod very pointedly on his foot. Her hand, hidden in a delicate-looking glove of teal lace, maintained a vise-like grip on his arm and made escape impossible. With her other hand she pretended to fuss with one of her elaborately pinned scarves to hide her answer. "Do try to smile a bit more vacuously, Simms. We're supposed to be royalty."

That, Simms thought, somehow made the entire situation worse. On any ordinary day, he was ferociously common, and in fact took great glee in relieving aristocrats and their devoted emulators of both wealth and dignity using hands scarred by many a fight and fingernails darkened with the dirt of honest—

well, mostly dishonest, these days—work. Being in proximity with this high-class ostentation was bound to give him hives. And that wasn't even touching on the issue of the array of expensive perfumes that made a nearly visible cloud at the bottom of the gangway they were fast approaching.

"I don't have to," he muttered. "We're not swimming in the piranha pool yet."

"You'd have an easier time if you didn't keep breaking character, you know," she pointed out.

They reached the bottom of the gangway. It was constructed of dark wood—no doubt expensive—well-polished brass, and covered with a canopy of perfect and nearly air-tight glass squares. It was also very long and swaying faintly in a way that Simms would have once found incredibly disturbing as a man who had spent his entire life with his feet planted firmly on the ground. Since his association with Captain Ramos, however, he'd spent far more time aloft than was probably truly healthy for a fellow's wits. He had little left to fear from airships like the *Titania*, which currently tugged gently against its mooring ropes thanks to the wind that howled just outside the glassed-in observation deck and airship port at the top of the Empire State Building.

The bottom of the gangway was blocked off by a crimson velvet rope and more importantly, a pair of guardsmen. They wore the uniforms of the Grand Duchess of New York's personal guard, the color of their jackets precisely matching the rope visible between them.

"Tickets, madam, sir?" the more senior of the two—this presumed from the healthy smattering of white in his mustache and what hair was visible around his shako—asked in a mostly polite tone.

Simms had a feeling the tone was only *mostly* polite because they'd likely already had to turn quite a few oh-I'm-so-clever-I'm-sure-I-can-bluff-the-rozzers desperate social climbers away.

"Oh, yes, of course, a moment if you please." Captain Ramos said, smiling up at the guard.

She did not often have to look *up* at anyone, with the sole exception of Simms and people built to match his rather intimidating proportions. Her current position wasn't due to unusual height on the part of the guard, but rather the appalling way she had contorted her own sturdy frame. She'd also wrapped herself in a volume of brocade normally reserved for upholstering large couches, but it had the artful effect of making her look like a rather plump dowager, quite unlike the tall and—by social standards—scandalously athletic figure she normally cut. A wig and the truly disturbing makeup that she had inflicted upon both of them completed the effect quite nicely.

Simms directed a long-suffering look at the guard as Captain Ramos pretended to dig through her clutch purse. This was not a look he had to fake; he'd been practicing for years. "We're not too late, are we?" he asked. For that, he did have to affect a more jolly—and fruity—tone than normally passed his lips.

The younger of the guards took a gold watch from his pocket. "Twenty minutes before launch off, sir. Cutting it a bit close, you are. The Grand Duchess likes things to be prompt."

He nodded, and from some hollow depth in his soul managed to dredge up a conspiratorial wink. "Was ready to leave the house ages ago, but the missus... Well, you know how they can be." Oh, but the ways in which that statement felt wrong were too numerous for someone of his education level to count.

"Ah, here they are!" Captain Ramos pulled an envelope from her little purse and offered it to the senior of the guards. He took it delicately and extracted the tickets, his expression unchanging.

Simms concentrated very hard on breathing normally.

"Lord and Lady Parnell-Muttar. Welcome aboard. If you'll turn left at the top of the gangway, there will be a man there to see to your wraps and escort you to the first class lounge." Then the guard, of all strange things, smiled as he offered the captain her tickets back. And it wasn't the polite smile of an underling, but something bizarrely genuine. "And may I say it's a pleasure to have you both aboard. I was hoping I'd get to greet you personally."

Captain Ramos smiled and fluttered, even as she subtly tried to crush Simms's foot under her heel. Hastily, he crafted his painted grimace into a broad grin. "Of course, of course. The pleasure is ours."

The younger of the guards hastened to unfasten the velvet rope and wave them up. As they started climbing the gangway, Simms desperately trying not to limp, the older guard called softly behind them, "We appreciate all you do for us, sir."

Simms waved a hand in what he hoped was a "no, think nothing of it, my pleasure" manner. As soon as they were nearly to the top of the gangway, indicated by the nose hair-charring concentrations of expensive perfume and the steadily growing volume of chattering voices, he hazarded whispering to the Captain, "What have I done for them?" It seemed the sort of thing he probably should know.

"You're a war hero," Captain Ramos informed him in an undertone. "And you single-handedly saved the crew of the *Venus Delphinia* as she sank to her watery grave."

Simms came within a hair's breadth of biting his tongue in half. He had personally been on the *Venus Delphinia* right beside Captain Ramos, and had in fact been a contributing factor to its sinking. "That's a bit crass."

"That's public relations, Simms." Captain Ramos tugged him forward and onto the richly carpeted deck of the airship, overriding his natural feelings of dread. More uniformed men waited there, though they were in much less ornate and sober jackets of deep indigo. "Smile prettily now."

"Yes, dear, you're quite right, quite right. The carpet is lovely." Simms stretched his lips into a rictus that approximated a posh grin.

"I don't think you're getting any better at this," the captain muttered for his ears and poked at his hand with the envelope containing the tickets. He hastened to take it, the heavy paper feeling awkward to his hand. "I really can't take you anywhere," she added, a bit more loudly, slipping her fan out from her little purse.

That, Simms thought, was really the opposite of the problem. In fact, she insisted on dragging him along like she was a kite and he her tail, whether he liked it or not. Only she never bothered to ask his opinion on the topic. This time she'd just shown up at his door while he was attempting to convince Dolly that his ties weren't suitable wear for her toys and informed him that they were catching an airship in the Grand Duchy of New York two days whence, and he was to see to the luggage. A very specific sort of luggage, split into several large familiar crates, the sight of which had filled him with equal parts anticipation and dread.

It was never a good sign for his blood pressure or potential lifespan when the captain thought they needed to pack their own glider.

"Yes, pet. But you do know how I adore these ticky little machines and their tricks, as unreasoning as that might be. You're quite an angel for putting up with all my little quirks," he said woodenly.

The disgusted look the captain directed at him from behind her ostentatiously lacy fan was reward enough. She tugged him left as the guardsman below had instructed and smiled sweetly at the steward who greeted them. Simms tried to smile sweetly too, into a very awkward pause that lasted until the captain poked at his hand again, this time with her fan.

Right. The tickets. "Would forget my own head if it weren't attached," he said, all teeth and forced jollity as he handed the envelope over.

THE FIRST CLASS RECEPTION was a fluttering, chattering mass of ladies in their finest dresses, accented with frilly bits of pearl-encrusted jewelry—that was the fashion this season, thanks to Lady Margot Shellstin of the Grand Duchy of Topeka—and husbands who had been stuffed into suits, colors carefully coordinated to complement and at times out-shout each other. The noise, the light, the kaleidoscopic spectacle of it all was a little much for Simms, now far too used to life in the abandoned silver mine of Devil's Roost. But any hesitation of his feet was overruled by Captain Ramos dragging him forward and into the hallucinatory heart of the colorful mass. It was follow or lose his arm, and he rather needed that arm for both punching and holding tea cups.

This was the moment Simms always dreaded. It was one thing to bluff common security men or even guards about their native class, but he'd always felt like he must stand out somehow from the moneyed classes, whiffing of poverty and a native disbelief in their assumed superiority. And after an unfortunate experience he had in the recent past with one Deliah Nimowitz, he even knew just how being singled out in such a fashion would work, from the spreading wave of appalled silence to the muffled little screams of dismay from the melodramatic ladies. Oh, yes, and the sounds of swords being drawn—that was always his favorite.

Much to Simms's relief, thus far the nobility plainly assumed he and the captain were of their class, even if their faces were not known. There was a raised eyebrow here and there, to go with all the curtsying and bowing, a bit of whispering behind fans, but Simms was a keen eavesdropper—among his other less savory skills—and he quickly discerned that the topic of discussion was which lord and lady they happened to be, not who had shoved that gorilla of a commoner into a natty suit and thrust him onto their delicate sensibilities. With that he relaxed, smiled—with carefully simulated mental vacancy—and managed to locate the one waiter bobbing gently around the room who was serving cold tea rather than wine so he could help himself to a glass. He poked Captain Ramos with the envelope containing the tickets until she took it back, thus freeing his other hand for the acquisition of carefully sculpted wedges of soft white cheese and several lovely little sausages from a silver tray.

Simms popped one of the juicy little sausages into his mouth and thought that this, at least, made the trip worth something. The rich really did occupy a different world from the one in which he'd grown up. Who would have thought that apple could belong in a sausage, let alone the odd little green bits he didn't want to think about too hard since they imparted a nicely sharp flavor.

He stuffed another sausage into his mouth as Captain Ramos introduced him to yet another lady as "Lord Parnell-Muttar" and mumbled something about being charmed. The lady in question, noting the smear of grease—if expensive grease—on his lips declined to offer her hand to be kissed. He almost wiped his lips on the back of his glove until the captain produced a handkerchief from her padded-out bosom and shoved it into his hand.

"I haven't eaten since breakfast," he muttered as she steered them farther into the ballroom. As if to lend credence to his claim, his stomach let out a loud, pleased growl around the bits of pork and beef he'd already given it.

"In this at least, you're acting the part quite well," she muttered back. "Just try not to eat too many of those sausages. I have to share a room with you later."

"You don't eat too many sausages," he muttered, well aware that was exceedingly weak as a retort, even by his own standards. He was about to protest a bit more loudly when Captain Ramos tugged him away from another waiter with a delightfully loaded tray, but one glance at her expression showed she was a woman on the hunt. Her expression was fixed into one of smiling politeness, but there was a sharpness to her gaze that Simms recognized well.

"Ah, and there he is," the captain murmured, steering them toward another brightly colored clump of overdressed people sweating money and a desperate need for relevance from their pores. The group stood near the floor to ceiling windows that filled out one entire wall of the observation deck, framing the smoke-hazed Manhattan skyline.

"Who?"

"Observe the man in bottle green surrounded by an odd combination of the shabbily dressed and lords with singe marks in their hair and grease stains upon their gloves. Academics on one side, idle tinkerers on the other, there. The cut of his suit is a bit off, you see? Not professionally tailored. I'd wager the fabric's poor as well, the way it's moving."

"Ah…" Simms took her meaning immediately. It was the sort of suit Captain Ramos had often pointed out as what a poor man wore to try to impress patronizing rich men. "So he's the inventor of the…thing." There had been a reason they were here, right? Other than the sausages.

"Thadius Clarkson, yes. Inventor of the alleged clockwork automated pilot. A coat that badly cut and he's still in with the first class passengers? I can't think of anyone else he might be."

Rather than go directly for the shabby fellow in question, the captain led them over to a nearby group. There was a minute of rapid fire introductions, bowing and hand kissing and fluttering, and then the conversation settled back to a discussion of which coming out balls were certain to be the best and which the most scandalous in the coastal regions. Simms didn't have to pretend at all to be bored and a bit lost, even as Captain Ramos made encouraging noises in the general direction of the conversation as she slowly shifted them over to one side of the group.

And there they were, in perfect position to eavesdrop.

"—tried to have the patent held, can you believe?" the man—Clarkson—asked, chuckling broadly at the murmurs of disbelief that bought. He had a bit of a ratty face, Simms thought, and a very nasal voice, the sort normally caused by having had one's nose broken multiple times. "So, of course, I couldn't allow that to stand. Damn Germans, always endeavoring thievery of the best efforts of the Duchies. If they were so far advanced in their design, they should have had the dashed confidence to file for themselves." He laughed again.

Listening to that laugh, thin and oozing with pomposity, Simms felt the not inconsiderable urge to flatten Clarkson's nose himself, just on principle. Pretending to be observing something out the windows, Simms tried to get a better look at the man's face. His much abused, rather crooked nose was underlined by a sparse and overly groomed mustache. Simms couldn't help but stroke his own rather more luxuriant growth—now unfortunately waxed by orders of the captain—and smirk a little behind his glove.

"You caught us all by surprise, though," one of the other men in that group said in a jolly tone. He was an older gentleman with hair gone mostly steel gray, his frame a bit rotund, one hand tucked into the pocket of his striped vest. He had a cigar in his other hand that he moved as he spoke, as if conducting some unseen orchestra. "I hadn't thought you'd still be in the business of difference engines. Not after Bremen."

The look Clarkson shot the avuncular fellow at that comment would have heralded a bottle being broken into an improvised knife in a more honest setting. "A true inventor never allows minor setbacks to interfere with the glorious process." He sniffed derisively.

Simms considered for a moment the many times he'd seen Captain Ramos working feverishly at some bit of machinery with hand bloody from skinned knuckles, her eyes gone strange and wandering from the effects of peyote in a face smeared with grease. He would never, ever, accuse the process of being at all glorious.

"Quite true, quite true. So I take it you were able to work out all those hiccups with the chain drive?"

At which point the conversation moved over to something far too technical for a man of Simms's education level and cheerful mechanical disinclination, though from the corner of his eye he saw Captain Ramos all but drinking it in, her eyes blazing with interest. Simms could only hope that the women in their little circle assumed it was directed toward their riveting discussion of the varieties of lace from the Grand Duchy of Galveston.

More sausages, Simms decided. It was his only chance at survival. As he scanned the ballroom for a waiter bearing a tray of savory salvation, he noticed that he and the captain weren't the only ones hovering nearby and doing a bit of eavesdropping. There were six other people he picked easily from the crowd, which meant they weren't trying to be in the least bit subtle. Most paid rapt attention—probably more amateur inventors. But one rather slight young man in a burnt orange and gold waistcoat, his brown hair slicked back in an unflattering style that made his entire head appear wedge-shaped, stared at Clarkson with unadulterated contempt and hatred writ large on his face.

Now that, Simms concluded, was rather unusual. People in first class usually excelled at hating each other while smiling. He nudged the captain lightly to bring her attention to the sour-faced fellow, but before he could say anything, the ship's gong rang out three times, indicating that they were about to cast off from the Empire State Building and begin their voyage.

That seemed to be the signal for Clarkson. He excused himself from his group and moved through the crowd to the small podium set up directly under the large portrait of the Grand Duchess of New York and her two terriers. All three sets of painted eyes seemed to glower disapprovingly at the assembled society occupying the ballroom.

"Ladies and gentlemen! Ladies and gentlemen, if I might have your attention!" Clarkson had to repeat himself several times before the room quieted. "As you've no doubt noticed, the glorious *Titania* is casting off and shall soon begin her most felicitous ascent. My automaton stands at the ready on the bridge, but I thought it best to let Captain Murray give the helm his deft and human touch one last time before the era of human imprecision officially comes to a close. I wish to inform you there has been a modest change of flight plans for our exhibition cruise, however." He held up his hands, smiling at the obedient murmurs of surprise. "Rather than move over the dark sylvan stretches of this fair duchy, we shall turn over the lusty expanse of the eastern waters and head out to sea so that you, honored guests, may appreciate the beauty of nightfall over the waters of the bewitching Atlantic as you take your dinner and be greeted by the sublime reflection of Helios's aurora to go with your breakfasts. But more importantly, we shall move far afield from the shining lineaments of the roads and rail lines. I wish you to witness the true complexity of my automaton as he navigates by mathematics alone!"

More applause greeted this pronouncement.

Next to Simms, Captain Ramos snorted, hiding her mouth behind her fan. "I'd be far more impressed if the thing *could* detect the lights or signals from the beacons and calculate anew from there. Flying a preprogrammed course over a place with no landmarks has the potential to be quite the dodge. It can all be reduced to velocities and times if the maps are sufficiently accurate."

Simms smiled sourly and muttered around his muttonchops, "I'd be far more impressed if he'd speak plain bloody English."

Clarkson continued blithely on, "And once our pleasure cruise is at its end, the clockwork pilot—overseen by Captain Murray—will guide us safely to rest at in the bosom of the Duchy of Charlotte's port!"

Docking an airship was no mean feat. Simms shot another glance at the captain. Her eyebrows arched up a little. "Should it provably happen that way, I will reconsider my opinion," she admitted a bit grudgingly.

"Now, if those of you with tickets illuminated around the edges with a gilded stripe would care to coalesce around me, we shall repair to the bridge for this momentous occasion. Other honored guests, please enjoy the ambrosial comestibles. We shall reconvene at dinner!"

Another glance at the captain and she flashed him a charming smile, tapping her lips with their tickets—which were, Simms noted now, decorated with a gold stripe along the edges.

"Oh, you're going, Lady Parnell-Muttar?"

Captain Marta Ramos smiled charmingly at the plump gentlewoman—Lady Margrave of Albany—who had asked the question. "I'm afraid so. A bit dull for my tastes, but"—here she let her voice drop to a conspiratorial whisper—"I do try to indulge darling James in his little whims, since he's then more likely to let me indulge in my passion for Zhonghua silks in return."

"Oh, yes. Then go, go." Lady Margrave made a little shooing motion with her hands. "This year's are particularly lovely, you'd best build up all the good credit you can!"

Marta bobbed a little curtsy and extricated herself and Simms from the group without further comment. The women closed the circle back in a moment later, the conversation turning immediately to the departed couple before they'd even gotten out of earshot. The ladies couldn't seem to decide if they were jealous of the false lord and his "wife" or not—it was quite the status symbol to go to the bridge, after all, but also would cut into valuable time better spent socially maneuvering and not concerning themselves with technical details they had sadly—in Marta's opinion—not been trained to understand.

Flashing the tickets as unsubtly as she could without actually bursting into song, she caught them up to the small group leaving the ballroom, placing them at the back. It put her in prime position to sort through the conversations of the rest of the group—mostly unctuous and ultimately shallow questions from would-be inventors aimed at Clarkson—while remaining safely ignored as they traversed the richly carpeted hallways and down stairs, all leading unerringly to the fore of the airship.

The hall leading to the bridge was surprisingly well decorated with an abstract golden design covering the walls and there were little alcoves at regular intervals containing statues of Roman gods or Zhonghua vases filled with fresh flowers. Even the duct work and conduits and that ran along the ceiling carrying pipes and wiring to the bridge were decorated to look like stately—if large—pieces of decorative molding, with the gratings done in frilly metalwork.

Marta had never had the chance to view the bridge of *the Titania* before—her previous business had been limited to the passenger cabins and cargo hold. With an appreciative eye, she took in the shining brass and polished wood paneling, the well-crafted dials and their pristine glass facings. While she could operate surrounded by any amount of grease and grit—and at times preferred to since shiny tended to give one away in certain situations—she could still appreciate a well-maintained machine, not to mention a smartly uniformed crew, none of whom smelled overtly of fermented beverages, chewing tobacco, or unwashed armpits.

Though in a pinch, she decided, she'd still rather have Lucius Lamburt, gleeful enforcer and part-time human, than any five of these airmen. He could open beer bottles using his teeth, or more often, using the teeth of others.

With a minimum of maneuvering—mostly running Simms into the more bored or timid-looking of the blue bloods—Marta moved them to the front of the little group. This was the part she had come to see, after all.

The automaton had been set up next to the polished ship's wheel, normally manned by the captain. It was not quite what she'd expected: a squat wooden cabinet with the top half of a man made of polished brass clockwork and more wood attached to the top, the entire array standing a bit over six feet in height. Someone had dressed the automaton in a uniform like that of the ship's captain, a navy blue peacoat with brass buttons and even the appropriate number of stripes of gold braid on its sleeves. She had little doubt that had rubbed proverbial fur in the wrong direction across the bridge.

The automaton's head was strangely bare, its machined dome of a head glittering brightly in the bright lighting. Around the automaton, the neatness of the bridge had fallen to disarray. The polished wooden cabinets were opened, spilling small steam pipes and wiring across the floor. Crewmen scrambled back and forth, attaching the wiring to labeled ports on the cabinet. Framing them all was the bank of pristine windows that afforded a one hundred and eighty degree view of the sky, rolling white clouds below like the breakers of waves and endless blue above and ahead.

"Ladies and gentlemen, may I present—" Clarkson paused, looking at the automaton and frowned.

He cast around. Marta craned her head to catch a bit of white to one side of the automaton—loose strips of fabric, and was that a feather? The remains of a jaunty hat, perhaps, recently shredded by someone displeased by this situation. Clarkson prodded the scraps from sight with the toe of his shoe. He gestured imperiously at one of the bridge officers, who was bent to attach the last few wires to the cabinet. The officer gave him a look of murder barely contained by a stiff expression, and handed over his hat. Clarkson climbed up onto the cabinet to slip the hat onto the automaton's head, flicking the brim with his fingers to tilt it at a jaunty angle.

"There!" Clarkson jumped back down to the deck. "May I present…the automated navigator!"

He pulled a theatrically large lever on the side of the cabinet as the little crowd applauded politely. The automaton jerked to life, turning its wooden head and precisely raising one hand to salute. This action drew a great many appreciative murmurs. Marta clapped politely since continuing to blend in the crowd was rather important.

"Captain, if you don't mind stepping aside..." Clarkson said.

Captain Murray, a bluff man with thinning gray hair who was the replacement for the former captain of *the Titania*—MacConnell had retired quite suddenly after Marta's last foray on the airship—took this in stride. He even shook hands with the automaton, the action accompanied by much clicking and whirring of gears from the machine.

For Simms's ears alone, Marta murmured, "Ask him what the cabinet is for."

"That is where the difference engine is stored," Clarkson answered, after Simms had repeated the question.

The man added in a slightly patronizing smile for good measure, which Simms did his best to encourage by looking utterly befuddled—bless him. Or that could be, Marta realized, because he didn't actually know what a difference engine was. She'd explained it to him on at least two occasions, but both times he'd seemed far more intent on less interesting activities such as dodging bullets and screaming.

"As you can see, all of the wiring for the instruments and engine control has been rerouted through the engine. This will allow it to perform all of the calculations without the interference of fallible and disorderly human interpretation. Present company accepted, of course," he added, with a glance at Captain Murray.

The captain smiled graciously, though Marta detected a bit of tightness around his eyes. He wasn't nearly so thrilled about being replaced by an automaton as he pretended. "Please, Mister Clarkson, have your machine take the wheel."

Clarkson flipped a series of comically large metal switches on the cabinet. After a moment of hesitation, the automaton turned and grasped the ship's wheel in its hands. There was much appreciative applause from the wealthy ticket holders, which Marta thought was a bit much considering the automaton hadn't actua*lly* done anything yet. Clarkson pulled a lever, and a regular ticking sound began to emanate from the cabinet.

"And there you have it," Clarkson announced. "My automaton has taken over navigation."

More clapping, and Marta took care to join in. Something about it seemed quite strange to her, however, as she listened to the mechanical rumbling from the cabinet. She didn't trust it, nor the slightly cracked smile on Clarkson's face, framed by his utterly hideous mustache. If the box, which presumably contained the difference engine that would calculate the course and all corrections, could simply be plugged into the ship's systems, why was there need for an actual automaton? Surely if it would be physically turning the ship's wheel—and the rudder cables seemed to still be in their original places, the deck panels hiding them unmoved—that would be just asking for the introduction of errors, wouldn't it? While she appreciated the aesthetic of a nice bit of machinery as much as the next person, or exponentially more if the next person happened to be Simms, it struck her as a lot of wasted effort that could only cause a loss of precision.

Clarkson gave them a few moments to marvel at the automaton adjusting the wheel a little bit here and there, though it seemed rather anticlimactic. The inventor cleared his throat. "Ladies and gentlemen, Captain Murray and crew, I have been assured our illustrious hostess in absentia has outdone herself. Let us away to dinner!"

"Captain and crew, you said?" one of the gentleman in the group asked, adjusting his spectacles.

Clarkson smiled slyly. "Of course, that's part of the proof! No crew is needed, not with the automaton to monitor all of the ship's functions and navigate on its own. To prove this to you, the crew will be joining us at dinner and even for dancing, with the door to the bridge securely locked so that you can be certain no one will interfere. It shall be a charming experience for all involved."

"Are you certain that's entirely safe?" the gentleman asked. For someone who had cheered enthusiastically mere moments before, he seemed reticent now.

"Not to worry, sir," Captain Murray said. "At my request, there's been an alarm installed."

"A completely unnecessary alarm," Clarkson hastened to add. "I would have thought it an insult, but I know it is difficult for some to trust the leading edge of technology."

Captain Murray smiled as if slightly pained. "Yes, yes. But at any rate, I assure you the alarm shall sound if our heading deviates at all."

The gentleman nodded. "I see. Very well then. Dinner, you said?"

Marta and Simms were among the last out, and they paused to watch the rather theatrical locking of the bridge doors with an almost comically large padlock and a length of thick chain. Clarkson held up the key with a flourish and presented it to Captain Murray with a bow that was just a shade short of mocking. Captain Murray and the crewmen standing around weren't ignorant to this subtle dig. Quite a few dark looks were exchanged as the captain tucked the key away in his waistcoat pocket. The strain to the jolly atmosphere wasn't helped in the slightest by a few of the wealthy passengers chuckling quietly at the show.

Only an idiot alienated his potential allies, particularly in favor of anyone who smelled so strongly of money. No one turned faster on a stumbling social climber than an aristocrat; Marta had used this fact to her advantage in the past. Many an inventor had put together an interesting engine and then hamstrung himself in full view of the benefactors he wanted desperately to impress. Ultimately, she was here to investigate Clarkson's difference engine, and now the inventor had helpfully decided to leave it completely unattended.

"Clarkson!" Ah, and there was the hatchet-like fellow in orange from the reception, waving one finger rather demandingly in the air. She took a quick glance back at Clarkson, and he looked an interesting combination of startled, frightened, and angry, which made his expression a muddle.

Then he pasted the rictus of a grin onto his lips. "Ah, sir. I'm so sorry you couldn't be on the tour, but the doors are now locked."

"Clarkson, this damn well isn't—"

"Of course!" he interrupted, waving frantically at the guards. Was this an expected altercation? One of them stepped forward to take the man's arm. "Please, sir, we will have this conversation at a more appropriate time. There are ladies present."

Well, lady. After a split second of consideration, Marta pursed her lips in disapproval. While she'd like to hear what the argument was about, it really didn't fit the part she was playing at the moment. She would have to do a bit of nosing around later.

The narrow-faced man had the good grace to look abashed. "Madam, my apologies. But—" Oh, was that a Teutonic accent to his English? And it seemed to grow worse the more flustered he became.

"No buts," Clarkson said. "I promise, I shall find you after dinner. Please, you have my word."

Marta doubted it was Clarkson's word so much as the increasingly firm hold the guard had on the man's arm that got him to move away silently, though glaring balefully all the while. Interesting, indeed. However, Clarkson's personal spats weren't her first priority. His supposed mechanical genius was of far more interest.

"My apologies, gentlemen. Lady. The trials of even such local fame as I might claim to be mine. I hope that unfortunate little fracas hasn't soured your stomachs for our evening repast." Clarkson laughed nervously.

"Of course not!" One of the other passengers patted his belly jovially. "Come, it's high time we ate. You can tell us more about your work then."

Marta spared a glance at the padlock as the group walked away and mentally calculated how long it would take her to pick it. The resulting number was ten seconds, plus or minus five. She wasn't particularly impressed.

"I don't trust it," Captain Ramos said.

They were in the cabin they ostensibly shared as Lord and Lady Parnell-Muttar, Simms having excused them from the after-dinner dancing, claiming his dear wife was quite exhausted. Really, it was a desire for self-preservation that had prompted his thoughtfulness. He wasn't much of a dancer at the best of times, and the captain took a perverse pleasure in dragging him around any available dance floor as if torturing him and making him smile while she did so would remedy his lack of rhythm and grace.

"You've often told me you don't trust anything," Simms replied, fumbling at his tie. He'd had to go with a different knot than his usual, one more popular with the upper class, and was having a hell of a time unraveling it. He glanced over his shoulder at the Captain, who was currently stripping off her shirt, and hastily looked away. "I really wish you'd warn me when you do that."

"Pish, Simms. Pish. I haven't the time nor patience for silly social mores."

Simms sighed. It wasn't that he really cared particularly. He'd seen Captain Ramos in nearly every state in which a person could exist. He just found the idea of talking *to any*one as they stripped off their clothing intensely awkward.

"What is it precisely you find so untrustworthy?"

"The entire setup of the device seems wrong."

"I thought it was a rather sharp looking automaton," Simms offered. "If you like that sort of thing."

Perhaps it was the influence of Captain Ramos, but he had developed a certain appreciation for a nice piece of machinery so long as it actually worked. And he did find the idea of automatons fascinating. Imagine, workhouses and dangerous factories a thing of the past, the work done by machines! Though his ever-present pessimism then hastened to remind him that such automatons were still in the realm of fiction, and if they were ever made they would probably be quite expensive. He had little doubt that the lives of lower class humans would be considered worth far less.

"It doesn't matter how nice the automaton looks. Any idiot can build a pretty piece of clockwork so long as it needn't think.

If all of the ship's inputs are run through the difference engine, why is an automaton even necessary?"

"Well, it is an expensive ship filled with rich people," Simms pointed out. "Perhaps they feel better knowing there's something at least vaguely man-shaped at the helm. People who aren't you get funny about that sort of thing."

"You may have a point," the captain admitted grudgingly. "You can stop covering your eyes now, Simms. I'm as dressed as you could wish."

By which she apparently meant costumed as one of the many maids employed by *the Tit*ania. "Feeling moved to do a bit of cleaning?"

"Hardly. Plausibility of place, Simms." She began to carefully scrub her face with a rag, removing all traces of Lady Parnell-Muttar. "Clarkson is likely to still be at the party. I thought I'd pop 'round to his cabin and have a look through his papers, since I'd rather like to know what he's doing with all that space."

"Not going to just pry open the machine itself first? Cut to the heart of the matter? Er...the difference engine of the matter?"

"Tempting. And the difference engine and I will have a date soon enough, make no mistake. But I wish to be acquainted with his design first so I won't have to waste time puzzling over the mess I shall no doubt find in that cabinet." She smiled thinly.

Simms nodded, finally stripping off his jacket and waistcoat. He glanced at the fully stocked liquor cabinet in one corner of the room. Suddenly, he disliked their ruse as first class all the more, for putting him the room with that much temptation. Normally it wouldn't be an issue at all, but spending a long period of time pretending to be someone else set his nerves jittering in a way that wouldn't deal well with being left to his own devices. He knew himself well enough to understand that.

And Captain Ramos, he thought, knew him just as thoroughly. She glanced over her shoulder, all the while carefully adding new shadows and lines to her face with a bit of makeup.

"Why don't you go to the cargo hold and check on our... shipment. If you smudge your face up a bit with the charcoal in my makeup kit and wear your normal clothes, you'll pass well enough as one of the stokers."

Simms nodded, feeling more than a little grateful. "I'll do that, then. Do you know where the crates are?"

Captain Ramos laughed. "I haven't the foggiest notion. And thus, you really ought to rectify that situation. Hopefully they've put them all in the same area at least. But it might be best to rearrange things a bit so that our things are nearest the loading area."

She was right. He knew the necessity of a speedy escape. But he also knew how damn heavy those crates were because he was the one who had moved them into place for loading to begin with, his face hidden by a thoroughly disreputable hat and a scarf that had smelled disturbingly of slightly off cream. His back twinged warningly at the mere thought.

"That's a lot of weight to shift."

"I have faith in you, Simms. Between brute strength and the winch they ought to have lurking in the depths of the hold, I think you'll do marvelously."

With that, she took herself from the room, her entire posture changing as she crossed the threshold. Simms gave her a few seconds to get down the hall before locking the door behind her and seeing to his own state of dress. With a task at hand, he was far too busy worrying about all of the horrific things that could go wrong between the cabin and his destination, let alone in the cargo hold itself, to let more self-destructive thoughts get a word in edgewise.

Much to his relief, no one stopped him on his way to the cargo hold, and he did pass by quite a few passengers on after dinner strolls, enjoying the view of sunset reflected upon a sea of clouds and distant water. As he was no longer in his fancy costume, they had the good grace to pointedly ignore him, which was really the ideal situation as far he was concerned. Rich people made him nervous.

The cavernous cargo bay was filled with the howl of wind, even though the great doors were closed. There was no need to make the bay air tight like the rest of the ship; it didn't need to be pressurized. Cruising along at an altitude somewhere north of 16,000 feet, Simms found the air quite thin. A bit of dizziness wouldn't bother him if he was just planning on poking around, but if he was to be rearranging the cargo for the sake of the captain's convenience, more air would be a requirement.

A row of breathing masks hung next to the door, lit by the steady yellow glow of an electrical lamp. He helped himself to one and slipped it over the lower half of his face, tightening straps and grimacing at the smell of stale breath and garlic. A tube ran from the mask down to a little brass bellows box hung on a leather belt, which he looped around his waist. Whomever his foul-breathed friend had been, at least he'd had the courtesy to wind up the box beforehand. Gears clicked and air flowed into the mask at the flip of the switch.

Thus fortified, Simms located the main switch for the entire hold—it was night and quite dark—and turned it on. More yellow light flared, almost blinding before setting down to a steady, rather unnatural glow that revealed cargo stowed in row upon row. Simms moved into the neatly stacked rows of crates, trying to locate the three large and exceedingly heavy ones that belonged to the captain. Thankfully, the cruise was a short one, set between two relatively close duchies. The neat rows plotted out on the floor with tie-downs and railings were barely filled, with crates stacked only three high at the most. It was enough to make parts of the hold a bit maze-like, but there was plenty of clearance at the ceiling to make use of the winch. Simms breathed a sigh of relief into the dank mask and began hunting through the rows.

The three crates each bore different freight marks and destinations, thanks to Captain Ramos's—sometimes justified— paranoia. Each did have a board on the side with a subtle pattern of dots hammered into it, something the captain expounded upon as the progression from some mathematical theorem or another, but Simms recognized them as a series of triangles and squares.

But, of course, the crates he wanted were scattered through the rows, and, of course, they were in the least convenient places possible and would all need to be moved. Grumbling to himself and idly picking at a splinter he'd acquired on a nasty board, Simms went to the far end of the hold and set to figuring out the controls for the winch. It was simple enough, gears and chains and a claw with straps for lifting crates, but it wasn't really intended for use by a man on his own.

Well, he thought grimly, at least it meant he wasn't alone in a room with a full liquor cabinet. That had always been a bad combination in the past, and the only ways he'd ever found to fight the temptation involved either Captain Ramos staring at him or the presence of his daughter, Dolly. He had far too many hazy memories of the bad years of the past when Dolly had looked at him with large sad eyes and asked to know why he smelled funny, followed immediately by a request if she could finally have a kitten now.

Thankfully, he was certain he'd be too tired to do anything but sleep by the time he'd rearranged the hold to his satisfaction. He took another walk down the rows of crates, mapping out the best escape route, and deciding which crates he'd be moving so that it would take the least effort. It all sounded excellent in theory, and he felt dangerously close to pleased with himself as he went to fetch the winch and get started.

MARTA KEPT HER EYES properly downcast as she made her way through the airship's halls. The first order of business was a trip down several flights of stairs to the windowless belly of the gondola, where the servants and minor officers were quartered. It wasn't the first time she'd made this particular trip, though perhaps thankfully, on this occasion, there was no corpse sprawling at the bottom of the stairs, as there had been during her last trip. Though really, that had been a fun enough diversion, and she wasn't about to complain.

This foray was necessary because she hadn't been able to get her hands on the passenger manifest before this trip and required the master lists kept by the chief steward. While poking her head into every cabin in second class might be informative as to the disposition of that slice of humanity and a chance to practice her lock picking skills, she knew quite enough backstabbing social climbers and her skills as a picklock were already without peer. Not that she needed even to pick the locks, as she'd had the good fortune to acquire a copy of the ship's master key during her previous voyage, and it seemed no one had bothered to change the locks. Something about Captain Murray perhaps not wanting to admit he'd let the key out of his possession in the first place.

Most of the servants were still engaged with cleaning up after dinner and seeing to the guests as they danced. The chief steward's office was dark, the door firmly shut. She unlocked the door with the master key and left the door open enough of a crack that she'd be able navigate the room. The list was simply pinned to a cork board on the wall, so she gave it a quick read, memorizing the number of Clarkson's cabin and committing to memory a few others who might be worth burglarizing if she ended up with a bit of spare time on her hands. Back on the passenger floor, Marta made herself as small and beneath notice as possible, rounding her back and keeping her hands clasped demurely in front of her. The uniform would do most of the work anyway.

Second class was quite empty, the passengers probably still enjoying their almost-as-good dinner and the dancing and drinks that followed. She headed for Clarkson's cabin and had reached to take the door handle when a man called out loudly behind her, his voice heavy with a German accent, "You! Is he in there?"

Marta's dismayed squeak was pure artifice, part of the character she'd decided to inhabit for this role. She covered her mouth with one hand and turned to face the man. "Begging your pardon, but who, sir?"

Ah, it was the narrow-shouldered man in the orange waistcoat again. Every time she saw him, he seemed determined to become even more interesting. Tatty engineers stuffed with burning resentment and jealousy were a fixture at events like these, and all that made this one remarkable at a glance was his rather slight build. Coupled with his unfortunately wedge-like haircut and his sharp features, he ended up looking like someone had drawn bloodshot, slightly googly eyes on a fire ax and dressed it up in borrowed orange finery. Because yes, it obviously was borrowed, everything was too big for him and held in at the seams with pins.

Perhaps she should have paid better attention because he was in something of a state. While before he'd been notable for his intensely sour expression among an otherwise merry crowd, she had put it down to annoyance at not being able to get past Clarkson's crowd of fawning pseudo-inventors. Now, looking at his red face and overly bright eyes, she began to think the issue one of more than simple annoyance. The scent of his hideous cologne had now been almost completely overpowered by the vinegary pong of alcoholic sweat, and it was a marked improvement on the atmosphere despite his thunderous expression.

A bad mood wasn't enough to make someone interesting, however. If that were the case, Simms would have been one of the most fascinating people on the planet. No, it was the streaks of grime she noted on his coat, rendered almost invisible by its dark color, the fuzz of pulled threads along one shoulder, and the thin angry red scratch across the back of his hand.

"Clarkson! Is that utter bastard in his room?" the man demanded.

Marta looked appropriately scandalized. "Sure I don't know that, sir. The whereabouts of a gentleman is no business of mine. And such language!"

At that rebuke, the man seemed to remember himself. He smoothed down his hair with one hand. "He's no gentleman, but I wouldn't expect you to know that." He hesitated. "Will you let me into his room, then?"

Marta compressed her lips in a thin line and crossed her arms over her chest, doing her best impression of an appalled schoolmarm. That seemed to be the tone this man would respond to. "I will do no such thing. The nerve of you to even ask! Sir."

"You have the key right there—"

"Of course I've a key if I'm to be cleaning." She turned on her heel to begin walking down the hall. "What do you take me for? I'll be reporting this to the chief steward, you had best believe—"

"No, no!" He took a couple of quick, unsteady steps toward her. "No. Please. Forget I asked. I shouldn't have. I forgot myself. Even servants have honor." His expression darkened for a moment. "Unlike Clarkson."

"It's not for me to judge the likes of you nor him, sir."

The man patted around in his pockets until he came up with his wallet. He dug out a few bills and offered them. "Please. Take these as an apology. I meant no offense."

For a split second, Marta considered the options. Continuing to be shocked at the man's nerve would be amusing, and would also be quite in character. But she didn't want him peremptorily running to any of the stewards to defend himself from a report she had no intention of making, and neither did she want to risk him following her and begging further for her mercy. She plucked the bills out of his fingers, tucked them into her apron, and then bobbed a curtsy. The curtsy had the added benefit of briefly putting her at an angle to see into his billfold, where a business card—hopefully one of his—was visible: *Gerhard Dominik Hartley, Inventor Of Clockwork Entertainments and Delights.*

"Thank you, kind sir. God save you."

And of all odd things, as if it was a spasm, he crossed himself. He opened his mouth to speak, and Marta hastily turned once again and retreated down the hall. To her relief, he didn't follow.

But to her annoyance, that also meant he was still in the hall with Clarkson's cabin. Marta rounded the corner and cast around for the nearest door, a little storage cupboard that proved to have just enough space for her inside among the mops and dust-cloths if she was compelled to hide. There was only one exit from the hall of cabins, and she could see it from this position.

Marta arranged herself next to the closet and began folding the already neatly folded dust-cloths, so she looked plausibly as if she ought to be there to the casual eye. From down the hallway she heard the sound of Hartley pounding on a door—presumably Clarkson's—and drunkenly demanding to be let in. She allowed herself a little huff of annoyance. She might be here a while.

Though perhaps Clarkson would show up and she'd have a lovely row to eavesdrop in on. She could only hope.

SIMMS REALLY SHOULD HAVE known by now that any time he felt optimistic about a situation, it was bound to go vomitously sour, like mixing large quantities of curry and cheap red wine in an empty stomach. His normal mode was one of morose pessimism, and it had served him well in the past. But no, he'd had to go and think that he had a handle on this little cargo moving assignment.

An interminable time passed, filled with swearing, splinters, and several skinned knuckles. Simms had begun to seriously question his own commitment to sobriety—really, what good would it do *if* that ended up being the thing that killed him?—by the time he lowered the final crate into place.

It was with relief he headed to the far end of the hold once more to stow his borrowed equipment. As he rounded a corner, a flash of bottle green caught his eye, obviously out of place at the end of one row. Simms froze and then ducked back, cursing quietly into his mask. The bottle green was the back of a coat belonging to a man—why did it look so familiar?—who must have entered the cargo hold while Simms was busy at the back. Considering the general roar incongruously produced by the thin air coupled with the sound of his own breath echoing in the breathing mask, a hundred people could have slammed the door while he was bashing around crates and he never would have heard.

Only what business would a hundred people have in the cargo hold? What business would even this one man have? He was obviously not part of the crew. They didn't wear anything close to that color.

That color. Where had he seen that color?

The man stepped back and half-turned. Simms ducked behind a row of crates. He hastily patted down his pockets and came up with a little knife—more a general tool than a weapon of potential murder—and used that as a mirror to try to peer around the corner. Thankfully, the man was not coming his way.

And really, had he thought of that? All on his own. He was rather pleased with himself. He'd have to tell Captain Ramos about this. He caught the impression of a pinched face and the line of a thin, ratty mustache—

Oh. Him. Clarkson. The inventor. Who then turned and proceeded down one of the rows of crates.

Well, this certainly crossed into the territory *of Things Captain Ramos Would Want To Hear About and Pray Tell, Simms, Why Didn't You Immediately Climb Into The Rafters So You Could Hang*

Upside Down Over Top Him And Observe His Every Move? Like hell he'd do that. But he would attempt to sneak a bit closer and see if he could catch a glimpse of what the man was up to. He was at least sufficiently changed in appearance from his time at the demonstration of the automaton, and the breathing mask was doing him the added service of hiding his muttonchops.

Simms crept forward. He wasn't by nature an overly stealthy person, but it also wasn't a difficult task to keep even heavy boots quiet when the surrounding environment howled with sound. Carefully, he extended his pocket knife a bit past the next corner, around a crate that was marked as holding a piano. Clarkson stood at the very end of this row now, turned to the side. Only his shoulders and coattails were really visible. The way Clarkson leaned back and forth, shoulders tilting and hunching, Simms quickly realized he must be having some sort of animated conversation with a person just out of sight.

Abruptly Clarkson froze, arms coming up—was he be*ing threat*ened?—then lunged forward.

The retort of a pistol echoed through the hold, sharp and unmistakable over the roar of the wind. Simms jerked back, flattening himself against the crates, breath suddenly coming quite faster. What sort *of i*diot fired a pistol on an airship? Simms wasn't even certain what thought was more horrifying: a puncture or the sudden reminder that Captain Ramos had once informed him that the gas holding them aloft was quite flammable.

And of course he hadn't brought his own pistol—well, if he was going to trust anyone to carry an instrument of fiery, screaming death on an airship, who could he trust but himself?—or even the machete Captain Ramos normally forced him to carry. He hadn't expected to come into armed conflict with a crate of crystal. He shifted his grip on the pocket knife and eased it around the corner again, but no one seemed to be coming.

Better, more heroic men might have taken that as an invitation to charge in, intent on affecting a daring rescue or perhaps a glorious citizen's arrest on a gun-wielding maniac. Slightly less gallant but infinitely more unhinged people—say, for example, Captain Ramos—might have gone running into the situation as well out of a desire to know what had happened because gosh, anything involving shooting was always so terribly interesting. Simms was not so burdened by any silly notions about himself or his goals in life. He had well-established allergies to being shot at, stabbed, and having crockery thrown at his head. He stayed put and counted to one hundred as measured a pace as he could manage.

No other sounds manifested, and no one moved past his position or even skulked across the crates that he could view in the reflection on his knife blade. There were plenty of other ways out from among the crates, however.

Simms, preceded by the laughable shield of his pocket knife, rounded the corner and headed toward the end of the row. Quietly cursing himself and then Captain Ramos for once again putting him in one of these situations, he peeked around the corner.

Clarkson sprawled face down on the floor, a dark pool of blood spreading out from under him. A worn leather wallet sat discarded nearby, sadly flopped open, one corner of it being slowly engulfed by the advancing red puddle. A pistol, a very small one, lay on the deck a few feet away.

The situation seemed clear enough. Simms took as deep of a breath as he could with the mask on and switched determinately into the mode of dry gallows humor that being around Captain

Ramos had caused him to long since perfect. It was really the best way to deal with these situations. He could feel all funny about it later.

Simms tapped the bottom of one of Clarkson's feet with the toe of his boot. No reaction at all, no indication that the man was either alive or about to reawaken into non-life. That was a relief. The reason for this stillness became apparent once he took a better look at Clarkson's face—or what remained of it. There was a terrible gash up the side of his neck, a hole in his chin, and the top of his head quite ruined. A stroke of luck, really, as Simms hadn't fancied having to saw off a ravenous non-man's head with the sharp but pathetically short blade of his pocket knife. He'd seen the rather horrifying process of reanimation before, and it involved a lot of twitching, as if nerves had gone raw in death and were curling up like snapped violin strings.

He quickly rescued the wallet before it was completely soaked through with blood, gingerly holding it by one corner using only two of his fingers. He might as well not have bothered. There was no money in it at all—hmm, had the man been robbed?—and the few slips of paper proved to be markers for gambling debts. Which might have also have been the reason for the emptiness of the wallet. Simms carefully put the wallet back down, since the space it had left seemed glaringly obvious even to his eyes. From the corpse's pockets, he unearthed a very questionable handkerchief, which he chose not to examine more closely, a pencil stub, and the key to the man's cabin. There didn't seem a point in taking any of those things.

He skirted the blood puddle, back pressed against a crate of custom crafted gears graced with the mark of T.G. Udole and Sons.

The pistol on the other side of the red smear was not only very small, it was a custom derringer, the sort that only carried two or three bullets and was intended to be concealed in a lady's handbag. The grip was even decorated with a pretty inlay of mother-of-pearl. Simms reached for the pistol, hesitated, and took a handkerchief with his pocket and picked it up with that. He took care to remove the remaining two rounds from the little pistol and pocketed them, and then tucked the pistol away in the recesses of his coat.

There was nothing else he could see, no bloody footprints on the deck, no conveniently dropped business cards or notes declaring that Clarkson, the bastard, had deserved what came to him and this was why, signed and in triplicate.

Damned cheeky of the murderer to be so unhelpful, in Simms's opinion.

IT TOOK SO LONG for Hartley to realize that no, hammering on Clarkson's door and roaring his name like a Teutonic lion in the midst of a tantrum would not get him to appear that Marta had begun considering either fetching a guard herself or just bashing the German over the head with a broom. Thankfully, before her patience had entirely run out, he gave the door one last kick, and then made his unsteady way down the hall. Marta ducked into the closet and clearly heard him muttering to himself about honor and vengeance as he passed by.

Well. That could provide an entertaining end to the evening.

Now was not the time to follow the disaster in the making, however. Marta hurried down the hall and unlocked Clarkson's door with her copy of the master key. She slipped inside and relocked it against the return of the determined Hartley.

Clarkson had already struck Marta as the sort who was incredibly impressed by his own intelligence. His stilted vocabulary and grandiose pronouncements indicated that nicely, without even requiring a detailed analysis of his more unfortunate wardrobe choices. He'd also sounded more than a bit paranoid, with his talk of patents and intellectual theft.

Thus, not knowing how much time she'd have to poke around in his cabin, Marta bypassed the safe and checked the supposedly more clever hiding places that people were wont to use, such as under the mattress and inside shoes. She found a pocket watch of iffy provenance that way and unearthed a set of ratty engineering plans rolled up and stuffed in the sleeve of a smoking jacket. The bottom and right hand margins of the plans were cut a bit unevenly, done by hand with a pair of scissors rather than a machine.

The plans, once unrolled, yielded not the machinery of a difference engine, but rather a reasonably clever puppet that could be run off commands inscribed on a brass cylinder. From the perspective of engineering, it wasn't a bad piece of design. It might even have a future in some sort of factory setting, she supposed. And Marta also did have to give Clarkson a bit of credit for producing a rather nice set of schematics, neatly drawn and so functionally clear that no additional written explanations were required.

All credit given was of course then promptly lost because he'd covered those artful schematics with all sorts of slapdash notes about bypasses and work-arounds for hooking the automaton into the bridge systems of *the Tit*ania. All of the instrumentation would be of no account. The automaton—puppet, really—would run its predetermined program unchanged. Definitely nothing a captain worth his or her salt would trust to fly a ship unattended. Perhaps it had the potential as an automatic pilot of sorts, but similar, far less clunky systems already existed.

While the evidence of pathetic fraud was quite satisfying, as she did so like to be right, there were still a great many questions that remained unanswered. Chief among them was the fact that the cabinet for the cylinder and systems in the plans was supposed to be a cube that measured two feet to the side, but the one on the bridge was considerably larger. What could be the reason behind that?

"What are you up to?" Marta murmured as she carefully rolled the plans up and tucked them under her skirts.

On the off chance she might find something interesting, she continued to riffle through Clarkson's tatty belongings. The safe yielded markers for gambling debts, vouchers for loans, and a ledger book that a cursory glance showed was dipped deeply in metaphorical red. He was obviously having severe money problems, which provided the base reason for this scam, not that she'd ever had a doubt on that account. Through the rest of the room she found a few pornographic etchings, some rather shameful undergarments, and all the trappings of a poor man who wished to be thought of as rich but would never quite reach that goal. She paused, inspecting a set of gloves, noting the cheap quality of the cloth and the small puckers in the stitching.

He might not even realize how far outside the rich classes he still was, treated like a fun pet who could do interesting tricks and play with fascinating toys.

Captain Ramos shook her head, and then went quickly through the room to make certain everything had been returned to its original position. People could be shockingly observant of tiny details while missing out on the larger picture, and it always happened at the most inconvenient moments. This would not be one of those times.

CAPTAIN RAMOS WASN'T BACK in the cabin when Simms arrived. He probably should have expected that. No doubt she'd be puttering around Clarkson's books and papers until she got a warning that he might be on his way back to his cabin—and as that quite literally could no longer happen, he might be in for an interminable wait indeed. Perhaps he ought to go looking for her.

The captain had long since hammered into his mind, however, that his wandering about and looking for her—"deviating from the plan" was how she normally put it, in her most smarmy tone—only tended to draw attention. And drawing attention was always a capital-letter-worthy Very Bad Thing.

But that also meant it was back to just Simms and a room empty but for the liquor cabinet, which was a distressingly physical presence for all its inanimate state. And he had just seen a man get murdered. For all his tough demeanor, that was a thankfully uncommon occurrence in his life. He wasn't terribly comfortable watching any human being get gunned down, no matter the state of their attitude or the grooming of their mustache.

After a few minutes of aimless pacing, in sheer desperation Simms actually picked up one of the captain's books, which was full of completely incomprehensible equations and diagrams. He tried to find comfort in the fact that had he even bothered to complete compulsory schooling, he still wouldn't be able to read this with any sort of comprehension. Penny dreadfuls were really about his speed, and he hadn't thought to bring any along since he hadn't felt like being mocked over his reading material. He dropped the book on the captain's pillow and returned to pacing. Little by little, his feet took him closer to the liquor cabinet as if the damned thing were exerting a magnetic force on him.

Before a point of crisis could be reached, however, the door opened and in breezed the captain. He'd never been so happy to see her before, even if the sharp sound of the door unlocking in the otherwise silent room had left him feeling strangely faint.

An un-servant-like grin lit the captain's face the instant she crossed the threshold. She straightened, hands pressed briefly against her back as if to relieve some great pressure. "Oh, Simms, the dirty laundry I have unearthed—"

He finally regained possession of his voice. Because yes, there was something very important he had to tell her. "—Captain, you really—"

"—the papers—"

"—this is important—"

"—and he's entirely a fraud, as I said—"

"—Marta, will you kindly shut up for a moment!" Simms didn't shout, precisely. He didn't trust the thickness of the walls or doors on a ship like this. But he so rarely bothered to use the captain's first name that sometimes he came perilously close to forgetting what it actually was.

And that was enough to bring Captain Ramos up short. She looked at him, eyebrow raised in a particularly sardonic expression. "Yes, Meriwether?"

He made a face and cleared his throat. "Things have gotten a bit more interesting."

"My sort of interesting or your sort of interesting?"

Wordlessly, he dug the derringer, still wrapped in the handkerchief, from his pocket and offered it to her.

Captain Ramos's eyebrows communicated a thorough surprise and puzzlement to him as she took the handkerchief and unwrapped the little pistol. Then, her expression became one much, much sharper. "A lovely present, but it doesn't really suit me." She checked to make certain the gun was unloaded and then held it up to her nose and sniffed delicately. "Who was involved?"

"Clarkson. Very thoroughly. All over the cargo bay thoroughly."

"Thoroughly in a very permanent way?"

"Very, very permanent."

Captain Ramos nodded. "You look like you could use a cup of tea, Simms. You can drink it while you tell me everything."

MARTA LISTENED TO SIMMS's description of all he'd done and observed, peppered with little pauses as he sipped his tea. He did a decent job of it, even. She only had to ask for clarification a few times, though she expected no less considering the length of their association. Having him organize events into a story also served to knit back together his somewhat frazzled nerves, which she considered a bonus. Simms wasn't the sort to have the vapors over something so common as a murder, but he did have a bit of a soft heart when it came to even thoroughly unlikeable people.

"And you're certain you didn't hear the door open at all?"

"Don't think I could have, between the racket that goes on in the hold and the breather bellows. I didn't see anyone pass by me, though. But there might have been other ways to get to the door."

Not helpful at all, that. Also not really Simms's fault. "You said that you saw him lunge at someone before he was shot, correct?"

"Yeah."

"How was he standing?"

"I don't know. He had his hands up, probably because someone was pointing a gun at him, and then he jumped forward."

This was the sort of detail that she really wished she could have observed firsthand because it was a subtle one. Marta turned sideways and raised her hands, the sort of universal gesture most people made when they were desperately hoping to not get shot.

"Was it more like this"—she stood up straight, even leaning back a bit, and looked strictly forward—"or like this." She tilted her chin down, as if looking at something below her eye level.

If Simms could recall that, it would at least give her an indication of the height of the attacker, or at least the height at which he'd been holding the gun. People had a tendency to stare at the muzzle when a gun was pointed at them—something about looking into the face of death, she supposed.

"Show me again?" Simms sipped his tea as she repeated her demonstration. She exaggerated a bit more the second time. "The second. He was looking down a bit. I remember that." He frowned. "A bit more than you were looking down, actually."

"Like this?" She looked down even more. Curious. Well, maybe the gun had originally been held at waist height. That wasn't uncommon.

"Yeah. And the last I saw of him, when he was jumping forward, he had his arms down, like he was grabbing in that direction instead of straight ahead."

"Hmm."

Marta envisioned the classic-concealed-threat-in-a-crowd pose of pulling a pistol from the waistband and then aiming for the kidneys, to keep it out of eye level. Yes, that seemed about right. Though why anyone would do that in a deserted cargo bay was questionable. Melodrama, perhaps, though that seemed far too neat of an explanation, and she didn't trust it in the slightest. A few hypotheses were all right, but drawing conclusions from so little evidence would be the sort of sloppy thinking she abhorred.

"Where did you say he was shot?"

Here, Simms squirmed a bit in his chair. "Right in the head. And he bled quite a lot as well. I...don't rightly know if that's normal or not."

"In the head...how? Dead center?" She tapped the middle of her forehead.

"No, not at all." Simms went on to describe the wounds, from soft underside of the chin to the ruined top of the head.

"Interesting." Indeed, when she visualized the sort of trajectory that would cause that kind of wound. "His attacker had the pistol at an odd angle indeed." It was more close to the sort of wound she might expect from suicide, but given what preceded, she rather doubted that would be the case.

"How do you mean?"

"Indulge me, Simms." She beckoned him to his feet. "In order to shoot you in that manner, I'd have to have the pistol so..." She held it in the vicinity of his neck, pointed almost straight upward. "Exceedingly awkward."

"They might have been wrestling for the gun," Simms offered.

"Mmm." It was possible, she supposed. She really did need more detail; it was all guesswork now, and she loathed guessing. "I'll just have to go have a look at him myself." That seemed the best solution. "Presumably he hasn't been found yet."

She'd just need to change into something a bit more masculine, since a maid had no excuse to be in the cargo hold. This thought on her mind, she took herself over to the trunk she'd brought with spare changes of costume and began to dig through it. She hadn't really planned on having to dress as a man on this trip, but Simms wasn't actually that much taller than her. She could make do with one of his shirts—

"—his cabin?"

Marta glanced over her shoulder at Simms. "What?"

"Were you not listening to me again?"

Marta sniffed. "Were you actually saying anything important?"

"I was asking if you found anything interesting in Clarkson's cabin." Simms gave her the sort of long-suffering look normally reserved for dogs with soulful brown eyes and excessively wrinkly faces.

All right, she had to admit that it was an important-ish question. Well, she already knew the answer to it since she'd been the one there, but Simms had this annoying habit of wanting to know everything that was happening. Rather like herself, really. The nerve of some people.

"Well, the bit of excitement you had in the cargo hold renders my own discoveries somewhat moot. I found the schematics for his so-called difference engine, and it's nothing more than a fancy puppet. It can't calculate at all. I'd thought to confront the man and engineer a bit of humiliation for him, but I've had that pleasure stolen from me."

She tapped her fingers on her chin, considering the new arrangement of things. Clarkson was no longer around to direct his machine, not that it had needed much direction before. It could prove far more problematic when it came time for Captain Murray to take control of the ship again.

"Though this potentially opens up a new, much more dangerous set of problems."

"The bit where there's a murderer running about?"

"No, I'd wager whoever did Clarkson in won't be hurting anyone else."

"Then what—"

The sudden clamor of bells cut him off: a general alarm. Well, that had happened much earlier than expected. Simms's hand jerked. Thankfully, he'd drunk enough of his tea that he didn't spill any on himself.

"What in the hell is that?"

"The new problem," Marta said, tossing Simms's shirt aside. The time *for* that change of clothing was now past, it seemed. "Get changed back into your borrowed finery, Simms. We're going to bluff our way onto the bridge."

THE ALARM CUT OFF abruptly midway through the two of them trying to scramble back into clothes that, by all rights, someone else should have been dressing them in.

Simms's hands stilled on the buttons of his shirt. "Short-lived emergency," he remarked.

The ship's gong rang four times. "Supposedly the all-clear," Captain Ramos said. "I shouldn't believe that for one moment. See to your tie, Simms."

"So paranoid, Captain." Simms grinned at her, and then found something else to look at as she hitched up her skirt to untwist one of her petticoats.

"It's almost as if I've been on this ship of fools before," she remarked.

The demands of costume followed by the necessary makeup, however hastily applied, meant that many of the other passengers, still dressed for the dance that promised to go long into the night, had stolen a march on them, crowding up into the hallway that led to the bridge and held at bay by polite but very stubborn uniformed crew. The first officer was out as well, reassuring anyone who would listen that the alarm had been a false one, and would they all please go back to their dancing or cabins, whatever suited them best.

Simms bulled his way through the crowd, grateful that the captain was watching his back and lending more material help in the form of sharp elbows a few well-placed shoves. As Simms shouldered an older, rather portly gentleman aside, the man caught his cane on a decorative table—had that been there earlier? It seemed a terrible place for it, the hallway wasn't that wide to begin with, and there was already an alcove with flowers and one of those ostentatiously decorative grates right overhead, wasn't that a bit much? Simms hastened to catch him and prop him up before he actually fell over.

"Sorry about that," he said, making certain the gentleman was steady on his feet before letting go of him. "Got knocked a bit sideways in the crowd."

The man sniffed. "Dashed mess, this. No way to run a ship. These people all ought to be in bed."

Simms made a wordless sound of agreement, deciding not to point out that he thought the gentleman ought to be in bed too and out of his bloody way right now, thank you very much. He wormed his way ahead, Captain Ramos behind him and breezily tossing out apologies and sounds of sympathy.

"Sir, please go back to your room or the ballroom," the first officer said, holding out a hand as Simms came up face to face with him. He spoke with the tired tone of a man who had repeated himself too many times and was well aware of the fact that no one was listening to him.

Just to the left of the guard lay the chain that had been used to secure the bridge door, lock open but pristine.

Captain Ramos tugged on Simms and he obediently leaned over to listen. "Tell him that you know it's a difficulty with the automaton." Ignoring his muttered, "Do I really," she continued on, "and your dear friend Clarkson has told you much about it, so you think you might be able to render assistance until the gentleman can be located."

Simms nodded and passed along that message with what he hoped was appropriately royal bluster. In a stroke of brilliance, he added, "And I don't mean to blow my own horn, dear boy," that was right, rich blokes called people "dear boy" in the most patronizing manner possible all the time, didn't they, "but perhaps you've heard of me. I am Lord Parnell-Muttar, and if that doesn't ring any bells, perhaps the *name Venus Delph*inia does?" As soon as the words crossed his lips, he had the uncomfortable feeling that if such a thing as hell existed, this alone would probably be enough to buy him a one-way ticket, even if he'd somehow managed to live a blameless life up until this moment.

That was the right thing to say, though. The harried officer's eyes widened and he waved Simms toward the doors, which meant Captain Ramos went along, clutching at his arm as if she were afraid she might be lost without it. The man in front of the doors opened them the barest crack necessary for Simms to fit his shoulders through. That alone was enough to give him a bad feeling about what might be on the other side.

The bridge was in disarray, shattered glass decorating the floor, the immaculate brass fittings pocked with dents. A black sky, void of all but the bright cutout of the moon and the indistinct fluff of clouds framed the wreckage. The automaton listed to one side, one of its arms missing. A fire ax discarded on the floor to one side left little doubt about the cause of the mess. Even more worrying, every pipe and cable that Simms recalled having seen earlier being attached to the automaton's cabinet were strewn across the floor, ends ragged. The door to the automaton's cabinet hung from a single hinge, revealing...very little. Mechanical detritus, but there wasn't nearly enough mass to account for the guts of a cabinet that size.

"Oh, that can't be good," Simms breathed, stopping in his tracks. "But if that's—What's flying the ship?"

"Right now?" Captain Ramos gave him a bright smile. "Nothing at all."

"Sir—" Captain Murray hurried to meet them.

Simms held up one hand. Fruity tones, he reminded himself, fruity tones. Hopefully fruity tones not colored by the sudden concerns he had about being in an effectively rudderless airship. "I'm here to render assistance, my good sir. Nothing more."

Captain Murray nodded, his gaze flicking to the captain. "This sort of havoc is perhaps not suitable for a lady..."

"Oh, fear not, sir. She's quite strong of stomach for one of her sex," Simms said in a tone of utter smarm. "And one must indulge one's wife in her little hobbies, don't you see? She won't be in the way." Despite the apparently dire situation, he still couldn't help but try to squeeze a little amusement from the role. He might as well have a good laugh if the ship was about to drop out of the sky and into the ocean.

"Have you caught the ghastly person who would do such a thing?" Captain Ramos asked, a little tremor in her voice as if to belie Simms's comment.

"Fear not, ma'am. We'll have him in custody shortly."

Simms didn't need Captain Ramos to tell him that Captain Murray was lying, and very badly, about that one.

Captain Ramos smiled vapidly and made a show of looking around, pointing at the fire axe on the ground. "Oh dear...you know, I think I saw Mister Hartley carrying that earlier, in the hall. He just told me it had fallen from its mounts and he was to give it to one of the crew. Perhaps you can ask him to whom he gave it? That might be your culprit." She smiled brightly. "Mister Hartley's such a helpful soul."

Captain Murray looked startled, but nodded, waving frantically to one of the guards. As soon as he'd moved away, Simms leaned down close to her. "Who the hell is Mister Hartley?" he muttered.

"Remember the man in the orange waistcoat at the reception? Looks a bit like a fire ax himself?"

"The one trying to set fire to Clarkson with the sheer power of his glare?"

Captain Ramos nodded. "Yes. Hartley."

"Right." He glanced quickly around. "Wait. Not right. Is there a reason we need to set everyone off on a wild hare chase?"

"This may not be a wild hare chase. When I saw Hartley earlier, he was hauling a grudge about rather than an ax, and looking a bit mussed. Pulled threads on his jacket and the like. And his shoulders are just narrow enough he could have squeezed into one of those conduits in the hall and crawled his way into the bridge."

"Now that's some determination." Simms thought of the table that had mysteriously appeared under one of the grates. Even going that short distance in such a cramped space, without towing a fire ax, would be impressive. "He must really hate Clarkson."

"Perhaps even enough to kill him in cold blood." Captain Ramos shook her head, cutting off the next question he'd been about to ask. "First things first, Simms. I rather like the bit where we don't crash into the ocean, and if you really gave it some thought, I reckon you'd agree. Let's have a look at the automaton. Go stand by it and pretend you're explaining how it works. There's a good fellow."

Simms did as directed. He had little doubt this was a ruse to let her get a closer look. Two engineers scrambled among the spilled wires and leaking pipes, their boots crunching on glass and bent gears. Judging by the expressions on their faces, the prognosis was grim. Simms didn't like it when other people were grim. That was supposed to be his job.

Another alarm went off. The younger of the two engineers crawled under a panel in the wall, cursing loudly as he sought to turn it back off.

"How bad is it?" Simms muttered to the captain.

"Hartley did quite the job of it. I don't think they'll be getting it in order any time soon."

"So we're adrift."

"They are," Captain Ramos said, her tone becoming pointed for all that she still spoke at a whisper. "We have our insurance policy in the cargo hold."

Simms frowned. "Co*uld* you fix it?"

"I suppose I could if I wanted, though that would quite destroy our cover I think."

He really wasn't certain how he felt about that, when stated so baldly. Neither the ship nor its crew nor its passengers had ever done anything to hurt him. Simms wasn't any sort of lover of the upper classes by any stretch of the imagination, but he'd also just had a sharp as a gunshot reminder that he hadn't yet hit a point where death could pass him by without putting another smudge on his conscience. And when he thought about it like that, he found he wanted to keep it that way.

The older of the engineers, a man with a neatly trimmed white beard now streaked with grease, finally noticed them. "Are you the one Captain Murray said might provide some help?" Another alarm, and more cursing from the engineer under the panel.

Simms looked down at Captain Ramos. "There are a lot of people on this ship to be drifting off to who knows what fate. So perhaps you could consider it a challenge...unless you think yourself unequal to it."

Captain Ramos sighed theatrically. "Then you'd best get to the cargo hold. We likely won't be welcome any longer by the time this is done." Before he could reply, she straightened, slipped away from his arm, and strode forward. "Actually, I'm the one who will be helping you." She held up one finger. "Don't even consider laughing, and hand me that spanner."

Perhaps it was the seriousness of her tone or the fire in her eye, but the older engineer mutely offered her the tool. He still did have the good grace to look away when she hitched up her skirts and squatted down to join the younger engineer under the bridge console.

Simms backed away and headed toward for the door. Captain Murray grabbed his sleeve. "I thought you were here to help."

"Well, I'm afraid it's more my wife's interest." Simms gave the man a sheepish smile. "She does like her little hobbies. As I said."

Captain Murray turned his head slowly to look behind him, where the two engineers had gathered around Captain Ramos, both obviously listening to her in all seriousness now. "Little hobbies," he repeated.

Simms shrugged, as if that were the answer to all possible questions. "Women. What can you do?"

"Madam...uh...lady...uh...I don't think—"

Marta waved a dismissive hand in the general direction the younger engineer, who was in the middle of stammering out protests. "If you haven't anything useful to say, hush."

The control panel was a mess of wires both neatly spliced and badly hacked apart. The former was obviously the work of attaching the so-called automaton to the ship's systems, the latter from the ax that had been used liberally around the bridge. A larger problem than the cut wiring were gears for the gauges, many of them now bent past all repair. Humming to herself, Marta used the spanner to free one badly mangled piece of metal from where it had been locking up the mechanism of a nearby set of gears. She tossed the bent gear out onto the engineer's shoe.

"We're going to have to do bypasses on all of these. Are there systems the captain can do without for piloting the ship?"

There was a long pause, a whispered conference between the engineers that she ignored as she worked to clear away the worst of the damaged parts. A different man spoke, presumably the older engineer. "We can do without the thermohygrometer and the variometer if need be. I've manual instruments I can put out one of the windows. Be like the old days, that."

"Excellent. That'll give us some spare parts to work with. Can Captain Murray make due with only one inclinometer?"

"Aye, think so."

"Even better." She tossed another mangled gear out from under the panel. "Does this ship use German or Imperial marking standards?"

"Mix of both, I'm afraid."

Marta slid out from under the panel so she could give the man an incredulous look. Even she had taken pains to standardize the controls for her own railcars and aeroplanes. "Is this the dark ages, Mister...?"

"Just call me Edmund, Lady. I'll get the schematics."

"Yes, you'd better." She turned her attention back to the younger engineer. She snapped her fingers at him until he stopped staring. "Your goggles, if you please. It's about to get a bit messy."

He pried the goggles off his head and handed them slowly to her. "Harrison."

Marta slipped the goggles on, noting the smudges of fingerprints with immense annoyance. "I'll keep that in mind for when you've been useful enough for me to bother with your name."

"Hey!"

"Hey yourself," she said as she crawled back under the panel. "If you want to be an engineer, you'd best get your knees dirty down here with me." After a moment of silence, he crawled under the panel next to her. "There's a good chap," Marta said, far more sweetly than she normally would have bothered, but she needed someone to start checking if any of the wires were live. Better him than her.

The state of the panels was not the worst mess Marta had ever worked through—and she'd certainly created more difficult messes herself in the past—but it was one of the more complex. She felt intensely relieved when Edmund returned with the schematics. The three of them bent over the drawings, which were laced with corrections and bypasses in myriad different hands, and laid out their course of action like a battle plan. Harrison had seemed to forget entirely at that point that she was a woman. Edmund hadn't seemed to much care to begin with, which she found even more gratifying. There were sensible people to be found on occasion, like priceless gems.

Too bad she couldn't just stick the man in her pocket and steal him away to the Roost. But she had a feeling Simms might object to that, and so might Edmund's wife, if the level of care she saw in the hand-stitched handkerchief sticking from his pocket was any indication of her affections for him.

After an interminable period of fiddling and cursing, at least the first panel, which was the most critical, had been put back in working order and an abbreviated set of instruments activated for it while Edmund got the rudder cables spliced into something approaching working order.

"That ought to do for this one. It's a bit ugly, but function over form." An alarm began to go off in the second panel, the shrill chattering of a bell. A swift kick stopped it. "We'll get to you soon enough."

Edmund laughed sharply. "If I didn't know better, I'd think you went to the Royal College. That's how we dealt with alarms there, too."

Marta grinned at him. "Some things are universal, my friend. All right, what's next…attitude control, yes?"

Really, from the moment she and Simms had entered the bridge, it had been unquestionable that she'd eventually end up to her elbows in the ship's nervous system. Clever of Simms to have framed it all as a challenge, though. She never had gotten the hang of turning those down. Intellectual fulfillment won over pragmatic survival every time, but there were certainly worse reasons to tweak the bony nose of death.

They'd only begun to work on the next panel when the bridge door opened and Hartley was marched in, held firmly between two large guards in the Grand Duchess's livery. The smile on his narrow face was a rictus of glee as he was brought to a halt before Captain Murray.

"What, no Clarkson?" he crowed. "That thieving bastard couldn't even stir himself for the ruin of all his dreams?"

"Oh, there he is, the man for whom I've waited all this time. Edmund, hold this for a moment, if you please," Marta said, handing him the spanner with the attitude of one who expected to be obeyed. He took the tool from her without hesitation. Marta had long ago noticed that when she entered this mode, the only two possible reactions to it seemed to be blind obedience or complete apoplexy. "If you can bend that gear a bit straighter, I think we'll get lift controls back, by the way."

Edmund nodded, sliding into her place under the panel. Marta brushed her skirts down as she strode, having given up on even pretending to be ladylike, over to Hartley. Ignoring whatever appalled pronouncement Murray was in the process of making, she grabbed Hartley's right wrist and jerked his hand up, sniffing at the fingers: alcohol, sweat, a bit of grease. Nothing more. She gave his fingernails a closer inspection, tightening her grip to the point of being nearly bone-grinding as he tried to jerk away.

"Lady Parnell-Muttar...I say!" Captain Murray said.

Satisfied, Marta let Hartley yank his hand back. He seemed the key to the most pressing question they faced, even if the lack of gunpowder residue on his hand indicated he was unlikely to answer the other, which was Clarkson's demise via petite handgun.

"What did you do with the mechanism in the cabinet?" she asked, jerking her head slightly toward the automaton.

Hartley laughed. "Nothing! There was nothing in there, nothing to fly this ship! He denied my consortium the patent *for* that? And stole my puppet designs? Bastard!" Suddenly, the paper roughly cut from the bottom of the schematics made a good deal more sense—as did Clarkson's slapdash writing against the backdrop of such otherwise neatly-made plans.

"I would not hand my ship over—" Captain Murray began.

"But you did!" Hartley interrupted. "To a fraud and a thief!"

"Gentlemen!" Marta interrupted them with her best authoritative bellow. "Thank you. Mister Hartley, three more questions."

"I don't—"

"*Three more questions*," Marta continued, eyes once again falling on the pulled threads that fuzzed the man's jacket around his shoulders. "And then you can return to your arguing. You entered the bridge by means of the air ducts, correct?"

Hartley stared at her, open-mouthed. "Yes. And a tight fit too, but worth it!"

"You what?" Captain Murray roare*d*.

"*If I may cont*inue!" It was definitely not a request. "You entered via the ceiling grate in the hallway outside the bridge, yes?" He could have moved the decorative table to stand on it and access the decorative grate that covered the duct along the ceiling.

"Yes, how—"

"How did you get through the grate on this side?" she asked Hartley.

"I gave it a kick and it popped right out." He sneered at Captain Murray. "Which just shows the sort of shoddy workmanship you allow on your bridge."

"You have endangered this entire ship with your vengeful stunt!" Murray bellowed.

"You endangered your ship by handing control over to a clockwork puppet!"

"It was no such thing. I watched Mister Clarkson's demonstration myself."

"Well, then, why haven't you called him down here to have him fix his marvelous device?"

"He hasn't been found!" Captain Murray paused, mouth open, eyes going a bit wide. "You have*n't* done anything to him, have you?"

"I couldn't find him either! He's probably hiding, like the base coward he is."

Marta let them bicker, considering both the entertainment value and wisdom of trying to direct Captain Murray's search toward the cargo hold. Bad idea, though. Simms would be in there, and it would probably look a bit suspicious if he were caught in proximity to a corpse while in the middle of constructing a glider whose only obvious use was escape. However, the search would eventually make it to the cargo hold. *The Titania* had a very finite allotment of hiding places. It was inevitable. That meant she needed to be as swift as possible on the bridge and throw a red herring or two in front of Captain Murray to buy a little more time.

She coughed discreetly, and then much more loudly when it didn't cause either of the men to shut up. "If you are looking for Mister Clarkson," she said, affecting the tones of an offended old auntie, on the off chance that it still might work even though the attitude was in direct opposition to her much more straightforward actions earlier, "I do believe I saw one of the young ladies flirting with him at the reception. I would not of course imply any sort of impropriety, but…"

There, that ought to do for a distraction. If they were trying to catch a couple in some sort of tryst, the exceedingly cold and rather loud cargo hold was not one of the places they would look until they had exhausted everything that was at least fully pressurized.

Marta left them to bicker. On the way back to check on Edmund's progress, she paused to look in the ruined cabinet, noting scratches, smudges of dirt, and the ghost of a scent— tobacco, of all things, and she knew that Clarkson was no smoker. With everyone else, including Edmund and Harrison distracted, she bent to sift through the rather small scattering of debris in the cabinet and discovered a cracked stopwatch, a few torn shreds of paper, and a shattered pencil. There weren't nearly enough mechanisms in evidence to provide the drive for a sophisticated puppet, but there were cracked levers and dangling, limp bits of rope.

"Oh, is it really so simple? I'm disappointed."

Turning the broken stopwatch over in her hand, she walked slowly around the bridge, this time looking for more particular debris. Too bad Hartley had made such a pig's ear of everything. The floor was one unending mess of shattered glass and twisted metal. But she eventually found just what she was looking for: a small brass screw, flat headed and too large to belong to any of the mechanisms in the control panels—and the panels themselves were put together with bolts. The screw pinched between her fingers, she crossed the short distance to the grate that covered the air duct letting out onto the bridge. Hartley must have been equal parts drunk, angry, and determined to squeeze himself through here. But as she'd begun to expect, the vent cover wasn't at all bent. Hartley's kick had knocked it loose because it hadn't been fastened to begin with.

But it had at least started the journey with one screw in it. And that screw had ended up rather carelessly discarded on the floor. Perhaps by someone on this side of the bridge, who had removed the vent cover to let him or herself out. Add to that the size of the controls, the space inside the cabinet, just the right size for a child or midget. Considering that the person who had resided in the cabinet had been in control of the ship at least until close to the time Clarkson had been murdered, she found herself hoping for the latter rather than the former. Children, in her estimation, were mysterious and sticky creatures best to be ignored until they had grown into something teenaged-shaped, and at that point they were to be avoided at all cost.

She couldn't help it, she laughed.

"What's so funny?" Edmund demanded, voice oddly hollow as it came from under the console.

"I do believe we were all taken in by one of the oldest tricks in the book," Marta said. "And then it turned around and bit its perpetrator. Deliciously just, I should say." She flicked the screw back into the wreckage and then dropped back down to her knees, holding one hand out for Edmund's goggles. "Do keep your eye out for a midget."

Edmund tried to sit up and only succeeded in bashing his head against the console. He cursed. "A... I must have heard you wrong."

"A midget," Marta said, once again considering the petite size of the pistol still in her possession. "He or she will be hiding in your duct work somewhere, I suspect. But don't worry. They are unarmed."

SIMMS WAS POURING SWEAT and breathing heavily into his bellows mask, though mercifully this time he'd grabbed one that didn't stink of garlic. He was also quite grateful that he'd rearranged the cargo earlier in the evening. Trying to do that and then subsequently construct the glider wasn't a task he could have done without snapping from the stress.

Nerves still drove him fast. Skinned knuckles and a split fingernail later, the glider was constructed and he sat by on a crate, waiting for Captain Ramos.

And waiting.

And waiting.

And waiting.

He was about to just say to hell with it and go looking for her—something that she'd sternly admonished him to never do, but *she* never kept him waiting this long on an escape. Then the woman in question entered the cargo hold at a sedate walk, a streak of grease on one cheek and her hair in complete disarray. She also looked decidedly smug, more so than normal.

Simms crossed his arms and directed his most disapproving of looks at her.

"Oh dear, Simms. You look quite constipated. Either we need to reconsider your diet or you're a bit upset."

"You told me to put together the glider."

"I did indeed."

"As if it were some sort of emergency."

"Not at all. As if it were insurance. Which it is."

"I expected you to come racing down the hall, guns blazing."

Captain Ramos laughed, throwing her head back. "If it would make you feel better, I can go back and try again."

Simms laughed as well, in spite of himself. Perhaps that was the reason they'd gotten along so well over the years. He wasn't the sort to hold on to his temper. "Don't tell me all my hard work is for nothing."

"Oh no." Captain Ramos paused to pull of her skirts, revealing a set of trousers beneath. She left the rumpled fabric discarded on a crate. "Even if I parted company with the bridge crew as the hero of the hour, I think it best if we avoid the uncomfortable questions that will begin to spring up like wildflowers after rain once the late and unlamented Mister Clarkson is at last discovered."

"So was it Hartley?"

"Surprisingly, no," the captain said. "Recall how you showed me the way Clarkson lunged? It seemed a bit low, considering Hartley's height, and the trajectory of the wound then makes no sense at all. And when he was brought to the bridge, there was no smell of powder to him, nor residue from the pistol you showed me. Which was also a bit small for him."

"Then who did it? I hardly think a jealous wife…"

"No, not with a mustache like that. You noticed the automaton's cabinet was empty?"

"Hartley didn't steal anything from it?"

"It was empty when he arrived with that ax. It was that revelation that made him go a bit mad, I think. No, it started the voyage occupied by a midget, who controlled the automaton. An old trick, but well engineered. Clarkson really ought to have stuck with clockwork, he was quite good at that."

"You're telling me that the midget killed him."

"Indeed—"

A woman cleared her throat firmly. "Little person." Simms surged to his feet, peering around Captain Ramos's shoulder. The captain herself turned around more slowly. Had she been expecting this? There, behind her, stood the aforementioned self-named little person, a tiny woman with curly brown hair shorn close to her head and rather elfin features, her arms crossed over her chest. She wore the same sort of clothes Simms had seen on children in workhouses, stained with gray streaks of dust and black smears of grease.

"Little person," the woman repeated.

"I beg pardon?" Captain Ramos inquired, still sounding damnably unsurprised.

"This entire stupid mess has been a circus, *but* I'm no sideshow," the woman said. "So the words you're looking for *are little person.*"

Simms was ever-so-slightly taken aback by that correction. While crime was most definitely a personal choice, what one got called by society certainly was not. He'd been treated to more than a few supremely acidic comments from Captain Ramos to that effect, often continuing on to a cold statement about the right to self-definition that men like him enjoyed and many other people lacked, which somehow had the effect of making him feel decidedly verminous. *So little person* it would be, if probably about to be appended with the adjective "murderous."

"Oh. Then I beg your pardon, Miss—"

"You can just call me Lisa for now, Captain Ramos."

A little flicker of surprise at that. Simms knew that while the name was well known enough, society seemed to be still in general denial of the fact that she happened to be a woman. Lisa must have been very clever to figure that out so quickly.

Captain Ramos continued on, "Lisa, then. Well, since you've decided to join us, would you care to explain why you decided to shoot your employer?"

Lisa's lips compressed into a thin, displeased line. "He was a liar and a cheat. I only even took the job because I was running into some...serious cash flow problems. Clarkson talked a good game and the timeline was short, which was what I needed. But I figured out early on he was going to try to weasel out of paying me, if he could. He had more debt than a leopard has spots. He thought I wasn't smart enough to figure that out." Her expression was caught between a frown and a sharp, angry smile. "A lot of people think that."

"Did you mean to shoot him?" Simms asked over the captain's shoulder.

Lisa shook her head. "People are normally worth more alive than dead. Even worthless asses like him. He just... He lunged at me. I panicked."

Somehow, that made Simms feel better. "Bad luck, that," he commented. Though then he immediately felt strange for having said so. He might have thrown a guard or two off a train, but he'd never killed someone by shooting them.

"I see," Captain Ramos said. "And what brought you out of your cabinet? I know that was before Mister Hartley tried to destroy the bridge."

"How do you know that?"

"Hartley found an empty cabinet. He might have been rather drunk, but he wasn't that drunk. So why did you take it upon yourself to meet up with Clarkson? Did you think to raise your price, now that he was inescapably dependent upon you to complete the scheme? There's no reason at all Clarkson might have called you from the cabinet, and no means by which he could have done so to begin with."

"Wouldn't you? Ask for more money? Demand it? The man was a pig."

"Perhaps." Captain Ramos flicked her fingers. "Did you try to go back to the bridge, after?"

Lisa grimaced. "I'm on this ship too, you know. No, it was—it was all gone when I got back. Like a bomb had gone off. You said it was Hartley?"

"Acquainted with the gentleman?"

"I've heard him yell a lot. That cabinet doesn't muffle things as nicely as you'd think."

Marta snorted. "That ties things up rather neatly. What an interesting confluence of lies coming home to roost. Well, good of you to come see us off." She began to turn away.

Lisa took a step forward. "I want to go with you. I want off this ship."

"No."

"What do you mean, no?" Lisa shook her head. "You're Captain Ramos. These aren't your people here. I'm more one of your people than they are."

"Be that as it may…no." The captain's tone was even more firm now. "Swindling the wealthy of their undeserved riches may be, indeed, something I consider a good bit of fun. But you placed this entire ship—including myself and my man Simms here—in very real danger with your scheme. I tend to take that personally."

"It would have gone fine if Hartley hadn't destroyed the puppet," Lisa protested. "I even watched him do it from the vents. Damn waste. Damn, stupid waste."

"It may have also not gone so fine when you decided to abandon your post to press your employer for a raise." Marta shook her head. "No. I shan't be throwing you to the tender mercies of Captain Murray's guards with my own hands, but you are not welcome on my glider. And you might want to find somewhere else to be, as I'm about to open the cargo bay doors."

"Do you know what happens to people like me in prison?" Lisa asked, her tone a little desperate.

Simms shifted uncomfortably from foot to foot. He agreed with the captain to an extent, but Lisa did look very small and vulnerable.

"I think you have a very good chance of escaping on your own," Captain Ramos said. "You're obviously clever enough, and accustomed to using your size to your advantage, I'd wager. If you're a bit lucky, they won't find Clarkson's body until you've landed."

Simms took a glance around the crates. One of Clarkson's shoes was just visible. "You didn't…"

"Oh, no, Simms. Couldn't have them poking about here while you were trying to work."

He frowned. "Seems a bit indecent."

"He wasn't a terribly decent person," Lisa said. She sniffed. Her eyes glittered with—oh hell, were those tears?

"Oh, please. Don't try to play upon my sympathies, I haven't any." Captain Ramos snorted.

"She really doesn't," Simms muttered.

"Fine." Lisa rubbed a hand across her eyes and straightened to her full diminutive height. Perhaps those hadn't been real tears at all. "But I won't forget this, Captain Ramos."

"And neither shall I. Don't hide in the ducts, I did tell them to look in there." Captain Ramos turned toward Simms and jerked her chin toward the glider. "I do believe our work here is done."

Simms nodded and stopped the bellows box, pulling the mask off and dropping it on top of the captain's discarded skirt. "All right. Open the doors and I'll see us gone." He dug into the pocket of his work jacket and pulled out his flight goggles, slipping them over his head. He hazarded another glance at Lisa, but she had already disappeared. He decided that any helpful advice he might be able to offer—all of which really amounted *to and don't get caught*—wouldn't have been well received anyway.

Captain Ramos gave the little glider its push start, as she was securely attached to it via a harness. Simms didn't have the nerve for that sort of thing, after a bad experience that had involved a rickety bridge and Captain Ramos after she'd been at the peyote again. Once they'd steadied out, she climbed in through the canopy and slid it shut behind her.

"Deja vu, this is," Simms remarked.

"I can't seem to be on that ship without someone getting murdered," the captain agreed. "They really ought to reconsider their clientele."

"Wasn't really the clientele this time."

"You know, I've never solved a crime committed by a little person before. I wouldn't have thought this particular voyage would fill such a void in my life."

Simms snorted. "I suppose I'm glad you're one step closer to completing your collection. This was all overpriced nonsense anyway if you ask me. Dancing about at ten thousand feet. I'd rather be flying like man was intended. Not trying to give it away to a bit of clockwork." He paused, sighing. "Except the sausages. I rather liked those."

About the Author

ALEX ACKS IS A writer, geologist, and sharp-dressed sir. Their biker gang space witch novels, *Hunger Makes the Wolf* and *Blood Binds the Pack*, were published by Angry Robot Books under the pen name Alex Wells. They've had short fiction in *Strange Horizons*, *Crossed Genres*, *Daily Science Fiction*, *Lightspeed Magazine* and more, and written movie reviews for *Strange Horizons* and *Mothership Zeta*. They've also written several episodes of Six to Start's *Superhero Workout* game.

Alex lives in Denver (where they bicycle, drink tea, and twirl their ever-so-dapper mustache) with their two furry little bastards.

For more information, see **http://www.alexacks.com**

ABOUT

QUEEN OF SWORDS PRESS

QUEEN OF SWORDS IS an independent small press, specializing in swashbuckling tales of derring-do, bold new adventures in time and space, mysterious stories of the occult and arcane and fantastical tales of people and lands far and near. Visit us online at **www.queenofswordspress.com** and sign up for our mailing list to get notified about upcoming releases and offers. Or follow us on Facebook at the Queen of Swords Press page so you don't miss any press news.

If you have a moment, the author would appreciate you taking the time to leave a review for this book at Goodreads, your blog or on the site you purchased it from.

Thank you for your assistance and your support of our authors.

CPSIA information can be obtained
at www.ICGtesting.com
Printed in the USA
LVOW13s0103290318
571577LV00011B/144/P